"I know my way out, Sarah."

He didn't look at her.

"I know you do. Thank you for the ride."

He turned to her, hands in his pockets, his gaze focused somewhere beyond her left ear. "It was no big deal."

And suddenly, she didn't want him to leave. Not yet, when she'd gotten a glimpse of the Aaron she used to know. "This was..." she said, "...almost like old times."

"Since when do you care about 'old times'?"

"What do you mean?" She leaned on the newel post at the bottom of the oak stairs.

"Your dreams were always bigger than this place, and you haven't been home in ages. I'm surprised you remember old times."

"I remember a lot more than you think." She took a step forward and inhaled his scent. Her emotions ricocheted from anger to frustration to confusion.

His blue eyes bored into hers. "So do I."

Dear Reader,

Growing up, I listened to my parents, grandparents and even great-grandparents recall their lives and describe growing up in a community where everyone knew their neighbors, people helped each other and the village truly did raise the children. Whether it was in Poland, New York City or a suburb, connection with one's neighbors stuck with me.

As a writer, I wanted to create that sense of community, but modernize it. I wanted diversity of all kinds. I wanted to tackle large issues on a small scale. And I wanted to show that no matter who you are, everyone can find their happily-ever-after.

Welcome to Browerville, a fictitious town in New Jersey with a thriving Main Street, bustling shops and diverse people. Join me at the Isaacson's Deli, a family-run business now owned by our hero, Aaron Isaacson. The smell of garlic and pickles permeates the air. The sounds of people ordering bagels, chatting over coffee and discussing the latest town gossip make you want to pull up a chair. And the hot man behind the counter is easy on the eyes.

That's what Sarah Abrams thinks the first time she steps back into the store after a ten-year hiatus. The power and promise of DC can't compare to the pull of her hometown, and as much as she tries to deny it, there is more than just the temptation of the best challah around to entice her to stay home.

So, grab a cup of your favorite beverage, put your feet up and dive into this second-chance romance. Bagels or challah are suggested, but optional. I hope you enjoy Aaron and Sarah's story!

Jennifer Wilck

Home for the Challah Days

—

JENNIFER WILCK

HARLEQUIN
SPECIAL
EDITION

HARLEQUIN®
SPECIAL EDITION™

PLEASE RECYCLE · THIS PRODUCT IS RECYCLABLE ·

Recycling programs
for this product may
not exist in your area.

ISBN-13: 978-1-335-59422-8

Home for the Challah Days

Harlequin Enterprises ULC
22 Adelaide St. West, 41st Floor
Toronto, Ontario M5H 4E3, Canada
www.Harlequin.com

Printed in U.S.A.

Jennifer Wilck is an award-winning contemporary romance author for readers who are passionate about love, laughter and happily-ever-after. Known for writing both Jewish and non-Jewish romances, her books feature damaged heroes, sassy and independent heroines, witty banter, yummy food and hot chemistry. She believes humor is the only way to get through the day and does not believe in sharing her chocolate. You can find her at www.jenniferwilck.com.

Books by Jennifer Wilck

Harlequin Special Edition

Holidays, Heart and Chutzpah

Home for the Challah Days

Visit the Author Profile page at Harlequin.com.

To Miriam—friend and critique partner.
This one's for you. I couldn't have written this
(and rewritten this and rewritten this, again) without you.

and

To Cathie—awesome agent. This story would have
never found a home without your belief in it.

Chapter One

Aaron Isaacson had no right to look this sexy.

Sarah's belly flopped, and she let out a quiet groan as she stood in the mass of people that passed for a line, four customers—or was it twenty?—away from the deli counter that had been in the Isaacson family for three generations. Aaron's short, reddish-brown hair gleamed beneath the pendulum lights suspended above him. Her fingers twitched, remembering the feel of running through those silky strands back in high school. As employees rushed past him, each waiting on customers who'd packed the store before the High Holiday rush, his close-cropped beard caught her attention.

That was new.

When she and Aaron were together, his face had been smooth, with whiskers barely sprouting along his firm jaw. She remembered the brush of his cheek against hers, the spicy smell of his skin, the way she'd shivered every time she was close to him. Warmth flooded through her. Now, at thirty, the dimple in his chin—the one she'd loved pressing with her finger—was hidden. Was it still a dimple, or had it developed into a cleft?

Why did she care?

The next customer stepped forward.

If she were in charge, there would be clear aisles with lanes for checkout.

Another customer moved to the side.

There really should be a straight shot out the door. It was almost her turn. Her throat dried and her heartbeat increased. She stared at the exit. If she made a run for it now, she'd be gone before he noticed her. She'd tell her mother they'd run out of *challah*. How important was it for the Rosh Hashanah meal? She straightened, preparing to make a break for it and hoping her mother wouldn't freak out, when Aaron's slate blue eyes pierced her.

Too late.

She trembled, and her breath quickened. The noise and bustle around her faded, and her vision tunneled until all she saw was him.

Recognition flashed a split second before he erected a wall—more impenetrable than the *mechitza* separating the men from the women in Orthodox temples. The woman in front of her moved to the side, and it was Sarah's turn.

Oh no.

She swallowed. They hadn't spoken in ten years. Surely enough time had passed, and she could tell him what food she wanted. She might even manage small talk. Or at least a hello. But before she could say the words, Aaron leaned over to a young girl behind the counter and whispered in her ear. The girl nodded, and without another glance in Sarah's direction, he walked away.

The yeasty smell of fresh baked bread and the pungent

odor of pickles and garlic—which had smelled good moments ago—now turned her stomach. Her neck burned with embarrassment. He couldn't even wait on her?

"May I help you?" The young voice interrupted her musings.

Sarah blinked and called upon the polished demeanor she'd perfected since leaving town. "I'd like to order two large round *challahs*, one with—and one without—raisins, please."

She sighed to herself. No Rosh Hashanah dinner was complete without round *challah*, symbolizing the continuation of life. Since she wasn't much of a cook or baker and didn't have time to learn with the demands of her job, her mom assigned the *challah* purchase to her. Isaacson's Deli made the best, and she knew if she ordered it today, it would be ready for next week's dinner.

She should have found another deli.

"Name?"

"Sarah Abrams."

The girl handed her a receipt.

With Aaron gone and customers jostling behind her, the only place she could go was outside. Dazed, she turned toward the door. She'd thought she was over Aaron. She'd never anticipated her body's reaction to him. It was muscle memory—or in her case, hormone memory. That was all.

But his cold shoulder? That hurt.

The warm New Jersey air wrapped around her as she stepped onto the sidewalk of Browerville. The small city was bustling. City? Not compared to DC, where she lived and worked. Still, it was more vibrant than she remembered. Between the balmy autumn weather, the updated shopping and business district and the upcoming holidays, it seemed like everyone was out on the street that afternoon.

"Sarah!" A familiar feminine voice called her name.

Turning toward the voice, Sarah found Emily—one of her oldest and best friends from high school. Both grown women now, they'd once known each other as well as they knew themselves. She smiled as Emily approached, noticing how little she'd changed—same glowing taupe-colored skin, same umber eyes that noticed everything, same curly, natural hair she always pushed out of her way. God, she'd missed her. Regret coursed through Sarah as she realized how awful she'd been at keeping in touch. She'd tried for a while but work and Matthew had gotten in the way. She never should have let a boyfriend prevent her from keeping in touch with her friends.

"Emily!" Sarah said, hugging her. "Oh my gosh, what are you doing here? I thought you worked in Philadelphia."

"I did, until last year. I got a new job in New York, and I commute from here. What are you doing here?"

"I'm home for the High Holidays," she said, hiding her surprise that Emily would choose such a long commute from their small hometown, rather than moving to a large city like New York.

"They're not until next week, though," Emily said.

"I work for a Jewish organization. I get the entire week off. Add to that some vacation time, and I'm here for close to two weeks."

"Wow, maybe I should get a job with you!"

Sarah laughed. "Are you free at all? I'd love to catch up with you. I've been a terrible friend, and I'm sorry."

Emily glanced at her ruby red phone before looking back at Sarah. Her friend's penchant for bright colors remained— her nails were as red as her phone, and her bright purple top added a splash of color to her gray, pinstripe pencil skirt.

"You won't win any friend awards." Emily's tone tinged with a cross between anger and hurt. "I've missed you. I've missed us."

"I've missed us, too. Maybe we can try again?" Sarah squeezed her hand into a fist, crumpling the deli receipt she hadn't yet put away, and digging her pale pink nails into her palms. "I wish I'd handled things differently."

After a brief pause, Emily's eyes softened. "I guess I haven't been much better."

Sarah pulled a business card out of her bag and handed it to Emily. "Here's my number. Give me a call, and maybe we can get together. If you have time."

Emily glanced at the card a long moment before nodding. "I will. I promise."

Her friend's hesitancy cut Sarah to the core, but she pulled her into a tight hug and squeezed a little longer than usual. "I hope you will. I'm staying at my parents' house."

When they parted, Sarah raced to the metered parking spot down the block, where she'd left her rental car. Now belted into her seat, she gripped the steering wheel and expelled a long breath. Between guilt at losing touch with Emily and the way Aaron blew her off, her stomach tightened and the bitter residue of her morning coffee bit at the back of her throat.

She'd thought she was over Aaron. She'd moved on, anyway—to Matthew Goldberg, the successful political lobbyist in DC who wanted to marry her. As soon as the holidays were over and she returned home, she'd give him an answer. She should've answered his proposal before she left, but she needed time to weigh her future with care. He'd been supportive, encouraging her to think before she spoke or acted.

A pang of longing for Matthew struck her. She wished he was beside her now, his arms wrapped around her and reassuring her everything would be okay. She shook her head. No—she had a decision to make, and she needed the separation to make the right one. While she'd known she might run into Aaron, she never anticipated her body's reaction to him.

And she hadn't anticipated his cold shoulder.

She threw her car into drive and pulled onto the crowded street, heading toward her parents' house. She smiled at the polite way other drivers waited when she flipped on her blinker for lane changes, rather than rushing ahead or hogging the lane so she couldn't get over. That would never happen in DC, which is why she'd sold her car and rode the metro instead.

Her phone rang with ABBA's "Money, Money, Money." She smiled, recognizing the ringtone she'd selected for Matthew, and touched the Bluetooth button in her rental car.

"Hi." She stopped at the stoplight. "It's so nice to hear from you."

"How was your drive?"

Sarah's heartbeat quickened at the sound of his voice. "Uneventful. How's everything with you?"

"I miss you. How is it being home?"

"Weird," she said. "But I'm not home yet."

"Town changed much?" Matthew asked.

She glanced at the midsize buildings surrounding her, the leaves on the trees in the park beginning to turn. Some of the signs had changed—the Italian restaurant where she'd celebrated her sixteenth birthday was now a laundromat, and the stationery store was now a Chinese restaurant—but the look and feel of the place was the same. "Not really."

"Gotta love small towns—*and* the people in them."

She frowned. "Hey, I'm from this town."

Matthew's voice usually pleased her, but something about his comment gave her pause. Browerville wasn't a small town in the middle of nowhere. It was a thriving, diverse place, forty-five minutes outside of New York

City. And as much as she once found it stifling, it was her hometown.

"And you're the best part about it." His smooth, rich baritone slid around her and filled the lonely cracks.

The light turned green, and she let out a breath before continuing down the street. Maybe she was too sensitive.

"I'll call you tomorrow," she said, turning onto her parents' street.

"Make it tonight. Please."

Her chest constricted and the air in the car stifled her as she pulled into the driveway. She was pleased he missed her, but what if she didn't have time? She was supposed to visit with her family—he promised he'd give her space.

"Sarah!" The front door to her childhood home flew open and her parents raced down the steps.

Her father reached her first, pulling open her car door and squeezing her in a hug before she could take off her seat belt. She breathed in his familiar soapy scent before turning and embracing her mother. Her eyes stung with a longing she hadn't expected at the scent of her mother's Dior perfume. A tight knot loosened in her chest. She was home.

"I've got to go, Matthew," Sarah said.

"Hi, Matthew!" her mother called out so the car's Bluetooth would pick up her voice. "Wish you could be here!"

While her father opened the backseat door and pulled out her luggage—his strong arms carrying both suitcases and a small bag with ease—her mother rushed ahead and opened the front door.

"Call me, Sarah," Matthew said. "I'll wait."

He'd said the same thing when he proposed. It had been endearing at the time.

"Okay." She swallowed and yanked back the car's parking brake.

"Come inside, Sarah," her father called. "We're dying to see you!"

Smiling to herself, Sarah exited the car and shut the door with a gentle slam. Matthew might wait, but her parents wouldn't.

Her childhood home, a two-story beige colonial, hadn't changed in as long as she could remember. The glistening windows, bordered by black shutters, still reminded her of eyes with long lashes. The trees in the front yard were well maintained, only taller and fuller than when she'd last visited.

Inside the front hallway, she squinted in the shadows and removed her light jacket. Hanging it on the oak banister like always, she followed her parents' voices into the sunny kitchen at the back of the house.

"Ah honey, it's good to see you." Her mother gave her another bone-crushing hug, then waved a hand at Sarah's black cotton top and linen pants. "But what's with all this black?"

Sarah looked down at herself. "What's wrong with it?" An image of Emily's brightly colored work outfit flashed through her mind. Her mother would've loved it.

"There's no color."

"Black is a color." Sarah sat at the kitchen table and smiled in thanks at her dad as he passed her a cup of tea. Although she didn't come home often—and never for such an extended time—when she did, this was their ritual. Her dad made the best oolong tea. Sarah inhaled the spicy aroma before taking a sip.

Her mom snorted inelegantly and ran a hand through her tousled salt-and-pepper curls before bringing her own teacup to her lips. "Let me make you something to eat. Pancakes? French toast? A waffle?"

"I'm good, Mom." Sarah remembered her mother's cooking—delicious, stick-to-your-ribs food. She couldn't afford to eat it now if she wanted to keep her slim figure. She'd made a lot of changes, her diet being one of them.

Her mother stared at her over the rim of her teacup. "So, how is your job and apartment? How's Matthew? I'm sorry he couldn't join us this year."

Sarah held back her own snort. Matthew hadn't ever joined them, despite the fact they'd dated for the past three years. "Matthew has too much work, Mom. Congress is in session, and he has lobbying work to do. Besides, couples need breaks occasionally."

"Breaks?" Her mother's eyes widened as though she'd suggested they watch a triple X-rated movie. "What breaks? Your father and I never needed breaks from each other. Is everything okay with you two?"

"Everything is fine. We're not like you and Daddy." A trickle of…something…slithered along her spine. Unlike her parents—who were like a matched pair of socks, always doing everything together—she and Mathew didn't mind doing things apart. And the last thing she wanted was to discuss Matthew or the marriage proposal. Her mother would have opinions with a capital O. "But he says hello. And as for my job, I love it."

Right, change the subject. If only her mother would bite.

Her father's eyes gleamed with pride. "You're making a difference?"

Her mother opened her mouth like she was about to say more, then closed it when her father interrupted with his question. Thank goodness for her father.

With a grateful smile, Sarah answered. "I am." Her chest expanded. "We're influential with the senators, and we're working to get them to back legislation helping women."

He nodded. "And you can afford all this time off?"

"I took three and a half days, and they give us off between Rosh Hashanah and Yom Kippur. It's fine."

Her mom rose and kissed her cheek. "That's wonderful, darling. Now all we need is to buy you some colorful pieces of clothing. And convince Matthew he needs to devote more time to you, not less."

Sarah's throat burned as she forced down a scalding sip of tea. If she didn't, she was afraid she'd spit it out. While her father was quiet, her mother was a force of nature, and she never gave up. Try as she might, Sarah rarely won an argument with her. And arguing about colors, or Matthew or discussing the marriage proposal, wasn't something she was going to do.

Aaron wiped the counter with a rag, scrubbing so hard he wouldn't be surprised if he wore a hole in the old Formica. Easing the rag away from the superclean area, he placed a piece of wax paper on the counter and grabbed two slices of rye bread. The din of the packed deli faded into the background.

Sarah Abrams.

His stomach clenched. Of all the people to walk into his deli, he'd never expected her. He'd hoped at one time that she'd change her mind and decide this is where she belonged. Dreamed about her for longer than he'd like to admit—how her long, dark hair brushed his chest when she leaned over and kissed him, how her soft lips teased his, how her olive skin slid smoothly beneath his hands. He'd even broken an engagement with another woman because he couldn't get Sarah out of his head. But expected? It had been ten years.

"I asked for pumpernickel," the wizened old man complained across the counter.

Aaron looked at the sandwich, swore under his breath and threw the rye slathered in mustard in the trash.

"Gloria!" He shouted down the line toward an older

woman with a brown apron covering her T-shirt and jeans. She patted the shoulder of the woman she was speaking to and strode over.

"Yeah?"

His six-foot frame towered over her, and she craned her neck to meet his gaze.

"Can you take over for me? He wants…" He turned to the customer. Age and disappointment conspired to make the old man resemble a shar-pei. Aaron shook his head and ushered Gloria forward. "Sorry, she'll make your sandwich. And it's on the house."

Wiping his hands on his apron, he weaved through the staff behind the counter. When he reached his tiny office tucked in the back, he shut the door and sank into the rickety-wheeled desk chair. He ground his teeth until his jaw ached. Other parts of his body used to ache when he was around Sarah in high school and college. They'd been inseparable. Her smile, with the one tooth a little crooked in the front, brightened any bad day. Her husky voice soothed him. Now, though?

Disappointment simmered. She'd promised him forever and broken his heart, walking away from this town—from him—without a thought for the people she'd left behind. And, when he'd tried to surprise her… It took him years to recover, but with focus and drive, he'd created a life for himself here. A good life, even if he was ultimately alone. He'd stepped up, shouldered the responsibility of this business and taken care of his family and friends. His steady and predictable life gave him purpose and satisfaction. He'd dated other women. He'd stopped looking for her at synagogue on holidays, stopped thinking every ring of the phone was her. He'd stopped waiting for her to walk into his deli and order *challah*.

Until today, when she'd done just that, acting as if she

had every right to be just another customer in line. Her
deep brown hair skimmed her shoulders. When they were
together, it had been curly. Her chocolate brown eyes were
more wary, but still big enough for him to drown in. Her
heels made her taller, but he'd bet she'd still fit against
his shoulder…

He slammed his hand against the desk, stormed out
of his office and up the back stairs to his apartment. She
wasn't the same, even if she was thirty, like him. She'd
changed, and he hated change.

His head ached, and his jaw was tight. He needed air.
Untying his apron, he reached for his sweatshirt with his
youth group logo on the back, the worn fabric soft against
his rough hands. At one time, they'd both worn sweat-
shirts from this youth group, attended events together…
He dropped it on the ground and reached for his Giants
one instead.

His phone rang, and he answered without looking.

"Hello?"

"Aaron? It's your mother."

He rolled his eyes. No matter how many times he told
her she was programmed into his phone, that he could see
who called when it rang, she insisted on starting her calls
this way. Of course, this time he hadn't looked, so his argument was moot. He wouldn't tell her, but still.

"How are you, Mom?"

"I'm worried about the catering order for the temple's
Rosh Hashanah meal."

His deli was catering it, as it had done every year for as
long as he could remember. His chest swelled with pride.
A long time ago, he and Sarah used to attend the meal together. Would she attend this year? Pride and nostalgia
turned to frustration. He shook his head. "Why? We've
got the same menu as we always do, I've ordered every-

thing for delivery, and I've got extra help coming in to help us prepare."

With his mother pulling away from the business to enjoy retirement, catering became another of his responsibilities.

Responsibility. He took it seriously and made sacrifices for it. Something Sarah never seemed to understand. He shook his head as his mother's words penetrated.

"I know, but I'd feel more comfortable if we could go over it one more time. And maybe you should have Jordan or Gabriel help you."

This was the first year his mother wasn't overseeing the event. He rolled his shoulders and tried to release some of the tension in his neck. She wasn't responsible for Sarah's return. And just because Sarah decided to pop into the deli unannounced, didn't mean he could take his frustration out on his mother. "I don't need their help, Mom. Let them focus on their own lives. How about you and I sit together after closing today to go over everything one more time?"

He could practically hear his mother's smile beam through the phone. It was his father's favorite thing—the wattage of her smile. She smiled with her entire being, and it was usually directed at his father. Despite not being able to see it, Aaron warmed knowing it was now directed at him.

"I would appreciate that, honey. Thank you."

"No problem, Mom. I'll meet you at the deli at eight."

He stared out the window of his apartment into the alley below. He wanted to get outside and restore his equilibrium. Clear his ex-girlfriend from his mind. However, he needed to go downstairs, especially if he was to go over the catering order with his mother later. Jogging down the stairs, he returned to the deli and maneuvered behind the counter.

"Aaron!"

Looking into the room full of shoppers, he spotted his

best friend, Dave, the man's bald brown head a beacon in any crowd.

He nodded. "What's up?"

"Grab a beer tonight?"

He reached behind him for an apron and tied it around his waist while listening to the order of the customer on the other side of the counter. Nodding, he leaned into the case and grabbed the turkey.

"Can't. Mom wants to go over the catering menu after closing."

"Again?" His friend leaned against the counter, eyebrow raised.

"It's the first year she's not in charge."

Dave nodded. "Guess she's having a hard time with the transition?"

"I can't blame her. It's our reputation, and she helped build it." Another thing Sarah never understood. She'd never taken his ties to home seriously, hadn't seemed to care he couldn't pick up and follow her to DC. Although he had two brothers who were willing to help if asked. Still, he was the one who'd always loved this place—the smells, the bustle, the satisfaction of providing a good meal. He was the one who wanted to carry it forward.

He slathered Russian dressing on rye, added the turkey and tomato and sliced the sandwich in two, before including a sour pickle with the order.

"What time will you be finished? Want to grab something afterward?"

Aaron eyed his friend. He looked casual enough as he leaned against the counter, but there was an intensity in his gaze that belied his easygoing stance. "I should be finished around nine. Want to meet at the Gold Bar?"

Dave nodded. "I'll save a bar stool for you."

On a Tuesday night, Aaron didn't think the place would

be crowded, but he nodded and tried to concentrate on the customers in the store. Except no matter how much he tried to focus on his customers and their orders, three questions replayed in his mind. Why was she here? How long was she staying? And who would pick up the *challah* she'd ordered?

Matthew's ringtone that evening sent a surge of pleasure through Sarah as she dried the last of the dinner dishes in her mother's colorful kitchen. She dried her hands on the red and teal floral dish towel and answered.

"Hi, Matthew." She walked as far away from the adjoining family room as possible so her parents wouldn't overhear her conversation.

She was twelve again. Wonderful.

"Hey, sweetheart. I wanted to hear the sound of your voice, so I thought I'd call you."

His sexy baritone flowed over her. "Working late?"

"As usual. And without the incentive of you to come home to, well…"

An image of their immaculate apartment flashed through her mind, so different from her parents' lived-in home, filled with photos, knickknacks and half-finished knitting projects her mother was working on. "Guess this will be a very productive time for you."

"It will, but I'll miss you. What are you doing tonight?"

She made her way upstairs to her bedroom.

"Sarah, wait a minute?" Her father called from the hallway.

"Matthew, hold on a second." She held the phone against her chest. "Yes, Dad?"

"I'm supposed to help move the tables at the synagogue tomorrow to set up for Rosh Hashanah lunch, but my back's bothering me. Would you mind going instead? I hate to ask you, but I also don't want to leave them shorthanded."

She nodded. "I wish you'd told me before you carried in my suitcases, though."

Her dad shrugged. "Those I can handle." He walked down the steps toward the family room.

When she was sure he'd left, she entered her bedroom. Kicking off her shoes, she settled onto the bed. "Hanging out with my parents and watching TV." Her parents were big fans of crime shows and challenged each other to figure out who committed the crime and why. Their antics were more entertaining than the show.

"Sounds nice. I almost wish I could have joined you."

A pang of loneliness pierced Sarah. These ten days would be the longest they'd been away from each other since they'd started dating. She loved being the center of his world, but she also recognized the need for a little space, especially when she had so much to think about.

"You know why I need the time alone, Matthew."

"Did you tell them yet?"

She closed her eyes. Matthew had surprised her with a marriage proposal. They'd talked about marriage before, but she always thought she had more time. She had a life plan, and while marriage was part of it, she hadn't expected a proposal quite so soon. She rubbed her stomach. "Not yet. I don't want their reaction to influence my decision."

"Maybe they'll help you make up your mind."

Matthew was the perfect boyfriend—with a promising political career, a lifestyle she'd grown to love and a habit of showering her with gifts to show his affection. But something had stopped her from giving him an automatic "yes." She hoped a vacation at home would help her sort out her feelings and be sure of her decision.

"Matthew, if we get married, it's because it's what we want, not what others want." She gripped the phone in her hand until its edges pressed into her palm.

"I know, sweetheart. I just hope you see in us what everyone else does. We're made for each other, Sarah."

"Then taking my time over such an important decision won't change anything. You surprised me. I thought I'd have more time to establish my career before getting married, so I need a little space in order to adjust and make the right decision." An ache began forming in her temples.

His intake of breath echoed through the phone. "You're right. I know you're right. I'm the one who told you to take your time in the first place. Forget I said anything. Take your time and make the right decision, Sarah. I miss you."

Hanging up the phone, she wondered what his idea of a "right" decision was.

Chapter Two

Aaron shucked his jacket as he entered the Gold Bar and wished he could shuck his mood with as much ease. This time of year was always hectic and with less than a week before Rosh Hashanah, the deli was packed every day. The work should have made him happy. Usually, carrying on the family business, connecting with customers and forging relationships with other small business owners fulfilled him. This year, the approaching holiday stress added to his feeling that something was missing. Meeting with his mother helped her but did little to relieve him. Her suggestion that his brothers help him only reminded him that their big dreams didn't involve the deli. They deserved their chance to follow those dreams. His dream had always been the deli. But the more he looked at his to-do list, the more items he added to it. The more he calculated the time he'd need to accomplish everything, the more he realized how little else he had in his life other than work. And for the first time, the lack of balance bothered him.

Maybe Dave would distract him.

"Hey, Aaron, thanks for putting me in touch with the liquor distributor," Mo, the bar owner, said. New to town, and to the United States, the Syrian immigrant's dream of opening a bar and making it prosper came true through sheer drive and determination. Hell, Aaron thought, if he made it through the rigorous screening process to come to the US, he could do anything. Admiration for the man surged through him.

"Happy to help, Mo. They're working out for you?"

Mo nodded. "Best prices and quality I've found. Drinks on the house tonight."

Aaron shook his head. "You've got a great place here, but you'll never survive if you give drinks away. Thanks, though." Mo put aside money weekly to sponsor the rest of his family, and Aaron didn't want to make his plan any harder.

He scanned the dim room. His friend sat at the end of the gold and black bar, saving a stool for him, as promised. Aaron slid onto it and flagged down the bartender. Pointing at Dave's drink, he held up two fingers. The bartender slid two mugs of beer along the bar to them. Aaron took a sip. The froth stained his upper lip, and he swigged another taste of the bitter brew before wiping his mouth and turning to his friend.

"What's up?"

"Crazy day." Dave shook his bald head.

"You're not kidding." He took a deep breath and relaxed. "Teenagers causing you trouble?"

Dave was a high school math teacher in town and liked to joke that the kids ensured his celibacy. Aaron knew otherwise. Dave was a *mensch*, and when he found the right man, would be an amazing husband and father.

"I've heard some troubling whispers."

Aaron cupped his hands around his mug. "What kind of whispers?"

"Hard to pinpoint. A little too much laughter at offensive jokes, less than tolerant speech. Nothing yet I can call anyone on specifically." He drank from his mug and shrugged, but his brown eyes were troubled.

"Could it be start-of-year posturing?"

"Maybe. I've made a few broad 'be kind' statements, and I hope that will be the end of it."

"You're right to be worried. These things have a way of taking off on their own if left unchecked," Aaron said. "But if anyone can handle them, you can. However, if you need to bounce ideas off someone, you know I'm always here."

Dave nodded. "I've got a great group of kids this year—all my classes, actually—but I've never dealt with anything like this. I hope I'm overreacting."

"Don't hesitate to speak up, and if you need to go to the school board and want backup, let me know."

"Thanks, I appreciate it. So…"

The pause stretched, and Aaron realized Dave hadn't yet gotten to the point of their meeting. He remembered the intensity of his gaze when Dave suggested a drink tonight. His chest tightened.

Finally, Dave broke the silence. "I heard Sarah's in town. I thought I'd warn you."

The beer he'd drunk sloshed in Aaron's stomach. His hand clenched around the mug handle. His scalp tightened. He swallowed and loosened his fingers one at a time.

"Your warning system needs a few tweaks. I already know." The bitter scent of the brew wafted about him, as did the murmur of voices in the room. Out of the corner of his eye, Dave's hand rested flat on the bar top. He focused on that image, rather than the others scrolling through his head—tempting images of Sarah that made pain slice through him.

"Have you seen her? Did you talk to her?"

Images of Sarah's dark hair glowing beneath the lights in his deli, her lustrous skin and big brown eyes, her very presence in his world, flashed. Regret burned a hole in his stomach. He should have at least said hello. "Why all the questions?"

"Because you're my friend."

Aaron arched an eyebrow. "You sound more like a *yenta* looking for gossip than a guy looking out for his buddy."

Dave's face flushed, and Aaron winced at his harsh tone. He hadn't meant it.

"I know," Dave said. "But when you acknowledged the news and went silent, I got carried away. Apparently, my students are rubbing off on me."

"Don't worry about it." Aaron turned around and stared into his beer. His friend was curious. In his place, Aaron would be the same.

"Are you?" Dave asked.

"Am I what?"

"Worried."

"About Sarah? Why would I be?"

Dave played with his beer mug. "I was there when you returned from DC that weekend. And I know how long it took for you to get over her."

Dave had been there for him, silent support as he got drunk and tried everything to get Sarah out of his head. If any good had come from Sarah's desertion and betrayal, it was the friendship it forged between him and Dave. *Maybe I should thank her for it.* He snorted.

"Don't deny how long it took you to get over her," Dave said.

"She ordered food for her family. I guess you can call

it the perils of having the most popular deli in the area."
He gave a half grin, knowing full well it did nothing to
convey cheerfulness.

Dave waved to the bartender. "You want another?" he
asked Aaron.

Aaron pushed his mug away. "I'm done. One glimpse of
Sarah isn't enough for me to have to drown my sorrows. I
doubt we'll run into each other again."

Sarah pulled her chestnut hair into a ponytail and
stretched her hamstrings before setting out on her early
morning jog. She ran through the sleepy neighborhood,
barely stirring at five thirty. Only the sound of birds chirp-
ing, and a few engines of New York City commuters disturbed the peaceful morning.

As she headed toward the main road leading into town,
a woman in a hot pink jogging outfit pulled out in front
of her. Sarah increased her speed. Something about the
body shape, the light brown hair swinging in its ponytail—

"Caro? Caroline Weiss!" Sarah called as she ran to catch
up.

The woman turned around, and Sarah squealed. "Hi!"

Surprise flashed across the woman's face as she jogged
in place. "Sarah Abrams? Are you actually here?"

Sarah nodded and a hint of guilt nudged her. "I'm in
town for the High Holidays. How are you?"

Caroline nodded. Her gaze shifted sideways. "Fine. Nice
to see you." She turned and started jogging away.

"Wait, Caro."

Caroline stopped, fisted her hands on her hips and bent
over. "What do you want, Sarah?" She remained facing
the ground.

"Want to jog with me? We can catch up…" She should
have been a better friend.

Caroline spun around and gazed into the distance. "You haven't talked to me in ages. Suddenly you're in town and you want to catch up?"

Sarah's heart thudded in her chest. She'd really messed up. At one time, Sarah and Caroline were inseparable. Members of the same temple youth group, they were part of a tight-knit friend group. But since moving to DC, Sarah lost touch with everyone. It wasn't something she was proud of, but it had happened. The stretches in between calls had grown longer, each conversation more stilted, until she'd given up.

And now it was up to her to fix it.

"I'm sorry," she said.

"It's going to take more than that to make up for dropping our friendship like you did." Caroline's eyes flashed with anger and hurt.

"I know," Sarah said. "I never meant to let such distance get between us. After Aaron and I broke up, I couldn't face home anymore and all the memories. Every time you posted on social media with the old group, with Aaron, it hurt too much. But I shouldn't have given up on everyone. Especially you. I should have valued our friendship more. I was wrong."

Caroline's nostrils flared. "Since when do you run?"

Caroline had always been a fitness freak, a star member of the track team. She'd received college scholarships to some of the top schools in the country but had stayed home and gone to community college because of her mom.

Sarah had been sedentary, until Matthew.

"I picked it up a few years ago. Matthew likes to keep in shape. We jog every morning before work."

"Your boyfriend?"

"Yeah. What are you doing now?"

"I'm a fitness instructor at the Jewish Community Center. Actually, I'm hoping for a promotion to program director."

Sarah smiled. "Wow, that's great. I hope you get it."

Caroline sighed. "I guess we might as well run together. Sure you can keep up?"

"I jog five miles every day, but if I hold you back…"

"No, I think you'll be fine."

The sun peeked above the horizon, and the two women jogged together in silence.

"You're pretty good at this," Caroline said as they turned onto Main Street. The stores and restaurants were still closed, and the sidewalk was quiet. She looked over at Sarah. "Guess you really have changed."

Sarah's face heated at the meaning behind the compliment. She paused at the corner and faced Caroline. "I really am sorry. I never meant to let such distance get between us. I should have made a better effort to stay in touch."

Caroline nodded. "I could have forced the issue. I was hurt when you disappeared from our lives."

"Will you let me try to make up for it?"

Caroline gave her a hug and bounced on the balls of her feet, her expression cautious. "I'd like that. I've missed you."

Sarah's eyes prickled with tears. "I've missed you, too. I haven't had more than a quick weekend here in ages."

"So, what gives?"

The two women continued their jog on a paved path leading off into the woods. The birch, maple and oak trees had started to change color. The brush on either side of the path lightened. In the distance, scurrying let them know the animals weren't thrilled to have their morning feeding routine disrupted.

"Matthew proposed."

Caroline stopped, mouth open. Her pale skin mottled with shock. "Wow. Mazel tov."

Sarah nodded. Caroline was the first person she'd told, other than her coworkers who had reacted in their predictable, DC-politics way, extolling Matthew's political future and what a wonderful life she would have as the wife of a politician who cared about people. They ignored what the changed timeline might do to Sarah's dreams.

Caroline looked at Sarah's left hand and reached for it. "Where's the ring?"

Sarah avoided her grasp, gripped the edge of her black cuff with her fingertips and pulled it over her hand. "I left it in DC with him. I haven't said yes. Yet."

Caroline pulled up short. "Why not?"

Would she understand? "We've dated for a little more than three years. He thinks it's time we got married, and I don't disagree."

"Sounds like a fairy-tale love story." Caroline had always been the most sarcastic of the group, and her tone proved some things hadn't changed.

But having the sarcasm directed at her stung. Sarah gave her a tiny shove. "He's got an amazing future in politics. He cares about the poor and helps draft bills in congress to protect and support them. He's smart and comes from a great family."

"So, other than his pedigree, what do you like about him?"

Annoyance flashed, and she tried tamping it down. "What are you talking about?" The woods were now silent, the two women scaring away any animals who might be tempted to appear. She wished her friend were as silent.

Caroline shrugged. "This isn't how the Sarah I remember would react to a marriage proposal. It doesn't sound like you're excited."

The Sarah that Caroline remembered had aged ten years. Didn't she understand? "Excited? A marriage proposal is serious stuff, Caro. I'm more logical now. I have to consider everything. This isn't one of your favorite ninety minute rom-com movies."

"You're right. It is serious. But tell me this. Do you love him?"

Sarah's chest constricted. She rubbed it, the black spandex smooth beneath her fingertips. She shouldn't be out of shape. Matthew was a big proponent of fitness, and she exercised on a regular basis. "Of course I do. I wouldn't consider his proposal if I didn't love him."

"Then what are you waiting for?"

Her side burned. For someone who ran five miles a day, this was weird. "I don't want to make a hasty decision. As much as love factors into it, love can't be the only reason I say yes. I need to think things through."

Caroline looked over her shoulder at her. "Race you to the trailhead?"

Not cool. First, she questioned her enough to make her breath catch, then she pulled ahead and now she wanted to race? Why did she like this woman again? Before she had a chance to respond, Caroline sprinted away. Never one to let anyone get the best of her, Sarah raced to catch up, and she pulled ahead at the last possible minute.

Satisfaction bubbled in her chest as she bent over, hands on her knees, and waited for her breath to even out. "Beat you!"

"Barely," Caroline panted. "Are you happy?"

Still trying to get her breathing under control, Sarah took up a slow jog and Caroline kept pace with her. "Why wouldn't I be?"

Caroline waved a hand over the length of her. "You're dressed like you're in mourning, you're not wearing your ring, you never come home and you haven't kept in touch. I want to make sure you're okay. This is me, remember? Maybe we haven't seen each other in a long time, but you can tell me anything."

Jogging in silence, Sarah considered Caroline's question, and her face burned. "I'll try to be better. I promise."

"You didn't answer my question," Caroline said.

A few early dog walkers approached them, and the two women moved aside to make room. The dogs pulled on their leashes, as if they wanted to join them, but the owners maintained control, and Sarah and Caroline continued on their way. Anger bubbled beneath the surface of Sarah's skin.

"My job gives me deep satisfaction. I love what I'm doing. DC is exactly where I want to be."

Caroline held her gaze.

Sarah let out a sigh. She'd promised to be a better friend and yelling at Caroline wouldn't help. But why did her friend doubt her? She needed a job where she could make a difference. Matthew understood and could help her achieve it. It was one of the things she found most attractive about him.

"Of course I'm happy."

"I'm not going in there," Sarah argued outside Isaacson's Deli.

"I'm not that cruel," Caroline said. "Aaron doesn't work Wednesdays. Although you'll probably see him at temple."

Caroline had suggested breakfast after their run, and although Sarah agreed, she stopped dead in her tracks when Caroline paused in front of Aaron's deli. It was bad enough she went there once. She wasn't doing it again. She joined Caroline at the door.

"I know," Sarah said, the memory of Aaron's icy stare changing to nothing burning inside her.

"In or out, ladies. I can't have you blocking all my customers."

Sarah stiffened at the sound of Aaron's voice. Caroline's mouth opened, and she shifted her glance over Sarah's shoulder.

"Hey, Aaron. Sorry. I thought Wednesday was your day off."

He held open the door and smiled at the other woman. "Caroline. No problem. There are no days off leading up to the High Holidays."

Sarah turned to him, and he stiffened, but he kept the door open.

"Are you coming in?" The timbre of his voice had deepened in the years since she'd left, his arm more muscular. Once again, his expression was blank, but his nostrils flared a little.

Sarah entered the deli, conscious of Aaron's presence behind her. His shoulders had broadened, and he'd grown a few inches. It was like walking in front of a bear and wondering if he was going to attack. The hair on the nape of her neck prickled.

She should forget about breakfast.

"Give me a second, and I'll help you out," Aaron called to Caroline.

A few people in business suits stood in line ordering breakfast, and some young mothers with strollers occupied a couple of tables in the back. Worn but clean linoleum floors, three large glass cases filled with meats and cheeses—separated so as not to mix the two—and baskets of breads and rolls. The only new things were the tables and chairs. The smells—garlic, grease and yeast, with the sharp tang of pickles. She inhaled, and her stomach rumbled. *Traitor.*

After chatting with the businesspeople, joking with the moms and making faces at the babies, Aaron walked behind the counter and turned to Caroline. "What can I get you?"

"Fried egg and cheese on a roll, please."

He smiled, and Sarah's breath caught. Once that smile had been directed at her. It changed his entire face. His blue eyes glowed and reminded her of the sun rising over Masada during her trip to Israel as a teen. His cheeks stretched and little lines appeared next to his nose—he'd never had those before, but somehow, they fit. She blinked. She was *not* admiring the smile of a man who refused to give her the time of day.

"You always order the same thing," he teased.

I guess she comes here often.

He wrote it up and reached for a roll. His arm muscles flexed as he sliced the roll and moved to the griddle, where he cracked two eggs. She looked away. The early morning air must be making her woozy.

"Well, I know what I like," her friend said.

Nostalgia for the old days hit her and her belly fluttered.

"What about you?" He directed the question to her, his expression shuttered. The laughter and ease disappeared. He was a man behind a counter.

"I'm not very hungry," Sarah said.

He examined her, his gaze traveling up and down her body, not in some sexy melt-your-bones kind of way, but more like a disappointed grandma who was offended by her offspring's refusal to eat.

"Guess that explains it," he said.

Taken aback, Sarah studied herself in the reflection of the glass case. Her black spandex leggings and top left nothing to the imagination. She should be embarrassed. But she'd thought they were going running, not running into an ex-boyfriend. And besides, she'd worked hard at keeping her figure trim. Matthew loved the way she looked.

"What's wrong with how I look?" She bit her lip, wondering why she even asked him. As though she needed his approval.

He seasoned the eggs and flipped them before answering. "Not a thing. Fits you perfectly."

Sarah shivered. Objectively, there was nothing wrong with what he said. But Sarah wasn't objective when it came to this man. And Aaron definitely meant something.

She played with the strap of her sports bra and ran her hands down to her waist, not breaking eye contact with Aaron. "Yes, it does, doesn't it?" Only when his cheeks above his beard darkened and his lids lowered, did she turn toward her friend.

"I'll meet you outside."

Five minutes later, after Sarah berated herself for rising to the bait, Caroline joined her outside the deli and handed her an iced coffee. "I thought you'd want one to cool off."

Sarah's eyes widened with longing. "Absolutely. Thanks. What do I owe you?"

"An explanation for what happened in there." She nodded toward Aaron inside the deli.

"So much for him being off on Wednesdays." She should have ignored the jerk.

"I can't believe he still holds a grudge. What's it been? Ten years since you two last saw each other?"

"When I came in yesterday, he didn't look pleased to see me, but I assumed he'd treat me like any other patron. Guess I was wrong." She took a sip. "Too bad he still makes an amazing coffee. You two seemed pretty friendly, though."

Caroline stared at her. "Aaron? We're just friends. So, what will you do now?"

Sarah fingered the keys in her pocket. "I'll spend time with my family and friends and figure out what to do about Matthew. It shouldn't be too hard to avoid Aaron."

Chapter Three

"Was that Caroline Weiss I overheard?" Aaron's mother asked as she walked into the front of the deli from the storeroom.

"Yup." He swiped the cloth across the counter for the hundredth time while he tried to forget about Sarah. At this rate, he'd have the cleanest deli in the county. Maybe the universe.

"Speak up, bub. No one likes a man who mumbles."

Aaron shook his head. His mother could hear Caroline from the other end of the deli, but not his response up close. He glanced over at her, sure she schemed about something, but unsure about what or why.

"She was in ordering breakfast."

"Alone?"

If only. "No, she was with a friend." *Please don't ask which friend.*

"I didn't hear anyone else with her."

If he told his mother about Sarah, she'd subject him to

the third degree. If he further said she'd walked out, his mother would accuse him of being rude to a customer, which he was. But said customer deserved it, even if the conversation veered in a direction he hadn't anticipated, and now left him imagining his hands on her slim body. Sweat popped on his upper lip, making his mustache itch, as he remembered her running her palms along her silhouette. He needed to change the subject.

"Can I do anything for you, Mom?"

"What time are you going over to the temple to set up the social hall?"

He was a smart man and a smarter son. This was a trick question. "What time would you like me to go?"

Pride softened his mother's voice. "One o'clock should be early enough."

They weren't due to start setting up until two. The temple employed staff who were paid to follow the floor plan, especially since it was the same floor plan they'd used since Aaron could remember. But he also knew his mother. She was a perfectionist and any perceived mistake, no matter how small, would puncture her like an arrow to the heart.

"I'll go right after lunch."

She reached over and cupped his cheek. "You're a good man."

He held on to her wrist and memories of her love and concern washed over him. This hand still held more strength than any he'd ever known. It had cared for him and his siblings when they were sick or sad. It had pointed the way when they were lost or wrong. And it showed love. He'd do anything for his parents. Always.

He rose and placed a kiss on the top of her gray head. "Let me get some work done before I have to leave."

Aaron arrived at the temple a couple of minutes after

one o'clock. He hopped out of his van, rang the buzzer to announce himself and walked into the temple. The lobby was welcoming, with flowers and Judaic art. There were photos of the rabbi, cantor and leadership interspersed with posters announcing upcoming events. Off to the side was a comfortable seating area in front of a set of doors. He entered those doors and was ushered into the administrator's office.

"Aaron, how nice to see you," Ruth Meyers said, winking at him. "Here to get an early start?"

He handed her a bag filled with her favorite sandwich. "You know my mom likes to make sure everything is perfect."

"She has nothing to worry about. Go on upstairs if you want. The staff will be here soon to get started. And I have a few volunteers coming as well."

"Great. We'll be done in no time. Thanks for all your help."

Aaron meandered upstairs on autopilot. This place was as much a part of him as his own home. He'd grown up here, become a bar mitzvah and confirmand here and someday planned to marry here. At one time, he'd thought his bride would be Sarah. Or Melissa. Now, he had no idea, and the uncertainty made him sad.

He entered the social hall. Its high ceilings and one wall of windows made the room appear large and airy. Decorated in shades of ivory and gray, it offered a neutral backdrop for any occasion. For the luncheon, with tables set with flowers, buffets filled with food and people mingling, it would be an appropriate start to the New Year.

Though he knew where everything would go, he walked the perimeter of the room, mentally double checking his plan, the same way he always did it. Hosting the temple's

Rosh Hashanah luncheon enabled his family to give back to the community, and it filled him with pride.

The doors swung open, and three men interrupted his perusal of the room.

"Hey, Aaron, we're ready for you."

As Aaron told them which tables went where, a voice behind him sent chills up the nape of his neck.

"Hi, I hear you need volunteers."

He turned around.

Sarah.

Sarah stopped short and swallowed the gasp that threated to escape her lips. Aaron's presence shouldn't have surprised her. This was his family's event. Still, when her father had asked her to take his place and help set up, he'd positioned it as not disappointing the temple or Mrs. Isaacson. Sarah had said yes, picturing an older woman directing people.

Not her son.

Didn't he have a deli to run?

A bump from behind made her realize she'd stopped midstride. Finding her composure—or at least pretending to—she continued her walk across the dance floor to where Aaron and some staff members stood.

"What are you doing here?" Aaron's voice was rough, his tone accusatory.

Sarah straightened her spine. "My dad was supposed to help set up, but his back is bothering him. He sent me instead."

For what seemed like the hundredth time, Aaron gave her a blank expression. Sarah's pulse pounded in her ears. Stay or go?

She was not letting this guy run her off.

"What can I do to help?" Her gaze bounced off Aaron's

stony features and skipped across the staff members, who smiled at her.

"We're moving tables into Aaron's configuration," one of them said. He pointed to the round tables stacked against the wall. Other volunteers walked into the room and soon, they all arranged tables according to the diagram.

It was mindless work, which suited Sarah fine because she couldn't concentrate on anything but the man in charge. The man who did his best to ignore her and make her feel unwelcome. But this was her temple, too, and she had as much right to be here as he did.

Memories assaulted her from every corner of the room— shul-ins with twenty to thirty youth group teens staying up all night laughing, countless social action projects spread throughout the room and Purim carnivals.

And the common denominator through all those things… Aaron.

He'd been her partner in crime, vice president to her president position in youth group and, of course, her boy-friend. As she constructed tables and placed them around the room, she wondered if she had been active as a teen because of Aaron, or if he was someone who made her activity more enjoyable? They'd kept a routine through-out high school. She'd bring the coffee, and he'd bring black-and-white cookies from his store. It wasn't some-thing they'd planned, but it became a tradition. And now, watching Aaron—taller, broader and stonier—set up the long buffet tables across the room, she longed for the sticky sweetness of the cookie.

Stupid memory. She didn't need the calories. Matthew would never approve. And she'd never fit into the clothes he loved her in. She brushed a hand across the stomach of her black skinny jeans, pushed up the sleeves of her black top and straightened the table she'd moved. Perfect.

Looking around, she noticed a slowdown in activity. Could they be finished already? With this number of volunteers, probably. She walked over to a man nearby.

"Are we done?" she asked.

He nodded. "I believe so. Hey, Aaron!" he called. "Need anything else?"

"Nah, we're good, Saul." He smiled at him, but as he turned toward Sarah, his expression hardened.

Saul walked away, but Sarah remained where she was. "What about tablecloths?"

"Don't worry about it," Aaron said.

Sarah looked around at the uncovered tables. "I'm sure your mother wouldn't want the tables left like this. Besides, if the linens don't have time to sit, they'll be wrinkled for the event. Do you want to risk her wrath?"

Although his stiff stance didn't change, a light flush reddened his neck and cheeks above his beard, giving her satisfaction. With a curt nod, he strode to a box and pulled out the linens. She joined him, and after a pause so filled with recrimination, she could practically hear the buzz, he handed her a pile. There were a few volunteers left in the room, and ten minutes later, all the tables were covered with ivory cloths.

"They should be steamed." Sarah stared at the wrinkles in the floor-length cloths.

"The temple staff will take care of it," one of the volunteers said.

Although she shouldn't care, Sarah glanced at Aaron for confirmation. She was here. She wasn't about to leave the job incomplete. Her dad wouldn't like it. And Aaron's mother was a perfectionist. There was no way she'd accept wrinkled cloths for her event.

He nodded, more toward the volunteer than Sarah. "That's right."

"I'll go, then," Sarah said.

The other volunteers smiled at her and said goodbye, joining her on the way out. Aaron was silent and remained in the room.

By the time she reached her car, Sarah was fuming. She and Aaron had broken up ten years ago, and he couldn't even bother with some mindless chitchat? Never mind common courtesy. No matter how much her dad might have needed her to do this, she wasn't about to put up with this kind of treatment. No more. She came home to be with her family, and that's what she'd do. She'd have to invent an excuse to avoid the luncheon.

Sliding into the front seat of her rental car, she fastened her seat belt and turned the ignition. Nothing. Frowning, she tried again. *Are you kidding me?* She tried once more before she got out and opened the hood.

"This is my reward for trying to do a *mitzvah*," she mumbled. Nothing in the engine looked out of place or problematic, not that she'd know. With a sigh, she reached for the hood.

"Problem?"

She screeched at the deep voice behind her, let the hood slam, turned and glared at Aaron, who stood a few feet away. God, he was gorgeous. With the light hitting him, his reddish-brown hair glowed red, like fire. Shadows accentuated the planes of his face. Arms folded across his chest drew attention to his biceps. She swallowed. Even *schmucks* could be hot. Not that she should notice.

"My car won't start." She reached into the car for her phone.

"Let me take a look."

"You're a mechanic, too?"

He raised an eyebrow. "Start the car when I tell you."

She swallowed a retort about domineering men who

thought they could tell women what to do. The only way she'd get away from this man was by getting her car started. If he could help her with it, it was worth her silence.

The open hood blocked her view of him, but through the crack between the hood and the engine, his hands moved. Powerful hands that had once moved over her body. Her skin prickled.

"Try it now," he said.

She turned the key. "Nothing."

"Hold on." He fiddled some more. "Try it again."

She did. "Still nothing."

He let the hood drop shut. "You'll have to get it towed and looked at."

No kidding. She nodded. "Thanks." Once again, she reached for her phone.

He walked away but stopped after a few steps.

He had a great ass. The close-fitting denim only served to accentuate it. *Okay hormones, enough already.*

Back still toward her, he raised his arm and ran a hand through his hair. "Come on. I'll give you a ride."

"No."

He turned, his movement slow, rigid, shooting her a look filled with exasperation. "What do you mean, no?"

"You're not giving me a ride."

"Why not?"

"I'll call my parents."

"Who will then ask why I'm not giving you a ride."

She shrugged. "So?"

He sighed. "I don't leave people stranded without a ride. Even you."

"Wow, I feel honored. What, are you afraid your mom will find out?

His Adam's apple bobbed, confirming she was right, and she stifled a laugh. "I'll tell them you already left."

"Get in my van, Sarah."

It was the first time he'd said her name since she'd returned to town. His voice dipped and dragged across the second syllable the way it had so many years ago, and her knees went weak. No one said her name like that, not even Matthew. She'd dreamed about his voice for years. Unable to fight him, and hating her weakness, she locked the car and climbed into his van. She fastened her seat belt and scooted as close to the door as possible. The inside was filled with deli aromas from their deliveries—garlic, yeast, pickles. Her stomach growled.

"Hungry?" he asked as he pulled out of the temple parking lot.

"No."

He smirked. "Right."

She was not letting him goad her into anything. All she had to do was get through one quick car ride. "I don't care whether or not you believe me."

"Good, because you're a terrible liar," he said. "At least in my presence."

What was that supposed to mean? "Take me home, please."

How many times had they been in this van together? Memories of kissing across the console, fooling around in the back and staring at the moon and stars while wrapped in each other's arms filled Sarah's mind during the silent, ten-minute drive to her house. Out of the corner of her eye, she stared at his hands gripping the steering wheel. Large, square and strong with a light dusting of hair and freckles across the backs. She remembered how she'd counted those freckles with kisses, and her cheeks burned. He'd always been a careful driver, and today was no exception. But despite the calm maneuvering of his van, his fingers were clasped tight around the wheel. She risked a peek at his profile. His jaw was clenched. Did he remember their past as well?

He pulled into her driveway and cut the engine, but still, he remained silent.

"Thanks for the ride." She unbuckled her seat belt and opened the door.

He nodded. "Need a mechanic?"

"I'll call the rental company."

Her front door opened, and her mom rushed out. "Aaron! It's good to see you! Come inside and say hello. It's been ages since you've been here."

Sarah's mouth opened, and she scoured her brain for some excuse so he wouldn't have to come inside. But her mind blanked, and she stood there like one of the whitefishes in Aaron's deli cases—mouth open, eyes glazed. This wouldn't do. Meanwhile, Aaron exited the van and approached her mother.

"It's good to see you, too, Mrs. Abrams." Straightening his shoulders, he walked with Sarah's mother into the house, leaving Sarah no choice but to follow.

Or abscond with the van. It was a reasonable choice. Tempting, too. Except she could imagine the headlines— "Jilted Woman Steals Ex-Lover's Van"—and the disproval on Matthew's face when he read them. Of course, she wouldn't have to decide about his proposal. Then again, she'd have a prison record and no future. With a sigh, she followed them into the house.

"So, tell me, Aaron, how are you? And your mom? I don't see her at the deli as often as I used to." Her mother pointed at the kitchen chair, and he sat.

"I'm busy with the deli. My parents have started to slow down. They're enjoying their grandkids and some time to themselves, when they don't pop in and make sure I don't destroy the place." He smiled.

Sarah inhaled. His smile lit his entire face and made his blue eyes glow.

"Oh, I'm sure they have complete faith in you."

Sarah remembered the faith and confidence Aaron's parents had shown toward all their children. But Aaron had always taken their faith to heart.

Sarah's mother put a plate with two stuffed cabbage rolls in front of him, and another plate with one in front of Sarah. "Eat, honey, you're too thin," her mother said to her.

Sarah shook her head. "No, I'm not, Mom, but thank you. How's Dad's back?"

She pushed the food around on her plate. Normally, she ate salads for lunch. Pulling the cabbage away from the beef, she scraped off some of the sauce before she stuck a forkful in her mouth. She closed her eyes in pleasure at its sweetness. God, she'd missed this. Opening her eyes, she speared the meat and dug in.

"Better, honey. Thanks for giving him time to rest. See, you do eat!"

Sarah let the comment pass.

"This is delicious," Aaron said. "I guess Mom hasn't been successful in getting your recipe?"

Her mother laughed. "No, despite multiple attempts." Her gaze moved between Sarah and Aaron. "It's nice to see the two of you together again."

The meat Sarah had eaten roiled in her stomach. She placed her fork on the table and pulled in three deep breaths. When she was sure of her composure, she looked up and met Aaron's glance. He looked about as pleased as she did. *Great.*

"Her car wouldn't start. I offered her a ride."

"That was very nice of you, Aaron," her mother said. "You always had a heart of gold."

His neck flushed, but he hid his expression behind a

sip of water. "Thanks for the lunch, Mrs. Abrams. It was great to see you again." He rose.

Her mother turned to her. "Sarah, you should walk him out. We'll see you at services, Aaron. Thanks for visiting."

Did her mother think she was five? She was a grown woman with manners. Of course, she *had* planned on letting him walk out alone. With a nod to her mother, she followed Aaron down the hall.

"I know my way out, Sarah." He didn't look at her.

"I know you do. Thank you for the ride."

He turned to her, hands in his pockets, his gaze focused somewhere beyond her left ear. "It was no big deal."

And suddenly, she didn't want him to leave. Not yet, when she'd gotten a glimpse of the Aaron she used to know. "This was…" she said, "…almost like old times."

"Since when do you care about 'old times'?"

"What do you mean?" She leaned on the newel post at the bottom of the oak stairs.

"Your dreams were always bigger than this place, and you haven't been home in ages. I'm surprised you remember old times."

"I remember a lot more than you think." She took a step forward and inhaled his scent. Her emotions ricocheted from anger to frustration to confusion.

His blue eyes bore into hers. "So do I."

Aaron focused on his van and counted the steps between him and it to keep from turning around and going back toward her—toward Sarah. His hands shook. He clenched them into fists and gritted his teeth to keep from screaming.

Inside his van, he let out his pent-up breath and drove away from her house.

When he was sure his van was no longer visible, he

pulled over, rested his forehead on the steering wheel and inhaled. The scent of her perfume filled his nostrils.

Why the hell had he given her a ride? His oldest brother would call it his knight-in-shining-armor complex. One twin would call him a glutton for punishment. The other twin would tell him he'd done it to show her he was a better person. His sister-in-law would laugh at all of them and say he was still attracted to Sarah.

His sister-in-law would be correct. He was more than attracted to Sarah. Thank God his sister-in-law wasn't here.

Why the hell did he still want the one woman who took his heart, squeezed it dry, stomped on it and returned it to him useless?

It wasn't because of her looks. She'd lost weight, straightened her hair and wore black. The Sarah he'd been in love with was rounder, colorful and natural. Not some two-dimensional magazine model.

It wasn't because of her personality. She was no longer the Sarah he'd once known. She was calm and quiet with perfect manners. The Sarah he'd fallen in love with filled the room with her laughter. She'd teased him without mercy, and he'd let her, just to see her face light up with joy. There was no joy in her expression now.

It certainly wasn't because she was home. He had no idea how long she was staying, but it was only temporary. Like their relationship. It was the one lesson he'd learned and learned the hard way. No matter what she might say to the contrary, her love for him hadn't been strong enough to stay here. Her dreams were too big for this place, and for him. She'd never sacrifice for him. The night he'd surprised her in DC confirmed his suspicions.

She'd changed.

So why was he sitting in his van on the side of the road,

like a pathetic weirdo, mooning over her? He didn't have an answer. Shaking his head, he rolled down the window to air out the van and headed to his parents' house.

"You're home!" His mother greeted him with a rib-cracking hug, as usual, and he shook his head. No matter how often he saw his parents, and it was at least once a day, she always greeted him like a long-lost relative.

"Tell me about the temple setup." She dragged him into the family room and pushed him onto the couch. "Pushed" was a little bit of an exaggeration. She was small and round, and he outweighed her by at least one hundred pounds. But she was his mother, and he let her guide him anywhere she wanted. "The tables have to be perfect. We want everyone to not only enjoy the food but *schmooze* and be comfortable."

"The room looks the same way it does every year." He reached into his pocket and removed his phone. "Here, I took a photo of it for you."

He handed her the phone and waited while she studied it, zoomed in and practically climbed into the phone while examining the room from every angle.

"It's perfect, Aaron." She patted his cheek. "How long did it take to set up? Did you have enough volunteers?"

"We were finished in less than an hour."

She frowned. "Was there traffic?"

"No, I had to make a stop first." Temple was ten minutes away, if you drove the speed limit. But he didn't want to tell his mother the truth.

"Oh no, did the temple run out of tables or chairs? Or supplies? We can't have this luncheon ruined. Please tell me we have—"

"I had to drop Sarah Abrams home, and her mother invited me in."

The look on his mother's face made him want to hide under the sofa. She looked like he'd perfected the recipe for brisket, which was already perfect, since it was hers. But if it could be more perfect, this is what she'd look like. "Oh, Aaron, that's wonderful! How is she?"

"Fine."

"Why did she need a ride home?"

Because God hates me.

"Her car wouldn't start."

"You fixed it, right?"

"It's a rental. They'll take care of it."

"It was nice of you to offer to drive her home."

He grunted.

"Was it good to see her?"

He'd never suffer through this questioning from anyone else. But his mother was…his mother, and he gave her latitude. And she didn't know about his secret visit to DC. So she had no idea how "not good" it was to see Sarah. He shrugged.

"You should give her another chance."

"She's not interested." There was latitude and there was masochism.

"She's here, Aaron."

He peered around his mother to see if there was some sign to indicate she'd taken a position working for a dating service. Nothing hung on the painted blue walls except family photos and some artwork his parents purchased on their last trip to Israel. "We're good as is, but thanks."

"As is? What's 'as is'? Why do you think she volunteered to help set up if not to see you?"

He hadn't given it a single thought. But now that his mother planted the seed, he couldn't ignore the question. Why did she come?

His mother wore a knowing grin, as if she'd followed along with his silent thoughts.

"Gotta go, Mom."

"Mmm-hmm."

Her laughter echoed as he shut the door.

Chapter Four

Ten minutes after Aaron left her house, Sarah was in her bedroom when the phone rang. "Hey, babe, how are you?" Matthew asked.

She slid her feet out of her shoes and sank onto her bed. The blue-and-green room from her childhood was filled with memories—photos of she and her friends laughing at a football game, a program from a school play she'd costarred in, her red rose prom corsage, stuffed animals, teen heartthrob magazines. She scanned them while holding the phone to her ear. She'd been such a different person when she'd lived here. It was hard reconciling the girl she'd been with the woman she'd become.

Matthew was her ideal, her life as she pictured it moving forward. He was easy and uncomplicated. It was good hearing his voice.

"I'm fine—my rental car, not so much." She filled him in on how it broke down, leaving out Aaron's rescue. Somehow, she didn't think he'd appreciate hearing that.

"I finally got a meeting with the senator's aide."

She lay in her bed and stared at the lines in the ceiling. She used to count them before she fell asleep. At one time, when she'd been in love with Aaron, she'd played "He loves me, he loves me not" with them.

"That's fantastic," she said. "When is it?"

"Tomorrow. Wish you were here to celebrate with me."

Me, too. "If the meeting goes well, we can celebrate when I get home." She envisioned the Michelin-starred DC restaurant he'd take her to, with champagne and a night of lovemaking afterward, and her heart raced with anticipation. He treated her like a fairy-tale princess.

"I'll hold you to that," he said. "So, what have you been doing?"

"I helped set up our Rosh Hashanah luncheon, went for a run with Caroline and Jessica and I are going out tonight to some new bar in town." Of all her friends from home, Jessica was the only one Sarah hadn't offended. She'd sent Sarah a text earlier that day, expressing pleasure she was home and inviting her out that night. Sarah had been happy to accept.

"A bar? You couldn't come up with any place nicer?"

Sarah laughed. "This isn't DC, Matthew, and we're not going into New York. The bar has karaoke, and a whole group is going. It will be fun."

"If you say so. Girls or guys?"

He'd never asked that question of her before. "Jess mentioned a group going, but I have no idea. Does it matter? We're catching up."

His breath was audible through the phone. "As long as that's all it is."

"Since when are you so possessive?" Her shoulders tensed at the idea of him restricting her movements. Didn't he trust her?

"I don't mean to be. I miss you."

Some of the tension eased. "I miss you, too. But you don't need to worry about me. What happened to trust?"

"You're right. I'm sorry. Hey, it's good you're keeping up with your running while you're home."

Sarah's head spun at the sudden change in topic. She should bring the conversation around again to trust, but she didn't want to get into an argument. She was looking forward to seeing Jessica and didn't want a bad mood to sour it. Maybe she was overreacting. She loved Matthew, and he deserved the benefit of the doubt. So, she paused and collected herself.

"I forgot how pretty the trails are around here," she said, deciding she'd run on one of them next time.

"I hope you're being safe."

"Always."

"Good. Call me tonight when you get home."

She shook her head. "It'll be late. We'll talk tomorrow."

"Okay. Have fun—but not too much." His laughter, laced with an edgy undertone, rang out across the line.

"No worries. I'll tell you all about it tomorrow."

Aaron ducked beneath the doorway of the new karaoke bar in town and waited for his eyesight to adjust to the dim lighting. What the hell was he doing here? His brother had dragged him here, insisting he'd have a blast.

He liked bars. He and his friends frequented one or two favorites in town. Those were quiet, though—unassuming places where everyone knew everyone else. And people he knew owned them. Reruns of *Cheers* flashed through his mind as he thought about them, and he shook his head. He was not Norm.

But this place. The owner was from New York. He'd met the man once at a town hall meeting. The guy reminded him of Jimmy Smits. He was friendly and donated to local causes. In fact, he liked the owner. But the place? It was made for singles and bachelorette parties and milestone birthdays. There was a stage with spotlights, a bar with fancy drinks he guaranteed were overpriced and pounding background music to fill the air until the singing started.

If you could call karaoke singing. More like people making fools of themselves.

God help him. The only reason he'd agreed was because he was in a lousy mood after seeing Sarah, and his brother had caught him in a moment of weakness. Even if there was more to life than work, he wasn't going to sing.

He waved to the Jimmy Smits look-alike and sat at a table for two.

A strong hand clapped him on the back. Aaron turned.

"Jordan." Aaron greeted his brother.

"You made it."

"No idea why." Aaron shrugged.

Jordan laughed. "I think you're secretly glad I suggested this."

His brother was nuts. They sat at a table and ordered two beers and a plate of nachos.

"Then you don't know me as well as you think," Aaron said.

"Come on, it'll be fun. You need to loosen up."

His brother was right. "You really come here and do this?"

Jordan took a swig of beer and pointed to the stage with the bottle. "It's entertaining."

"Hearing other people butcher songs is entertaining?" Aaron shook his head. "I don't like when talented artists cover other singers' songs. Why would I like random people doing it?"

Digging around in the pile of nachos, Jordan found one

to his liking and stuffed it in his mouth. "Lighten up, big brother."

"Okay ladies and gentlemen," the announcer's voice interrupted. "Get your song requests in!"

A group of people rushed the host, and Aaron shook his head. Maybe he could beat the crowds and leave now. Before his ears started bleeding. But that would mean ditching his brother, and he'd never do that. He sighed.

"Got a song you want to sing?" his brother asked.

"Nope."

Jordan laughed and settled into his seat.

The first group on stage was a bachelorette party. The six women butchered Madonna's "Like a Prayer."

"Really?" Aaron groaned when the song finally ended, and the giggling mass returned to their table.

"Come on. The ladies were nice to look at."

He wasn't here to look at ladies. The thought brought him up short. Since when wasn't he interested in looking at women? When had he become such a downer?

A guy and a girl sang "Private Eyes" by Hall & Oates. They stared into each other's eyes as if they were the only two there. The guy caressed her face, the girl stepped closer to him, until there was barely space between them. They gyrated together, arms and legs in sync and everywhere.

"I think they need a room," Aaron murmured.

"Jealous?"

"Nope. You?"

Jordan looked at him sideways. "Maybe a little."

"So, go up there and sing. I'll bet half a dozen women will come up to you afterward."

Jordan nodded. "Maybe. Hey, isn't that Sarah?"

Aaron's stomach clenched as he stared at the group onstage singing The B-52's "Love Shack." Why did he keep running into her? Did the universe have something against him? Three other women sang with her, but his gaze kept straying back to Sarah. A quick glance around revealed he wasn't alone. A shaft of jealousy shot through him, competing with a surge of need to protect her. She wore a formfitting, black mini dress—her apparent color of choice—with little left to the imagination. Under the spotlights, her small waist accentuated the outline of her breasts and her long legs. He suppressed the urge to race up there and cover her with a blanket. Or a table. Without meaning to, he let out a growl, and as soon as the song ended, he strode toward her.

"What are you doing?" He stood next to the stage exit, arms folded across his chest.

Her eyes wide, she moved to walk past him, but he blocked her way.

"Singing," she said. "Let me pass."

Her perfume filled his nostrils, and he nearly staggered with need.

She glared at him. "Why do you care?"

"All the guys in here were staring at you."

Her face flushed and she glanced around. "Again, why do you care?"

His pulse pounded in his ears, and he wanted to yell. But he couldn't yell here, not without making a scene, which he was pretty sure he was already making. Not to mention that she'd asked a damned good question and he had no plausible answer. With another growl, he turned around and stomped to his table.

Jordan stared at him. "I think we should go and sing."

"Why the hell would I do that?"

"Because you need something to release all that energy."

Before he could protest, Jordan dragged him up to the host and thrust the songbook at him. "Pick something."

Aaron shook his head. "No."

"Then I will."

Aaron grabbed the book and pointed to the first song he saw.

Jordan smirked. "Pretty appropriate, I guess."

The host cued "Cry Me A River" by Justin Timberlake, and Aaron was forced to follow along or look like an idiot on the stage. Not that he didn't already. He and his siblings had sung in their temple choir growing up. Their voices were passable—better than some, worse than others. But as he sang the words flashing across the screen, he couldn't help keeping one eye on Sarah.

She sat at a table with the three other women, one of whom he recognized vaguely from high school. A spotlight shone on her, giving her dark hair blue highlights. She stilled as he sang about finding out what she'd done.

He didn't realize how appropriate the song was until the lyrics poured from his mouth, along with the hurt he'd felt at her betrayal. His heart thudded at the memory of seeing the man enter her apartment building, their silhouettes in the window and the man's head as it tipped down to kiss her. He tried clearing away the image, but it burned anyway.

His weekend surprise had been ruined.

Aaron's pulse quickened. His life plans had been altered irrevocably. He thought he'd gotten past the hurt, but seeing Sarah now brought everything back, especially when she stood up to him. How could she have done what she did, changed so much, yet sit there unaffected? He'd now run into her three times, and she'd yet to apologize.

When the music stopped, everyone in the audience clapped except Sarah. Maybe she wasn't as unaffected as he'd thought.

Good.

"You coming?" Jordan laid a hand on his arm, bringing him back to awareness.

Aaron nodded and followed him off the stage to their table at the other side of the room.

"Enjoy yourself up there?" Jordan asked.

"No."

"Funny, you seemed pretty into it." Jordan leaned back in his chair. "Oh look, she's going up again."

This time, only one friend accompanied Sarah. He recognized the woman, Jessica…something. After a couple seconds, the music cued, and they sang "Somebody That I Used to Know" by Gotye.

Sarah swayed as she sang, her motions mesmerizing him. Her hips undulated back and forth, and his mouth dried. He couldn't take his gaze off her.

Jordan leaned over and whispered in his ear. "She's singing for you, you know."

Startled, Aaron listened to the lyrics, about treating her like a stranger and cutting her off.

What the hell? She left, not him. He'd tried to convince her to stay, to find a job here, and she'd refused. He rose, determined to confront her, but Jordan stopped him.

"Easy, brother. You don't want to make another scene."

Aaron looked around, noticing for the first time how all the women in the room were joining in. His brother was right.

"Plus, we have enough sins to atone for on Yom Kippur. You don't want to add to them."

He glared at his brother. "She's baiting me."

"Or you sang, and she responded."

"I'm not the one who should apologize."

Jordan shook his head. "You will be if you don't sit."

With his pulse pounding in his ears, he sat, irritated at

his brother, but whether it was for defending Sarah, bringing him here in the first place or being right, he didn't know.

Two more groups butchered songs before he'd had enough. Stalking toward the stage once again, he cut in front of another group and demanded his chance.

"Um, sir, you need to wait your turn," the host stammered.

Aaron glared at him and the other group, thankful his size gave him an edge.

"That's okay. He can go first," one of the people in the group said.

"Let him have a turn," a drunk guy shouted.

With a nod, Aaron pointed at the song he wanted, grabbed the microphone and stood on stage. The introduction to Marvin Gaye's "I Heard It Through The Grapevine" played and he waited for the words. He needed to get this right. He watched her once again as he sang about seeing her with someone else.

Sarah paused, her drink halfway to her lips as she listened to his song. Aaron's heart beat with satisfaction and his testosterone flared as the other men in the audience got in on the game. They joined in as he sang about how she should have told him she loved someone else.

Sarah mouthed something to her friends, flung her chair away from the table and left the bar before he finished singing. Now, with her gone, he somehow became one of those pathetic singers he'd tried not to be. His voice cracked as he finished the song, and without another word, he returned to his table, oblivious to the deafening roars from the men in the room.

"Maybe now you'll talk to her?" Jordan asked.

"What do you mean?"

"That was your passive-aggressive way of letting her know you're pissed. She knows. So go talk to her."

"I'm not pissed," Aaron said, his beer tasting more bitter than it should. "I'm uninterested."

"You're also a liar."

"She's probably gone." He rose anyway and headed outside to see.

It took him a minute or so to find her, and when he did, he swore to himself. He raced along the sidewalk and tapped her on the shoulder.

She paused a moment before realizing it was him, then spun away from him.

"Hold on," he said. "You shouldn't walk at night alone."

"Again, why do you care?" she asked over her shoulder.

"Because it's not safe."

"Ha." She snorted. "This town is perfectly safe."

Aaron's temples pounded. "I don't care if you're used to DC. Women shouldn't walk alone in the dark. Where the hell are your friends?"

"Chauvinist much?"

He folded his arms across his chest and stared at her. Her panting made her chest rise and fall. Against his will, he was drawn to her. He gritted his teeth and focused on her mouth. That was worse. Her delectable lips were pursed. He remembered how sweet they tasted. Now was not the time to remember any of that.

"Where are your friends, and why aren't they with you?" he ground out.

She folded her arms and glared at him. "Still inside. *They're* having fun."

"You looked like you were enjoying yourself."

"Were you watching me?" One side of her mouth quirked in a self-satisfied smile.

His shoulders tightened. "You were performing for the crowd, not hiding under the table."

She looked away. His hand itched to draw her to him, but he made a fist and ignored the pull.

"Why did you come after me?" she asked.

"Why did you leave?"

"I'm not in the mood to play games." She flicked her hair off her shoulder, anger sharpening her movements.

"That's not what your song choice said."

Shit.

Aaron's vision tunneled as if observing himself from far away. In the middle of the sidewalk was the last place to let out his feelings—feelings he'd thought were long ago laid to rest. Hell, he'd proposed to Melissa. True, he'd been unable to go through with the wedding, but he'd thought he was long over Sarah.

"It's karaoke. You're really going to read into what I sang?" she asked.

"Considering what you were singing, I don't think reading into them is far-fetched."

"So, I should read into your songs?" She arched an eyebrow. "Okay. You were trying to send me a message."

"And if I was? What would you do then?"

"I'd say you were an idiot." She spun around and began walking away again.

"Wait a minute." He moved in front of her, grasping her arm. "You don't get to call me names and walk away."

"Why not? You get to glare at me, when you bother to acknowledge my presence, and then escape. At least I'm talking to you."

"You call this talking?" He knew he should let go of her arm, but her warmth penetrated through the fabric of her light coat and her scent tantalized him. Though he couldn't stand her, he also couldn't let go of her.

Once again, her eyes flashed, their long lashes fluttering as she widened them. "Words. Coming out of the mouth. Talking."

Standing beneath the glow of the streetlight, he couldn't stop staring at her lips. They were plump, like he remembered them. His heart raced faster, and he stepped closer. Her mouth opened into an *oh*, and her pulse fluttered in her neck. For the first time since she'd come to town, he wanted to kiss her.

All the reasons he shouldn't flooded his brain.

She'd left.

She'd betrayed him.

He was over her.

But one by one they petered out. His pulse pounded in his ears. Her scent filled his nostrils.

He slid his hand behind her neck and crashed his mouth onto hers. Every nerve ending in his body fired. Desire filled him. And…

"No!" She pushed him away, chest heaving.

Before he could do anything, she turned and ran down the street. Away from him, once again.

No, no, no. She wiped the back of her hand across her mouth, but the imprint of Aaron's lips on hers remained as she sat in her dad's car in the parking garage.

She shouldn't have kissed him.

She hadn't. *He'd* kissed her.

And it was glorious.

Chills ran along her spine, her stomach housed a kaleidoscope of butterflies and she resisted the urge to lick her lips to see if they still tasted like him.

It didn't matter if they tasted like Aaron, chocolate and truffles combined—if that was even a combination that tasted good. Because Aaron and his lips were off-limits.

She was engaged to Matthew. Or almost. Matthew, with his cool composure, his drive to be a successful influencer in Washington, DC. His support of her dreams.

Matthew was everything Aaron wasn't. And Matthew was the one she was supposed to think about.

Not Aaron and his luscious kisses.

Luscious kisses?

She groaned.

No, no, no.

Are you okay?

The text from Jessica pinged.

Nope. Yes, I'm fine. In my car. Going home.

Okay, drive safe. See you soon?

Yes.

With a deep, shaky breath, she started the car and drove home.

Much later, long after she'd gone to bed, the ringing of her cell phone jolted her out of a fitful sleep and a dream about a bullfight between Aaron and Matthew.

"H-hello?" Her voice was scratchy, and her head pounded.

"Meet me outside."

"Aaron?" She squinted as she pulled the phone away and checked the time.

"Meet me outside."

"Aaron, it's five o'clock in the morning. I'm still in bed."

"Get out of bed and come outside."

"No, it's too early."

"If you don't come outside, I'll pound on your front door. And your parents will wake up and they'll want to know why I'm at your house. And I'll be forced to tell them about last night. Is that what you want?"

Oh God. "No."

"Then come outside."

She sighed. "Give me fifteen minutes."

"Ten."

She had no idea why she humored him. Yes, she did. It was early, she hadn't slept well and she hadn't had her first cup of coffee yet. Plus, she didn't want anyone knowing about last night, and she wouldn't put it past Aaron to make good on his promise to out her to her parents. She threw on a pair of black leggings and black zippered jacket, and she laced her sneakers and snuck downstairs.

A car sat in her driveway, idling. She opened the door and climbed in.

"Two minutes to spare," he said. "Good job."

"Why are you here?"

He put the car in reverse and pulled out of her driveway. "Because we need to talk." He handed her a cup of coffee. "It's a little early for black-and-whites."

Whether it was him telling her she was right, or the promise of a caffeine fix or his memory about the cookies, she didn't know. But she sipped the coffee and waited to see where Aaron was taking her. Outside, it was still dark with only a few cars on the road. They drove for ten minutes until he pulled into a parking area on the edge of a lake and community park.

"Come on." He got out of the car.

She followed, clutching her coffee. As teens, they'd often hung out here on warm summer evenings, dipping in the water, walking the trails and planning their futures. Had he taken her here because of the memories? Or had he turned into a killer while she was gone and planned to hide her body? He led her toward a picnic table, dropped a paper sack in front of her, then pulled out two breakfast sandwiches and handed one to her. At least he'd feed her first. The buttery smell wafted around her, and she withheld a groan of delight. Probably not a killer.

"Don't you have to work this morning?" She took a bite.

He nodded. "Later. Do you ever wear anything other than black?"

She glanced down at her clothes. "You gave me ten minutes."

"You came into my deli wearing black. You wore black at the temple. And last night you were wearing a black dress."

"You noticed."

Heat emanated from his gaze, and she tried restraining her satisfaction. He wasn't supposed to be attracted to her, nor she him. But it was flattering, nonetheless, in an "I told you so" kind of way.

"Never mind." He stared into the distance, and she used the opportunity to study him. His profile had hardened in the years since she'd known him. His face was all sharp angles and planes. The close-cropped beard softened those angles a little, but not much. He wasn't soft, not by a long shot.

He turned to her. "So, let's talk."

Her stomach plummeted. *Not about the kiss, anything but the kiss.* She channeled everything she'd learned in DC about coming across as calm and unruffled, folded her hands on the table and waited for Aaron to continue. The breakfast sandwich she'd eaten three bites of sat like a badly made matzah ball in her belly. As the silence stretched, she swallowed. "Go on."

Aaron ran a hand over his face. "You and I have a history."

"We do."

"But that's in the past. And as angry as I am, I think

it's better for both of us if we move beyond it. As for that kiss—"

She leaned forward. "Wait, *you're* angry? Why?"

His body stilled. "I know you've changed, Sarah, but playing stupid isn't a good look. Not for someone as smart as you."

Sarah closed her eyes. When she opened them, nothing had changed except the sky was a little lighter. "We broke up years ago. The distance was too much. But that's old news."

Especially since he'd let her go without a fight. Their calls and texts became fewer and more stilted until he'd admitted the distance was too much. He said he'd never leave his family and New Jersey, and they broke up. He never even gave her a chance to come up with a compromise or alternative.

His jaw flexed in the waxing daylight. "Jeez, I never knew you'd be this dense."

She jumped off the bench. "What the hell is your problem? We broke up ten years ago, and you disappeared off the face of the earth. No, I don't know why you're angry since you won't tell me. But let *me* tell *you* something." She stalked toward him and poked him hard in the chest. "Attacking me is not the way to have a conversation."

Spinning around, she stomped toward the trail that led around the park. So much for the calm and collected attitude she'd tried to perfect in DC. Her blood pounded in her ears.

"Sarah, wait!"

Now he said it. *Ten years too late, bud.* She kept walking. A long shadow approached, and his footfalls were next to her. She stuffed her hands in her pockets and kept moving. If he wanted to talk, he'd have to keep up with her.

He jumped in front of her and forced her to stop. She stared at his square fingers as they made fists at his sides.

"You're right, I shouldn't have attacked you. I'm sorry."

"We have to find a way to exist together," she said. "Because as much as I'd like to avoid you, it's not possible. We're going to the same synagogue for the holidays. We're in the same town." She hadn't expected they'd run into each other so often. Then again, this was her first time back home, and he was apparently more involved in the community than she'd realized. "I don't want to have to avoid an entire swath of my life to keep the peace."

Aaron stared off into the distance. His chest heaved and he clasped and unclasped his hands. Finally, after silent minutes passed, he turned to her. "How about we call a truce?"

Chapter Five

The numbers in the deli's accounting ledger swam before Aaron's eyes. He couldn't get Sarah out of his mind. How could she not know why he was angry? He'd seen her kiss another man. What was left to say? And speaking of kissing, the kiss he and Sarah shared last night. He still tasted her on his lips. His body still hardened when he thought about her. Hell, it hadn't been anything but hard since.

But he couldn't talk to her about the kiss because he'd have to confess he still possessed feelings for her after all this time. He thought he'd gotten over her. That's why he'd pursued a relationship with—and almost married—Melissa. Obviously, he hadn't. What kind of a desperate *putz* did that make him? And how could he possibly compete with Sarah's dreams? Even if he could, it wouldn't be fair to her.

Could he be friends with her? The colorful, joyful person he'd known had changed. She wore black. She was reserved, except when she was angry. Then a spark of the old Sarah returned—flashing brown eyes, ruddy olive cheeks. The spitfire he remembered. Not that he wanted her anger directed at him, but it was an improvement over the aloof Sarah she'd become. With the truce, would he adjust to her new personality? Or would he be able to evoke the old Sarah? And did he want to try? His pulse raced at the thought.

For the rest of the day, a low buzz of energy hummed beneath the surface. How much fun would it be to see if he could uncover a little of the old Sarah underneath the polished new one?

Later that afternoon, as he wrapped up work for the day, his phone rang.

"Hey, *Bubbe*, how's my favorite grandmother?"

"*Oy. Boychik*, I'm your only grandmother."

"Which is why I can call you my favorite without any guilt."

The older woman's thready voice rasped in a combination of a laugh and a wheeze. "I thought I was your favorite because I warn you when your mother and aunt are up to something."

"That, too."

"Good. They're up to something."

He sighed. "What now?"

"You know that Cohen girl?"

Aaron's mind drew a blank. There were a lot of Cohens in his world. "Can you be a little more specific?"

"Belongs to your synagogue."

"*Bubbe*, you need to give me more than that."

She groaned. "You know, she's a bank something or other, wears big earrings, has short, curly hair?"

"Stephanie?"

"Yes, that's her!"

"What about her?"

"They think you should date her."

"*Bubbe*, they think I should date a lot of women." Sarah first and foremost.

"True, but how many of them are they thinking of inviting to their Yom Kippur break fast?"

He slumped in his chair. In addition to sponsoring the temple's Rosh Hashanah luncheon, his parents hosted an "intimate" break fast after Yom Kippur for about thirty of their closest friends. Apparently, the Cohens, whose daughter was Stephanie, were about to be included.

"Are you sure?"

"Your mother and aunt are playing matchmaker. They're planning to throw you two together."

"Fan-damn-tastic." Stephanie Cohen was not his type. At all. Her voice grated on him, she was more concerned about not chipping her manicure than anything else and he couldn't hold a two-minute conversation with her.

"Watch your language, *boychik*!"

"Sorry, *Bubbe*." Now he'd have to figure out a way to convince his mother and aunt not to invite the Cohens.

"You can make it up by visiting me. This place is filled with old people. We need some young blood."

He laughed. The senior facility his grandmother lived in was beautiful, and she had a ton of friends. In fact, he'd bet her social life was better than his. "I'll try to visit tomorrow before temple."

"Good. And bring that Sarah girl with you."

His hand jerked, and he gripped his phone to keep from dropping it. "Excuse me?"

"You heard me, *boychik*. Only one of us is old enough to have hearing issues, and it's not you."

"How do you know about Sarah?"

"Please, I may live with old people, but we have the best

network of spies around. The CIA comes to us for advice. Besides, your mother told me."

"Ah."

"So, you'll bring her when you visit me tomorrow?"

He ran a hand through his short hair. "I have to see if she's available."

"Remind her I'm not getting any younger. I love you, Aaron."

"Love you, too, *Bubbe*."

He stared into space. Between his grandmother's desire, and his mother's and aunt's matchmaking plans, he needed a plan to head them off. Just because he and Sarah called a truce, didn't mean she liked being in his company. However, his grandmother wanted to see her. Having Sarah around would also help him foil his mother's matchmaking. And more importantly, maybe it could renew a friendship he'd missed.

He hated subterfuge. Dialing his phone again, he whispered a prayer for luck.

"Hello?"

"It's Aaron. Are you free for dinner tonight?"

There was a big difference between a truce and a dinner date, and none of the fashion sites Sarah frequented had a satisfactory suggestion about what to wear. Coming to a truce with the man whose presence had tied her in knots since she stepped foot into town meant no longer worrying about running into him. Having dinner with him, however, was an entirely different issue. They'd talk, which meant avoiding minefields. They'd spend time together, without *being* together. Her stomach clenched. Matthew had been jealous of her going to a bar with her girlfriends. What in the world was she supposed to tell him about having dinner with an ex-boyfriend?

She shook her head. Matthew would have to deal and appreciate she told him about it at all—which she'd do afterward. She was reconnecting with lots of people from her past. It was only natural she'd reconnect with Aaron. And maybe she'd be more inclined to visit again if she didn't have to worry about him.

Speaking of whom… He was picking her up in a half hour for dinner, and she didn't know what to wear. If she were in DC and going out with Matthew, it would be a no-brainer. Black cocktail dress, pearls, heels. But here, with Aaron, that wouldn't work. She pulled out a pair of black linen pants. Reaching for a black shell, she paused. Tilting her head, she peered into the back of her closet and spied a heather blue blouse left over from her days at home. She'd forgotten all about it. Pulling it forward, she studied it. Simple, with a V-neck and three-quarter sleeves, it was pretty and light. Most of all, it wasn't black.

Her phone rang, and she smiled at Caroline's number.

"Hey, Caro, I'm getting ready to go out with Aaron." She glanced at herself in the mirror and examined her makeup.

"Did you kiss him?" Caroline's voice was distant and cold.

Her face reddened. It was amazing how fast the skin reacted, she thought as she turned away from her reflection. "Technically, he kissed me. But how did you know?"

"Sarah Abrams, if you think you can ignore us for years, then waltz in here and break his heart, you're crazy!"

Sarah winced. "Wait, hold on. There was no waltzing. Not even a *hora*. He kissed me before I could react. I didn't ask him to, nor did I want him to. So why am I the bad guy?"

"Jessica said the two of you kissed, and after what you told me about you and Matthew…"

Sarah sputtered. "You thought I'd go ahead and taste test another guy to make sure I was picking the right one? We've not seen much of each other in ten years, but you *know* me. How could you even believe this of me?"

"Well, when you put it that way." Caroline cleared her throat. "I'm sorry."

"You should know I'd never do that." She sank onto the bed.

"Have you told Aaron you're engaged?" Though her tone had gentled, the question alone left little doubt whose side she was on.

"I'm not engaged yet. And no, it hasn't come up."

Caroline sighed. "Sarah, you need to tell him. Especially if he still has feelings for you."

"I don't know if he does. I think kissing me was a spur-of-the-moment reaction."

"Aaron doesn't do spur of the moment. You need to tell him. Tonight, before things go too far. Trust me, I was there when you left."

"Okay, I will."

By the time Aaron pulled into her driveway, she was ready with a plan to tell him about Matthew. With a quick goodbye to her parents and a thanks to her dad for getting her a replacement rental car, she met Aaron outside as he unfolded himself from the front seat.

Wow, he looked good. The blue chambray shirt highlighted his eyes and emphasized his wide chest. Tan jeans fit him well. She swallowed. She wasn't looking down there.

He stepped toward her, and the fresh scent of soap and mint surrounded her.

"You look great." He ushered her to the passenger side of his car.

She wanted to say he smelled great, but that would be

weird. Or if not weird, would hint at things she shouldn't hint at. She stiffened as an image of Matthew flashed in her head.

"You okay?" he asked.

She and Aaron were old friends before they'd been a couple. They'd declared a truce. It was perfectly fine for her to eat with him. As long as she kept her thoughts about how he smelled to herself and let Aaron know she was almost engaged. But first, she needed to pull herself together.

"I'm good." She flashed him a smile. "I like your shirt."

His cheeks flushed, and he closed her door before going around to his side and climbing in. By the time he turned to her, his eyes twinkled. "And I like yours. It's not black."

"I thought you'd approve." She froze. Seeking his approval felt weird. She'd always had more confidence when she lived here. It was different in DC.

He nodded. "I do."

Somehow, knowing she had his approval didn't feel the same as having Matthew's. She looked out the window as she contemplated the difference. Had she turned into someone who needed approval?

"I never asked you where we're going for dinner," she said.

"I thought I'd cook."

Her jaw dropped.

"Don't look like that," he said. "It's no big deal. We can eat out if you'd rather."

"No, it's fine." She shook her head. "I remember how well you used to cook."

"I remember how adventurous you were when it came to food," he said, pulling into the parking lot behind his family's deli.

She'd been adventurous about a lot of things. It was she who'd suggested cliff diving at a local park, she who'd loved heading off on a spontaneous road trip, she who'd dared her friends with bets and drinking games. But that was then.

They entered a private door and walked up two flights of stairs to his apartment. It was as large as the entire deli below with exposed brickwork, a fireplace and high ceilings. Brightly colored paintings hung on the walls, and black-and-white family photos covered every available furniture surface. The warmth of home surrounded her like a familiar blanket as she entered.

"Oh, is that your nephew?" She pointed to a family photo on a shelf across the room.

"Yeah. Zachary is married with an eighteen-month-old son, Tyler. He's a chubby ball of laughter."

Sarah smiled. "And your other brothers? Are they married, too?" One by one, she picked up a variety of photos of Aaron's family, studied them and replaced them where they were displayed.

"Nope, much to my mother's disappointment, the rest of us are single."

"And none of them wanted to work the family business?"

He shook his head. "They have degrees they need to put to good use.

He'd always taken family responsibility seriously. "You didn't answer my question."

"I can handle it on my own."

Same as ever. "How are your parents? I didn't see them at the deli."

"They're good. Taking it easy now, letting me handle most of the work. My dad helps out on the weekends and my mom oversees the catering but has turned over most of the day-to-day work to me."

She followed Aaron into the kitchen. Whatever he was cooking smelled delicious.

"And your grandmother?" Sarah asked. "Is she still alive?"

"She plans to live forever, and pretty much runs the senior facility where she lives. I'm visiting her tomorrow. You should come. In fact, she asked for you."

She bit her lip. A truce meant being cordial. It could mean dinner together. Visiting family, however, might be going a little far. "I'm not sure what my plans are tomorrow."

Looking at her over his shoulder, he held her gaze a moment before nodding and adjusting the flame.

"That's what I told her. Dinner will be ready in about twenty minutes." He pulled a plate of cheese out of the refrigerator and led her into the living room, then placed the plate on the coffee table where a basket of crackers already sat.

"I love this." Sarah smoothed her hand across the polished finish of a distressed wood door that been repurposed and made into his coffee table.

"Thanks. My sister-in-law helped me with the place. She said I needed more than a bachelor pad. She's right, but don't tell her I said that." He winked.

"My lips are sealed."

Aaron looked up from the cheese he was arranging on a cracker. His blue-eyed gaze zeroed in on her lips.

Bad word choice. "Can I get a glass of water?"

He blinked before walking to the kitchen. "I have wine if you'd prefer. Or soda. Also, beer."

She hadn't drunk a beer since Matthew. He liked wine and had taught her about different vintages, always choosing their bottle for them. She scowled at herself—she didn't need his approval for everything.

"I'd love a beer, thanks."

Aaron returned with two bottles of Stella Artois and

handed one to her. He hadn't changed, and the knowledge left her with a smile. They tapped the necks together.

"To our truce," Aaron said.

"To our truce."

"Tell me about your job in DC," he said.

"I work on social justice campaigns with Jewish organizations and try to get congressional support for the causes they represent." It's how she'd met Matthew, on one of her first trips to the White House, but she left out that information. Somehow, she didn't think Aaron would appreciate it.

"Such as?"

She smiled, pleased at his interest in the one achievement that filled her with the most pride. "Right now, I'm working on criminal justice reform, specifically for women."

"You were always passionate about those things." He grinned. "I'll bet you're fantastic at your job."

"Thank you." Her chest swelled at his words. "So are you."

He stared at his lap, his grip tightening around the beer bottle. Did he regret staying home and working in the family business? Were his other brothers unwilling to help, or had he pushed them toward their own careers? He'd always stressed the importance of family responsibility to her. Had something changed?

"You do a great job helping your family," she added.

"I know." His shoulders straightened. "My family needs me, I have a great community and our business is doing well."

She wanted to ask if there was anyone special in his life, but she didn't know where the question fell in their truce, or if it did. However, it would be a great lead in to telling him about Matthew. "So, are you dating anyone?"

"No." The oven buzzer beeped, and he rose. "Dinner's

ready." He removed a dish from the oven—a beautiful baked salmon with a pecan crust. Corn chowder came off the stove and fresh bread accompanied the meal, as well as a salad.

"Wow, I'm impressed." Sarah sat at the dining table. "And this table is cool!"

Obviously handmade, it was a large-paned window, covered with a glass overlay.

"Again, my sister-in-law," Aaron said. "And don't be impressed until you taste everything."

Sarah took a bite of each thing and moaned. "It's good!"

He gave a simple nod, but his neck flushed. "I'm glad you like it."

They ate for a few minutes in silence. Sarah savored the explosion of tastes on her tongue, while she searched for a new opening. His quick "no" to her question about a girlfriend didn't lend itself to continuing the subject. She should have mentioned Matthew when she'd talked about her job, but that opportunity had passed. She'd have to find another way.

"You know, you could open a restaurant," Sarah said.

Aaron bristled. "I'm happy with the deli as is."

"I didn't mean anything by my suggestion," she replied in a low voice. "Your deli is fantastic. I meant it as a compliment to your cooking."

He softened. "Thank you. I'm sure you're used to fine dining in DC."

She nodded. "It's true I've been to a lot of fancy restaurants, but I haven't eaten anything this good."

Talking about DC was tricky. And there was Matthew and his proposal to mention, which suddenly seemed more complex. Especially since Aaron got prickly about things.

"So, what are you plans tomorrow?" he asked.

"My mom and I are supposed to go shopping, but I'm not sure about the timing."

"I'm visiting my grandmother in the afternoon around three. Only an hour or so. She would love to see you. Like I said, she asked for you. So, if you're home in time…"

This was the second time he'd mentioned the visit. She remembered Aaron's grandmother from her high school days. And it was, after all, a *mitzvah* to visit the old. Plus, maybe it would open up a way to mention Matthew.

"I'll talk to my mom and let you know. I'm sure she doesn't want to be out long because of synagogue tomorrow night anyway."

"Great. I'll pick you up."

When they finished dinner, she brought the dishes into the kitchen, despite his protests.

"You cooked," she said. "I clean."

"You're my guest." He maneuvered in front of the dishwasher and tried to take the plates from her hands.

"That's ridiculous." She faked left and opened the dishwasher door before he recovered. With a sigh, he stepped back and let her load.

"Fine, but I'm not letting you wash dishes," he argued.

"Then I'll dry."

He glowered at her, but she laughed him off, grabbed a towel and tapped her foot as she waited for him to turn on the tap.

"You're impossible, you know that?" Though the words were a grumble, there was a distinct twinkle in his eye.

"Yup." She'd missed this banter. She and Aaron had always had a natural rhythm, and the years hadn't diminished it. Call it chemistry, or comedic timing or knowing each other all their lives. They worked well together. She didn't have this with Matthew. At least, not yet.

When the last pot was dried and put away, the counters wiped clean and the table spotless, she turned toward the door.

"You should take me home," she said. "If I'm going to make plans with my mom, I don't want to get home too late."

He grabbed his keys and followed her out the door. In the car, she relaxed against the seat as he drove the short distance to her parents' home. Once in the driveway, he turned off the ignition.

"Dinner was great," she said. "Thank you for cooking for me."

"It reminded me of old times," he said.

She swallowed and turned toward him, wondering how she should respond. "I like our truce."

"Me, too." He reached across the console and brushed strands of hair away from her cheek. His hand was warm, and her heart pounded at his proximity. His lips parted as he leaned toward her. She remembered his kisses from years ago, and she knew what they were like now, too. As much as her body wanted him to kiss her, she couldn't allow it to happen. She was with Matthew. Aaron's last kiss had been unexpected, perhaps forgivable. Another one wouldn't be. Caroline's warning not to hurt Aaron flashed through her brain.

"I have a boyfriend," she whispered.

Aaron stiffened, his gaze searching hers. The air in the car, charged a moment ago with sexual tension, shifted. Surprise crossed Aaron's face before he banked it.

"I'll see you tomorrow," he said.

As she watched his car pull away, the cool evening air cleared away all traces of desire. They were friends, nothing more, and once she left and returned to DC, they'd probably never see each other again.

His life was here.

Hers was in DC. With Matthew.

* * *

"Sarah. Earth to Sarah. Hello?"

Her mother waved a hand in front of her face as they stood in the clothing store at the local mall.

Sarah jerked. "Did you say something?"

"I said, I think this blouse would look beautiful on you. Where were you?"

"Sorry, Mom."

"I didn't ask you to apologize. I asked where you were in that head of yours."

She was with Aaron, in his car last night, wondering if he was going to kiss her. She was yelling at herself for betraying Matthew in her mind, although she was innocent, and for not telling Aaron about Matthew's proposal. And she was once again wondering why she was having such a hard time getting to a "yes" for Matthew. But how was she supposed to say any of this to her mother?

"Were you thinking about Matthew?" Her mother held the blouse she somehow thought Sarah would like. As if a blouse would solve her problems.

"Yes." Sort of.

Her mother nodded. "I'm sorry he couldn't join us for the holidays. You must miss him."

Of course, but differently than she'd expected. "Show me the blouse again."

Her mother held it up. It was pale pink with darker pink, coral and blue stripes. "It would look beautiful with a black skirt."

She was right. It would. An occasional pop of color would be okay. "I'll try it on." She took it into the dressing room. As she admired herself in the mirror, her phone rang.

"Hi, sweetheart," Matthew said.

Her cheeks heated at his timing. "Hi, babe. Happy New Year, a little early."

"Same to you. What are you doing?"

"My mom and I are shopping. She found this pink and peach and blue blouse for me. I'm thinking of wearing it tonight."

"Doesn't sound like you, but if you like it... I miss you. Are you enjoying your time home?"

She frowned at her reflection. Maybe it was a little busy. "Yeah, it's nice to be here. I've kind of forgotten what it's like."

"I'm glad," he said. "Services tonight?"

"And tomorrow. You?"

"Probably tomorrow. I'm trying to finish some things here, and I'm not sure I'll be done in time."

"I'm sorry you're busy," Sarah said. "My parents both wish you could have joined us. So do I." Somehow, seeing people from home would have been much easier and less confusing with Matthew by her side.

"Next time, Sar. *Shanah Tovah.*"

She frowned. *"Shanah Tovah."*

She hung up and replaced the blouse on the hanger.

"So, what do you think?" her mother asked as she exited the dressing room. "Did you like the blouse?"

"I think I'll stick to what I already have."

Her mother sighed. "I miss seeing you in color."

Aaron had said the same thing. But if she bought the blouse, would she ever wear it after tonight? She usually stuck to more sophisticated, muted tones.

"I know, Mom. But if I want to be given important work, I have to look polished."

With an arched brow, her mom shook her head. "I would think you'd need to be intelligent and capable—which you are."

"That's true. But you also have to look the part."

"At temple?"

They left the store and continued walking through the mall. "What's the point of buying something I'll only wear once?"

"All right," her mother said. "I give up. But maybe don't wear black to visit Aaron's grandmother. She might think you're there for her funeral."

Chapter Six

The familiar smell of the assisted living facility—a little stale, but with food and flower scents competing to cover it—made Aaron shudder as they entered. If he could, he'd have his grandmother live with him, but the ninety-year-old woman was stubborn. She insisted she enjoyed living at the facility and refused any option which might make her a "burden" to her family.

A part of him respected that about her. Another part thought she liked being the ruler of the roost. She bore it well, like the queen she thought she was. Most of the women tried to get her to join their row for exercise, make up their fourth for mah-jongg and sit out on the patio together to gossip in the nice weather. The single men vied for her attention, inviting her to join them at meals or watch TV together. While many would have liked to have her place of esteem, few resented her because she was always gracious and friendly—unless someone ticked her off, in which case, they should watch out.

His grandmother sputtered as he and Sarah walked down the hallway.

"Absolutely not!" Her voice was surprisingly firm, and he didn't envy the person she spoke to. "The last time that woman arranged the mah-jongg groups, poor Betty was left playing with three experts who scared her so much she only agreed to join in again last week. I will not allow Marge to bully anyone, even if she tries to hide it in game groups. Make sure you let me see the list before it's posted."

She slapped her flip phone shut as Aaron and Sarah knocked on her open door.

"Aaron! I'm happy to see you!" She held out her stick-like arms and Aaron entered, leaning and enfolding her in a gentle hug.

"Oh, you can do better than that, *boychik*! I won't break."

Chuckling, he squeezed a little harder until she gave a contented sigh. "Much better." She looked across the room, her wrinkled face glowing. "You brought Sarah to visit me! Come here, *shayna madel*, and let me look at you."

His grandmother called Sarah beautiful, and he agreed. Her dark brown hair was glossy, her skin smooth. She'd selected a beigy-pink top over her regular black, and he'd joked with her in the car for expanding her wardrobe's color choices. She'd told him it was "taupe," and the entire conversation had brought some color to her cheeks. Her black pants molded her ass and did things to his insides. Things he shouldn't contemplate but did anyway. With a shake of his head, he turned his attention to the conversation between his grandmother and Sarah, who was explaining about her life in DC, her job and her boyfriend.

Sarah had a boyfriend.

When she'd told him that last night, he'd been too

stunned to say anything. Back home in his apartment, he'd spent most of the night wondering about the guy and whether he was good enough for her. Aaron automatically resented the guy, but he couldn't fault Sarah for having someone. After all, he'd dated plenty during the ten years they'd been apart. Hell, he'd almost gotten married. He'd let the subject drop this afternoon when he'd picked her up. The last thing either of them needed was a reason for more tension.

But now, he wanted more information.

"He works in the congressional office for Michigan's junior senator," Sarah was saying. "And he plans to go into politics himself one day."

Aaron's lips curled in distaste, and he turned away to hide his reaction. He wasn't a fan of politics, but someone in that position would be helpful for Sarah's dreams.

"My, my, he sounds important," his grandmother said.

Sarah blushed. "He's busy."

Too busy for Sarah? Was there dissatisfaction in her voice? He shouldn't hope, but he did anyway.

"Is that why he didn't come home with you?" his grandmother asked.

Under normal circumstances, he'd intervene so Sarah didn't feel set upon. But these were not normal circumstances.

"He doesn't get time off for Jewish holidays the way I do," Sarah explained.

If she were important to him, why wouldn't he take time off to come with her? Judaism was important to Sarah. Shouldn't it be important to the boyfriend?

"That's a shame." His grandmother patted her hand. "Maybe next time."

"I hope so," Sarah said.

"Sadie, who's this?" His grandmother's friend Ruth

toddled in and stared at Sarah like most people looked at a salami sandwich.

"Ruth, you know my grandson, Aaron, and this is his friend, Sarah."

As if given permission with her introduction, old people wandered into his grandmother's room en masse. The women wore bright, flowered housedresses, and most sported a shade of purple-red dyed hair one had never seen wild in nature. The men were bald or pasted their three strands of hair across their age-spotted heads. They sucked hard candies and smiles stretched their wrinkled faces. His grandmother preened at the attention. Despite their aged looks, they asked pointed questions, one after another— did she have a boyfriend, a job, a home? Why was she here? When was she leaving? How long had she known Aaron? Would she be interested in their own grandsons?

Aaron began sympathizing with her, but she handled the questions well, and his grandmother ran interference when they got too pointed.

"No, Morty, she's not going to date your grandson. The boy barely makes a living." His grandmother turned to Bessie. "And you know very well your grandson prefers men."

Sarah turned to Aaron, amusement brimming in her gaze. He'd missed their silent conversations, where each knew the other's thoughts without saying anything.

They stayed another twenty minutes while a distracted Aaron allowed Sarah and his grandmother to handle most of the conversation. As they prepared to leave, Aaron gave his grandmother a kiss. She pulled him close and whispered in his ear. "If you want to make a move, now is your chance."

He rose, coughing. Subtle, she was not. Plus, there were

still too many questions to which he needed answers. Like, why had Sarah let him kiss her if she had a boyfriend?

"Bye, Grandma. *L'Shanah Tovah!* Happy New Year!"

"*L'Shanah Tovah*, Aaron. And Sarah, too. Thank you both for visiting."

Aaron was silent on their walk to the car and while he held the door open for her once they reached it.

"Thanks for bringing me," Sarah said. "I enjoyed spending time with your grandmother. And I love her friends."

Only when his seat belt was fastened, and the car started did he speak. "How come you let me kiss you?"

Her skin flushed, and she fisted her hands in her lap. She raised her chin. "If I'd known you were going to, I would have stopped you. Like I did last night. But you caught me by surprise. However, it can't happen again. We're friends, Aaron. Nothing more."

"I'm not the kind of man who poaches, Sarah."

"I'm not the kind of woman who cheats on my boyfriend."

He let out a deep breath and gripped the steering wheel, staring at the road in front of him. They stopped at a traffic light. The center of town was busy as the day neared its end.

He studied her, brow raised. "Then we're good."

"We're good," she agreed.

He stared at the road in front of him. *Shit.*

Sarah dressed for the *erev* Rosh Hashanah temple services that evening in a cream silk blouse, a brown knee-length skirt and a matching short blazer jacket. A string of pearls and black-and-brown heels completed the outfit. She studied her reflection in the full-length mirror hanging on the other side of her bedroom door. She looked polished and understated. And boring.

She should have bought the blouse.

"You look beautiful, sweetheart." Her father kissed her cheek as the three of them headed out to the car.

"She does, but would look better in color," her mother said.

Before Sarah could respond, her father touched her mother's arm. A silent conversation took place between the two of them, making Sarah's heart ache.

She wanted that. Would Matthew give it to her? She tried to remember her own silent conversations with Matthew. They must have had some, but she couldn't think of any.

Her mother nodded at her father, then turned to her. "I love you, Sarah."

"I love you too, Mom."

At the synagogue, they joined the rest of the congregation in the sanctuary. Despite the years and the lack of assigned seats, the same families sat in the same rows that they had in her childhood. Her family sat in the third row from the front on the right-hand side. The remainder of those in that same row were friends of her parents, their extended families and people who joined in the intervening years. Someday, if she and Matthew married and had children, they'd fill in the rest of the row. Unless they attended their own synagogue for services. She shook her head, unwilling to think about losing a tradition she hadn't known she'd missed.

Sarah smiled and nodded to everyone who greeted her, was introduced to those she hadn't yet met and exchanged pleasantries until the robed choir walked up the center aisle.

The rabbi—in her white robe, white-and-silver-stitched *tallit* and matching *kippah*—followed the choir and stood on the *bima*, facing the congregation. The cantor, dressed in the same manner, walked over to the choir before she also turned and faced the congregation. Conversations ceased. The cantor raised her arms and she and the choir chanted a *niggun*—a wordless melody, meant to infuse the congregants in the sanctuary with the spirit of the holy days. The tune was a lovely minor key repetition with a soaring melody. Sarah listened, enraptured as always.

When the choir finished, the rabbi chanted the familiar prayers spoken every *erev* Rosh Hashanah. Because the eve of the holiday also fell on Shabbat this year, the regular Friday night prayers were interwoven into the service, but these carried different melodies due to the holiday. All in all, the differences were distinct enough that Sarah paid attention, instead of letting her mind wander.

After the service ended, everyone left the sanctuary. Because the social hall was set for the luncheon tomorrow, the *oneg*—the festive *challah*, wine and dessert after the service—was held in the hallway, library and study center to accommodate everyone.

Out in the hallway, Caroline and Jessica made a beeline for Sarah.

"Oh good, you're here." Caroline squeezed her in a hug.

"Did you think I wouldn't be?"

Caroline shrugged and exchanged a look with Jessica. "I wasn't sure. I heard you were seen with Aaron so I thought you might spend the evening with him."

Sarah frowned. "Thanks, Jess."

"I'm sorry, I didn't know it was a secret."

It wasn't, but Jessica had never been good at keeping quiet.

"Don't blame her," Caroline said. "My cousin was visiting my grandmother, who knows Aaron's grandmother, and saw you visiting her earlier today."

Sarah shook her head. "Of course. Wow, the gossip line is strong."

"You better believe it. So, what's going on with the two of you?"

Sarah eyed the crush of people milling near them and shook her head. "I'd rather not discuss it here."

"After the karaoke scene, I knew it!" Jessica squealed, her short brown hair bouncing around her face in her excitement.

Caroline arched an eyebrow. "So, there *is* something going on? Have you told him about Matthew yet?"

"I told him I have a boyfriend. And I'll thank you not to try to create some exposé about me, Jess."

"Hey, I report what I see," Jessica said. "You two were like rival alpha lions trying to determine who would run the pack."

"I think you're getting your metaphors wrong, and I know you're exaggerating." Sarah snagged a mini black-and-white cookie from the table and munched. The sweet icing she remembered so well melted on her tongue, leaving a vanilla aftertaste. "But I will say I'm glad we've reached a truce and things are out in the open. It's a lot easier not having to worry about running into him." Of course, she still hadn't told him about Matthew's proposal.

"I want to hear about this," Caroline said. "What are you doing after the luncheon tomorrow?"

"Hanging with my family. Why don't you come over? I know my parents would love to see you." Turning, she nodded at her parents as they approached. "Speaking of which…"

"Caroline!" her mom exclaimed. "It's good to see you. *Shanah Tovah.* And Jessica! You're home!"

"Only for a few days," Jessica said. "I have to return to the paper in New York."

"How's your job going?" Sarah's dad asked.

Jessica's eyes glowed with pride. "I've moved up to investigative reporter."

"That's terrific," he said. "We're proud of you. And you, too, Caroline. Give our regards to your family, Jess."

A brief flash of longing crossed Caroline's face, and Sarah's heart squeezed. "*Shanah Tovah* to you as well," Caroline said. With a wave, she walked away.

Sarah turned to her parents. "Caroline is coming to visit tomorrow afternoon if it's all right. Jess, are you coming, too?"

"I'll try. I'm not sure what the family has in mind. But if not, I expect to be filled in later. If you'll excuse me, please, I have to say hello to the Abramowitzes." Blowing a kiss, she waved to Sarah's parents and walked away.

Sarah's mom smiled. "Oh, that reminds me of when all of you were teenagers. The chatter I'd hear from your bedroom…"

"Wait, you listened?" Sarah turned to her mother, her eyes wide, as they headed out of the temple.

"Of course I didn't listen, Sarah," her mother said at once. "But I can't help if some of what you said reached me. You weren't very quiet."

They approached the crowded doorway filled with congregants accepting paper grocery sacks with lists of needed food items for the hungry.

One of the men handed Sarah's father a bag. "Don't forget to return this, full, on Yom Kippur. We go without food by choice that day. The hungry don't have that luxury."

With a nod, her father accepted the bag and the three walked outside.

She couldn't believe her mother had heard their conversations. She'd remind Caroline and Jessica to keep their voices lowered tomorrow. The last thing she wanted was her mother involved in any discussion about her private life.

If Sarah thought Aaron looked good in jeans, it was nothing compared to how he looked in a suit the next day in synagogue. Tall. Broad. Straight out of a movie. She swallowed. "*Shanah Tovah*, Aaron."

"*Shanah Tovah*, Sarah."

His parents and family were with him, and she gave hugs and New Year wishes to everyone.

"It was nice of you to visit my mother," Aaron's mom said.

"I enjoyed seeing her again."

"I hope we'll see you at the house one of these days," his father said.

"Of course," she said. "I'll come visit before I leave."

The crowd moved as one toward the sanctuary, leaving Sarah no more time for conversation. They found their seats—the Abramses in their same seats from last night, and the Isaacsons in their customary seats a few rows back on the left.

Last night, the sanctuary was filled. Today, there were even more people, and they filled the annex as well with services streaming on screens so everyone could see.

"I'm glad we don't have to sit in those uncomfortable chairs." Her father passed her the special High Holy Day prayer book.

He said the same thing every year, always waking them extra early and making sure they arrived forty-five minutes before services started to claim their customary seats.

Fifteen minutes ahead of the start of services, the rest of the congregation—those who cared less about where they sat—arrived, scanned the full sanctuary and moved into the annex.

"I like sitting here so I can see and hear better," her mother said.

Their friends joined the conversation, the older ones agreeing with her parents and the younger ones rolling their eyes and stifling laughter along with Sarah. She turned to see how full the sanctuary was and her eyes caught Aaron's.

He nodded and, despite the innocence of the glance, her face heated. Their conversation yesterday had disturbed her. She needed to speak to Matthew, keep things open and honest between them—especially at the start of the High Holidays—and explain to Aaron how serious she and Matthew were.

At the same time, she didn't want to make an issue out of nothing. She and Aaron had declared a truce and it was only one kiss. Old friends kissed each other all the time. But they were more than old friends. They had a past with a capital P. And the kiss wasn't a simple buss of the cheek. They'd locked lips, and a part of her had enjoyed it.

Before she could carry the thought any further, the service started. Once again, the rabbi and cantor wore white robes, white-and-silver *tallitot* and *kippot*. White, the symbol of purity and renewal. On Rosh Hashanah, Jews pray for a fresh start and a chance to renew themselves in the eyes of God.

Sarah looked at her clothing. She hadn't worn white, but her customary muted colors. This time her suit was black with a gray silk blouse beneath her jacket. No one around her besides the rabbi and cantor wore white either, and she'd bet they wore their typical colored clothing beneath their white robes as well. It was the symbolism that mattered.

She listened to the rabbi lead the prayers. She doubted

God would care what colors she wore if she prayed with sincerity.

And are honest with Matthew and Aaron, a voice in her mind whispered.

She sighed.

"Everything okay?" Her mother turned and looked at her.

Sarah nodded and focused again on the rabbi. The congregation rose as the ark holding the Torah scrolls was opened and they joined in the *Avinu Malkeinu* prayer, asking God for compassion, life and happiness. It was one of Sarah's favorites and helped her focus her mind on the holiday. The rabbi removed the Torah and carried it around the sanctuary, allowing the congregants to line up and touch the holy scrolls. Once she made her way throughout the entire sanctuary, she read the day's Torah reading, which told the story of God visiting Abraham and Sarah and promising them a child. For obvious reasons, Sarah had always loved this story of her namesake. Beside her, her mother squeezed her hand.

The rabbi's sermon focused on change. Sarah listened with interest as the rabbi incorporated personal stories, challenges to the congregation and words of wisdom from the Torah and Talmud, another holy Jewish book, to prove her point.

She smiled to herself as she thought about the appropriateness of the topic. Matthew wanted to marry her. Talk about change! No matter how well-suited they were for each other, if she said yes, her life would face significant changes. Matthew challenged her to do better. He'd shared his map of how their life would be—she at a Jewish organization lobbying congress, and he rising through the political ranks. She loved him and wanted to share his life. And the changes, no matter how scary, would be worth it.

When the service ended, everyone melded into the social hall for the catered lunch. Crossing the threshold, Sarah's body filled with warmth as she took in the room. She was home. The feeling was weird because she hadn't been here in a while, hadn't had the time. Instead, she'd joined Matthew at a DC synagogue where they'd schmoozed high-ranking politicians, lobbyists and business executives. That synagogue was flashy and oozed power. This one was filled with memories. This synagogue oozed friendship, family and love.

She looked around the room she'd helped set up. The tables were piled with mouthwatering deli platters, colorful salads, various textured breads and bagels and sinful desserts. People waited in line for the buffet while the rabbi and cantor mingled.

"Can I make you a plate, Rabbi?" Sarah asked as the woman approached. "I know you don't have much time to eat before you start the afternoon service."

"Oh, thank you, Sarah. It's nice to see you here. Your parents talk about you often." She leaned over and bussed her cheek, then offered a conspiratorial wink. "I've already got a plate put aside in my office. I'll mingle a little longer before I disappear and put my feet up."

Sarah's father approached with her mother and grinned at them both. "Sounds like a good plan, Rabbi. Marvelous service."

"Thank you, Bob."

"Sarah, you remember the Cohens, don't you?" Her mother weaved an arm through hers and pulled her toward an older couple.

"Of course!"

For the next twenty minutes, Sarah filled her plate while her parents reintroduced her to their friends. Each congratulated her on how sophisticated she looked and how successful she was. Silently, she thanked Matthew for his influence on her appearance. The success, though, she owned.

"You must be proud of your girl," an older woman said to Sarah's mother.

Her mom beamed. "Very. She's doing important work and making a difference."

"Keep it up, dear," the woman said.

"I will. Thank you."

She smelled Aaron's soapy scent a second before he approached them. She set her plate on a nearby table.

"Don't let me stop you from eating," he said. "That's a crime for a deli owner, you know."

"Ha." She picked up her plate again, took a forkful of Israeli salad, chewed and swallowed. "Better?"

"Only if you actually tasted it and liked it," he said.

"It's delicious."

"Good. Interesting sermon today."

"I found it especially meaningful based on my life right now. But the rabbi's sermons have always resonated with me."

Aaron folded his arms across his chest. Sarah focused her gaze on his face, rather than his well-sculpted muscles.

"I'll admit to not listening to them very well when I was younger," he said. "But I listen more now."

"I hope so. Otherwise, you'll have to add her to your list of repentance." Sarah grinned.

"Oh, you think I have a list?"

They leaned against the wall, both taking mouthfuls of food between speaking. Warmth radiated from Aaron's body, making Sarah wish she could spend hours talking to him.

"It wouldn't surprise me if you did," she said.

"And what about you?" He cocked a brow. "Do you have one?"

He didn't admit to having a list, although he didn't deny it, either. She wondered what was on it…and who. He cleared his throat and brought her attention to his question. Did she have a list?

"I always have a list of things I need to improve or wish I did differently." Or not done. Like kiss Aaron. Ugh, she needed to apologize to Matthew.

"That would be an interesting list to read." His tone was lighthearted, but an underlying edge belied his easygoing manner. His blue eyes darkened—more sapphire, less sky.

Sarah thought about when she'd arrived, and how he'd accused her of something. She still didn't know what, but they'd declared a truce and she'd never found out. Did she want to pursue it? The packed social hall wasn't the place. Although no one made it obvious, being with Aaron—the two of them standing alone against the wall—would certainly draw attention. Synagogues, no matter how big or small, were founts of gossip, despite the Jewish law against it. Human nature won out. A deep conversation with the potential of deteriorating into conflict would only make the situation worse. She'd have to postpone it for another day.

"I'll bet yours would be interesting, too," she said.

His eyes lightened again, and his shoulders relaxed. "Touché," he said, taking her empty plate and stacking it below his.

"Want a drink?" she asked. "I'm thirsty."

"Coke or Pepsi," he said.

She walked to the drink table and poured him a Pepsi and herself an iced tea, before returning with both drinks to their spot against the wall. Except now it wasn't "their spot" anymore. Others joined them.

"Sarah, it's nice to see you." A man about her age held out his hand.

She handed Aaron his soda and then shook the outstretched hand. "Hi, Mark. It's nice to see you, too. It's been a long time."

"Probably since high school," he said. "I didn't come here often during college. Let me introduce you to my girlfriend." Turning to his right, he placed his arm around a redheaded woman with an open expression and a quick smile. "Abigail, this is Sarah."

Sarah smiled at Abigail. "Hi, it's nice to meet you."

"Likewise."

"So, Sarah, what have you been up to?" Mark asked.

She gave him a brief overview of her job and life in DC.

"Sounds like an important job. Exactly what you were looking to do. And it's amazing you and Aaron have kept up your relationship."

Sarah's chest swelled with pride at the same time heat flooded her cheeks. "Oh, no. We... I..."

"We're friends." Aaron interrupted.

Mark's face reddened and he stammered, "Oh, sorry. I thought with the two of you standing alone over here... Well, never mind."

"Aaron, what do you do?" Abigail interrupted.

Sarah tuned out the conversation as she struggled to relax. The question shouldn't have thrown her for such a loop. She should have said she had a boyfriend in DC. An almost fiancé. Aaron looked at her, as if expecting her to make the correction. Instead, she'd floundered.

Why?

She'd lived in DC for ten years. She'd been home approximately five days. Yet the longer she was here, the more she found herself slipping into her old ways. And trying to mix her old and new ways together. Was it the place? Or the people?

Or could it be her?

Rosh Hashanah was the Jewish New Year, but it was

also the time to begin self-evaluation. She always became contemplative at this time of year, figuring out who she was, what she'd done well and how she could do better. And of course, reflecting on whom she owed apologies. Therefore, she shouldn't be surprised at the direction of her thoughts.

Except she was.

Chapter Seven

Sarah returned from temple, changed out of her clothes and was putting the finishing touches on her hair and makeup when the doorbell rang. With one last peek in the mirror, she raced down the stairs to answer.

"I've got it," she cried as her dad rose from his chair in the family room.

Opening the door, Sarah gave each of her friends a hug before craning her neck for a look over their shoulders. "Caro. Jess. Your parents couldn't make it?"

"They send their regrets." Jess smiled and spoke over Sarah's shoulder to her mom as she came out of the kitchen. "My mom said she'd call you to make a date to get together."

"Great, can't wait to see her. Have fun, girls!" Her mom returned to the kitchen, and Sarah ushered Caroline and Jessica into the family room.

"So, tell me everything," Caroline said. "I want to know all the details about you and Matthew and Aaron."

Sarah put her finger to her lips, remembering her mother's comment about overhearing their conversations. "You make it sound like a love triangle. Besides, I want to hear about the two of you. What's going on in your lives?"

"I've been paying off my mom's medical bills and working." Caroline's expression was shuttered, and Sarah suspected she was withholding information. Should she pry?

"I'm working at the paper," Jessica added.

"No boyfriends?"

"I'm living vicariously through you," Caroline said. "Which is why I want all the details."

Jessica's eyes narrowed and a bitter frown formed.

"What about you, Jess?" Sarah asked, wondering about her friend's unusual bitterness.

Jessica cleared her throat. "Nothing worth talking about. Now don't change the subject. What's going on with you and your two men?"

Sarah's eyes widened. "Aaron and I are just friends. Matthew wants to marry me."

"How wonderful!" Jessica said. "I assume you'll want a big, splashy announcement in the papers, right? Wait, did you dream of a veil or a floral headband? I can't remember now."

Sarah cringed inwardly. Matthew would want to alert the press. For some reason, the idea made her uneasy.

"She was the veil," Caroline said. "I was the floral headband. And yeah, you'd think it was wonderful, wouldn't you?"

Sarah ran her hands across the leather sofa, its cool, smooth surface somehow soothing. "Yes, I *think* it is."

"Think? What's to think about?" Jessica asked.

"Remember how we used to sit here and plan out all of our dream weddings?" Caroline asked.

"Well, you two did. I'm going to elope." Jessica's expression held a look of desperation that Sarah wanted to ask about, but before she could, Jessica continued. "When's the wedding?"

"I haven't given him an answer yet."

Caroline leaned forward. "Tell her why not."

She clenched her hand into a fist behind her back. "Because I told him I needed time."

"For what?" Jessica said.

"He totally surprised me. I mean, when we first started talking about it, I told him I wanted to wait to get married until I was further along in my career, until I felt more settled in DC."

"Settled?" Caroline asked. "You've been there how long?"

She'd been there since college graduation, but she still didn't feel that deep sense of home, like she did when she was…here. "DC has a different vibe. It takes a long time to get accepted into the circles I need to be in."

Jessica and Caroline exchanged a look.

"A surprise proposal can be romantic," Jessica added. "I thought you wanted that."

It could be. She used to want that. She just thought Matthew understood her needs better. She smiled. "He took me to this beautiful neighborhood with a view of the Capitol and pointed to the apartment he's going to buy. He gave me roses…" The scent had overwhelmed her, as had his plans. "It's a big decision." She paused, trying to modulate her tone. "I always thought I wanted to be swept off my feet. But marriage is more than that. So, I don't know."

"Matthew doesn't sweep you off your feet?" Caroline asked.

Her body tensed. "He did. He used to. He's sophisticated. I was amazed he was interested in me. He'd take me out to these expensive restaurants, show me what to order—what to wear—and introduced me to all these important people. It was amazing. But now?" He was everything she thought she wanted when she first arrived in DC. She stared out the window, wondering where the spark was. "No relationship can maintain that forever. I thought coming home would help me decide, but it's making me more confused."

A worried look passed between her two friends.

"Do you love him?" Caroline asked.

"Yes." She pressed her lips together.

"Then what's to think about?" Jessica asked.

Yeah, what's there to think about?

Goddamn her inner voice. Her temperature rose. "Everything. We're a good match. We both want the same things. He's been a great influence on me and he's a good man."

"This doesn't sound like the romantic Sarah I know," Jessica said.

She sighed. That Sarah was long gone.

No, I'm not. I'm right here.

"What do you want?" Jessica asked.

Sarah sighed. "I have what I want. A fulfilling job. A beautiful apartment. A good life."

"You know, I always admired your independence," Jessica said. "You were the first one who left home, went after what you wanted and seem to have gotten it. Is Matthew part of that? Because marriage is about more than transactions."

Sarah's teeth pressed together until her jaw ached. She drew in a deep breath and shook out her shoulders. "Don't you think I know? I don't see how you can judge someone you haven't met." Abruptly, Sarah stood, her hands gripped together. "Excuse me."

She left the room and returned with three glasses of wine, along with a renewed attempt at remaining calm.

"I'm sorry I snapped. I know you were trying to help, and I'm grateful—truly."

"So, how are you and Aaron?" Caroline asked.

Sarah had just taken a sip of wine and inhaled sharply, choking it down the wrong way. Her eyes streamed and Caroline patted her back.

Her mother rushed into the family room. "Are you all right? I heard choking."

Nodding, but unable to speak, Sarah waved her mom away. When she could inhale without coughing, Caroline moved back to her end of the sofa. After another moment, Sarah wiped her face and turned her attention to her friend.

"So, that's how it is," Caroline said.

"No, it's not." Sarah closed her eyes.

"Want to try again? With feeling this time?" Jessica added.

Sarah opened her eyes and glared at her friends before glancing down at her blouse and noticing the drops of wine stains. She brushed at them to no avail. "Ugh, I've got to change. Come upstairs with me."

The three women went upstairs to Sarah's bedroom and shut the door. Sarah changed out of her stained outfit and into a purple T-shirt and a worn pair of jeans.

Caroline smiled. "There's the Sarah I remember!"

"Yay, you're back," Jessica said.

Sarah plunked onto the bed. "You two are unfair." Her inner voice contradicted her, but she shushed it. "Okay, there might be something there with Aaron, but only because we have a history."

"Are you sure?" Caroline asked.

"He kissed me. And I liked it." Sarah slumped. Just like that, everything she'd thought she wanted had changed. She covered her face. "God, I'm too old for this kind of conversation. I sound like I'm in high school."

"You didn't dress like that in high school." Caroline pointed to the pile of clothes on the floor.

Sarah threw a pillow at her friend. "You didn't drink like this then, either."

"Not in front of your parents." Caroline raised her wineglass. "But seriously, what are you feeling?"

With a sigh, Sarah lay back on the bed and stared at the cracks in the ceiling. She used to think those cracks were a map and they'd lead her to her future. Now, they looked like a maze.

"I don't know." Her voice came out as a wail. Lowering her voice, she continued. "I shouldn't be interested in him. I have Matthew. And it didn't work with Aaron last time."

"It was ten years ago, Sarah," Jessica said. "You've both grown."

"He let me leave."

"You wanted to go," Jessica corrected. "You got a great job in DC, and everyone could see how excited you were about it. What kind of man would he be if he'd held you back?"

A valid point, she had to admit. "And what kind of woman would I be if gave up my dream for a man? I can't stay here. He won't leave. Nothing has changed. The separation killed us last time. Why do you think I stayed away so long?"

"Have you talked to him about it? Asked him why?" Caroline asked.

She shook her head.

"So, you *are* in high school," Caroline said.

"Ouch!"

"You can't assume you know what he would do," Jessica said. "You have to talk to him."

Easy for her to say.

She ran her fingers along the edge of the wineglass. "He's

not the only one I have to talk to. I have to talk to Matthew, too."

"Look, I don't know Matthew, but I do know Aaron," Caroline said. "So do you. You know he doesn't play games. He's the straightest shooter there is. In fact, that was one of the things you used to like best about him. And it's not fair to him not to be upfront about your feelings. It's not like you to do this."

Then why hadn't he contacted her in all this time?

Sarah covered her face with both hands. "I know. I'm not a game player. I don't leave guys hanging, wondering what I'm thinking. I'm smart. I don't investigate strange noises alone."

Caroline snorted.

"I came home to get some space from Matthew and figure out what I wanted," Sarah said. "I didn't expect to still have feelings for Aaron, and it threw me. I really thought I was over him. But I'm not going to sit around, passively wondering and not doing anything about it. First thing is to talk to Matthew. Then I'll have a conversation with Aaron. And then I'll make up my mind."

Aaron had just returned home—after spending the last hour throwing pieces of bread into the water and symbolically casting his sins of the last year away in a ceremony known as *taschleich*—when his phone rang.

"Aaron, it's Steve. Can you return to the temple? We need help."

Shrugging into his T-shirt, he grabbed a sweatshirt and raced down the stairs. "On my way. What's the problem?"

"Someone shattered one of the stained-glass windows and spray painted a swastika on the side of the building."

Aaron's heart pounded in his chest. Bile rose in his throat. The symbol was enough to strike fear and loathing in every Jew who saw it. And someone had had the gall to paint it on a house of worship?

A burning need to get to the temple overwhelmed him. He pressed the gas pedal to the floor and made it to the synagogue in half the time it should've if he'd travelled the speed limit.

Police cars blocked the entrance to the parking lot. Cops huddled next to the building. The rabbi and cantor stood on the grass, shaking their heads and speaking to the police chief.

As Aaron approached, a uniformed officer stopped him and requested identification. He pulled out his driver's license as Steve walked over and vouched for him. The officer waved him through.

"Thanks for coming quickly," Steve said. "I called a bunch of volunteers to help out."

"How did this happen?" Aaron climbed out of his car. "This is our synagogue, our home. And I was here a couple of hours ago."

"We all were."

The rabbi walked over and gave both men hugs.

"I can't believe this," Aaron said.

The rabbi pulled in a steadying breath. "We always face threats this time of year, unfortunately, which is why we have a police presence during the services. But I never expected to need them afterward."

"Any idea who did it?" Aaron asked.

"Right now, no. Chief Forsyth assured me he'll do everything he can."

Aaron knew the chief. About ten years older than him, he'd been a great student and star athlete in high school. He'd gone into the military, gotten married and raised a family here. This town was his community—every part of it. He knew the man would work hard to find the vandals.

"The police are going to review our security camera feed," the rabbi continued. "As soon as they're finished over there, we'll start cleaning up. You'll stay?"

He nodded, and she squeezed his arm and returned to the taped-off area.

Aaron paced. Rage bubbled inside. One of the holiest days of the year. They should be celebrating. Cleaning anti-Semitic graffiti and stained-glass shards shouldn't be part of the plan.

He thought about all the hate on the news. It was always in the background lately, a distant hum, until it hit home. His stomach churned. He stared at the brick building with the wide rear entrance to the religious school, the sanctuary's stained-glass windows on the left side—now broken—and the lowered blinds covering the office windows on the right. If he concentrated hard enough, he could hear the raised voices of the congregants praying, the children laughing in religious school. Images filtered through his mind like a beloved home movie. His connection here was personal. Never mind the hundreds of parties his family had catered. He'd made his first menorah out of cardboard in preschool here. His chest swelled with pride when he remembered learning to chant his bar mitzvah prayers. He'd bonded with Jewish teens during youth group and fallen in love with Sarah.

Sarah.

She belonged here.

He scanned the mass of volunteers who'd congregated but didn't see her. His head began to pound. He reached for his phone but paused before calling the number he still knew by heart. She'd left, made a life, forgotten all about them. Sure, she was home for the holidays, and the vandalism would devastate her, but it wasn't the same. Her roots had been pulled and planted elsewhere. He slipped the cold phone into his pocket.

His friend Ben walked over to him. "I can't believe this happened."

Aaron shook his head. "I'd like to get my hands on whoever did it."

"It was probably some kids," Alan, an older man in the men's group, said.

Aaron swung around, fists clenched. "I don't care how old they are. They should know better."

Steve grabbed his shoulder and pulled him away from the others. "Hey, easy there."

Aaron took several deep breaths and nodded. "Sorry, Alan."

Alan held up a hand as if saying, *It's okay.*

Aaron turned to his friend. "I'm pissed."

"I am, too. But we can't turn on one another or take it out on each other. We need to be unified against this. And we have to know what happened and why before we rush to judge."

"I'm not sure I can, Steve." *How could anyone be rational at a time like this?* His pulse pounded in his ears.

Steve's brows rose. "You're usually the levelheaded one."

"Not with something like this. I don't care who they are or why they did it. They need to be punished." Aaron's breathing grew harsh, and his voice rose with each word. Around them, people stared.

"I know you're angry, Aaron. I am, too. But you need to manage it, so it doesn't get in the way of fixing things."

Steve was right, but he struggled to calm himself. This place was his escape from the stresses of real life. For the first time, it was the cause. Walking away, he paced the parking lot. By the time he'd gotten ahold of his emotions and trusted himself to be calmer around everyone, the police were wrapping things up and the chief had already left.

The cantor approached the group. "Thank you all so much for coming and showing your support. It means a lot. The police said we can clean the graffiti, and if you all don't mind, we'd like to get started now. It's the holy days, and, well..."

"I've got a power washer in my car," said one of the men.

"I've got the chemical remover," said a woman. "I stopped at the store on the way over when I heard what happened."

There were more volunteers than necessary and with everyone pitching in, the cement wall was clean in less than an hour and the broken window was boarded up for repair later. Finished for now, the rabbi drew everyone around and led them in a prayer of thanksgiving.

"Thank you all for your assistance and love today," the rabbi said after the completion of the prayer. "I'd prefer drawing attention to acts of love and kindness, rather than hate, so please, let's not dwell on this. Instead, let's let the police handle it."

Aaron thought about the rabbi's words and sentiments. Thankfulness, kindness, love. He was still filled with so much anger that he didn't know if he could get to that place. And part of the reason was because the woman he most wanted to turn to wasn't there.

Chapter Eight

Sarah gripped the phone late that afternoon and listened to Matthew describe the policies he was working on. Usually, she asked questions and offered suggestions. But this time, although she'd been the one to call him right after her girlfriends left, she couldn't muster suitable enthusiasm.

Her mouth dried as she waited for him to stop talking so she could discuss their relationship. She needed to tell him about the kiss, apologize and hope by some miracle that he forgave her. Only then could she address her doubts with him. Walking into her mother's cheery kitchen to get a glass of water, she took in the yellow walls, warm oak cabinets and red and blue accents. She'd smiled each morning as she came down for breakfast and bathed in the charm the room offered. Her own kitchen was stark—black granite countertops, top of the line stainless steel appliances and pale gray walls. It screamed sophistication but left her emotionally empty.

"Sarah, you're quiet," Matthew said. "What do you think?"

She swallowed a gulp of water and placed the still full glass on the counter. "I think it sounds good."

"Good? You're usually more talkative. What's going on?"

She stared out the kitchen window at the dark landscape. "I think we should talk."

Matthew was practically her fiancé. Not only did he deserve a faithful partner, but a truthful one. Her parents would be married thirty-five years this coming March, and their entire relationship was built on love, trust and respect. Sarah wanted a relationship like theirs. That meant admitting her mistake.

"That sounds ominous, since I thought we were talking now."

Her stomach clenched. "I have to tell you something."

Concern deepened his voice. "You know you can tell me anything."

"Aaron and I... He kissed me." Dread formed in the pit of her stomach. "It didn't mean anything, and I'm sorry, Matthew."

She said the last part quietly. Oh God, it sounded worse than it was, although it wasn't great to begin with. If she were in Matthew's shoes, she'd be crushed. Her eyes filled with tears. She was a terrible person. She didn't deserve him.

"What do you mean, he kissed you?" The words were measured, like when he asked why someone hadn't supported the bill he was pushing.

"He...he leaned over and kissed me. I didn't realize it was happening, and when I did, I stopped it." She touched her mouth, remembering the feel of his lips on hers.

"I don't understand. Why did he kiss you?"

"I don't know. We were arguing, and it just happened." She closed her eyes.

"Didn't you tell him about us?"

"I told him I have a boyfriend." Shame burned through her. She should have told Aaron about Matthew first.

"But not a fiancé."

She remained quiet.

"He kissed you anyway?" Disbelief echoed in his voice.

"I told him afterward." The more she spoke, the worse it sounded. How could she do this to the man she loved?

Silence stretched between them. She was about to break it when he finally spoke. "Did you do anything to provoke him?"

"Provoke him?" Her voice rose. "Of course I didn't. I never would!"

"Sarah, do you love me?" Matthew asked, his voice urgent.

"Yes. That's why I told you. I don't want us in a relationship with secrets, and I want you to trust me. I know it sounds laughable right now, but I promise, nothing happened other than that kiss. It will never happen again, and—"

"I believe you. And I forgive you."

"You do?" She waited for relief to course through her.

"Of course. You didn't have to tell me, and you did. And you didn't encourage him. Would I have preferred it not to have happened? Yes. Do I understand, though? Yes."

She must've found the most understanding boyfriend in the history of boyfriends. Still, a niggle of doubt tickled her. "Why?"

"Why what?"

"Why do you understand? Why aren't you angrier?" Shouldn't he be angry? She would be furious.

Matthew sighed. "Look, you and Aaron have a history. Obviously there's attraction between you two. And a kiss—well, it's just a kiss. It happens. I don't like it, and if I were with you, it wouldn't have happened. But I wasn't. And it's better you had this time alone, to see what Aaron is truly like."

Was he suggesting Aaron was the kind of man to kiss women who were engaged to someone else?

"Don't worry," he continued. "It's why I encouraged you to take this time to think before you accepted my proposal. I wanted you to be sure I was the right man for you. You and I have the rest of our lives to form the bond you and Aaron had."

She frowned. Telling him was the most difficult thing she'd ever done, yet she didn't feel any better. Her stomach was still in a knot.

"Why are you silent, Sarah?"

"I…I don't know. I guess I didn't expect you to be understanding." She couldn't imagine Aaron ever being this understanding when they were together. Then again, when they'd been together, she never would have kissed someone else.

"What else is bothering you?" Matthew asked, his voice deep with concern.

How like Matthew to get right to the point. She'd always liked that about him—his logical, analytical mind was great for identifying a problem and creating a solution. It's why he'd make a marvelous politician.

Worries she'd kept buried bubbled to the surface—the different person she was here, her parents' marriage, her friends' concerns, Aaron.

"I don't think I can get married right now." The words fell out of her mouth almost on their own. "I feel guilty about kissing Aaron, even if you're okay with it, and I don't want my guilt to be the reason we go ahead with it."

There. She'd said it.

Her body trembled, like the only thing keeping her standing was her concerns. She held her breath and waited for his answer.

"We're not getting married right now, Sarah. A rushed wedding will make people wonder. We'll have an engagement of at least a year, which will give you plenty of time to get over feeling guilty and get ready."

He was a brilliant man—was he purposefully misunderstanding her?

"Why do we need to have such a long engagement? Why can't we wait another six months, get engaged and get married three or six months later?" she asked.

"You know the best planners need at least a year's notice to reserve. It's why I need you to make your decision as soon as possible. If we don't get on their calendars right away, we'll have a terrible time planning our wedding. Not to mention the venue and the food and the band… We need the best, and we can't expect the Washington elite to come to a subpar wedding."

Would marrying her be "subpar" if they did something small and intimate? Wasn't marriage about the two of them and their love for each other?

"We don't need to get married in DC, Matthew," she began. "We could get married here—"

"You're kidding, right? We need our wedding to set the tone for the rest of our lives, Sarah. And that life is in DC."

"I care about you, Matthew. About us and our love for each other. All the other stuff is irrelevant to me."

"You need to care about it, Sarah. Our life will be under a microscope."

"But it isn't yet. Shouldn't we focus on the two of us to start? Solidify that and move on to what the rest of society will come to think of us?"

"We make a great couple. We balance each other out, we have good connections and we enjoy each other. All that's left is to get married."

Sarah's heart sank. Matthew had never cataloged their couple attributes like a grocery list before, and although he was correct in everything he said, hearing it made it sound so…cold. No wonder her friends expressed disbelief when she discussed her plans with them. Is this what she sounded like?

Looking at it in this new light, Sarah realized their engagement sounded more like a business arrangement than a love match. And despite Matthew's understanding, he hadn't once said he'd loved her through the course of their conversation. It occurred to her, now, that she couldn't remember the last time he had.

"Do you love me, Matthew?"

"Where is this doubt coming from? You know I do. Maybe you should come back early, and we can plan our wedding. I'm not sure being home is the best thing for you. Returning to your life here, to me, will get you past this sudden insecurity."

Was that all it was? The small voice inside her said no.

Matthew interrupted her thoughts. "Sarah, we're perfect together. You know it, and I know it. Come on. In all the dreams you've had about getting married, have any of them ever involved you and me in some small, backyard ceremony?"

Whenever she'd pictured her wedding, it had been this fuzzy dream, a kaleidoscope of lace and flowers and rings, like Caroline and Jessica had said. When she'd talked to them about it as a young girl, she'd described the dress in detail—long train, sweetheart neckline, tight bodice, flowing veil. But the groom? In high school, she'd pictured Aaron. But recently, the groom had grown fuzzy, and she'd assumed it was Matthew. Closing her eyes, she thought about marrying him—the grand synagogue they belonged to filled with people and flowers, the music echoing in the sanctuary, her parents walking her down the aisle. And at the end of the aisle was a man. As hard as she tried, she couldn't see a face. It had to be Matthew. Who else could it be?

"Exactly," he said, his voice filled with warmth. "You're nervous, sweetheart."

"You're probably right." *About so many things.*

"So, does this mean you're saying yes?"

Over the phone? This isn't how she'd imagined accepting a proposal. Not to mention that she still had reservations.

"No."

"Why not?"

She sighed. "Because I need to know you're marrying me for me, not for what I can bring to your campaign." He started to speak but she kept on going. "And I need to be sure I can continue my work and be fulfilled on my own while I support your campaign."

"You're everything I've ever wanted in a wife. How could I not marry you for you?"

"There are lots of women who could check off your boxes, Matthew."

He barked a laugh. "None who check them off the way you do. You challenge me and inspire me. You're adaptable and learn quickly. You're gorgeous and smart. What more could I want?"

It wasn't sweet, flowery language, but it was all Matthew.

"Is it enough for you?" *Is it enough for me?*

"Of course it's enough for me, Sarah. As for you being fulfilled in your job, I've told you from the beginning—

I love what you do. Of course, once my career takes off, you won't be able to work as many nights and weekends that you do now, since it will impact our private life, but at least for the near future, there won't be any changes."

She stilled at his words. "Are you saying I'll have to resign?"

"Not right away, Sarah. There will be plenty of time for you to make the mark you've always wanted to. And, when I'm ready, you'll be able to support me, like the other political wives do."

She pulled in a deep breath and considered his side. Her job involved a lot of outside-of-work activities, and it made sense he'd want to spend more time with her. But what he described sounded less like he wanted to spend time with her and more like a perk of his job. The knot in her stomach tightened.

"Look, I don't want to rush you," Matthew added. "I mean, I do, because I want to start the rest of our life together, but I understand you need to give our marriage careful consideration. I just… Don't dawdle, okay? Take the time you need, but don't take too long."

She hung up the phone in a fog. She'd hoped she'd feel better about her relationship. Maybe it was being at her parents' home. Matthew was different from everyone she knew here, and the difference was glaring. What she found attractive about him—his coolheadedness, his logic and his drive—sounded cold and calculating now. He had a plan, and he followed through. His plan included her, and she should feel thrilled. But suddenly, his plan and hers sounded very different.

Aaron paced the confines of his apartment the next morning and fumed. His sleep had been fitful, and his anger had surged through the night. It didn't matter that they'd removed the graffiti. It didn't matter that they'd come together as one. Someone out there was filled with enough hatred to vandalize their synagogue. Someone in their local community.

He clenched his fists. His apartment was too small. He needed to get away and clear his head. Flinging open the door, he jogged downstairs and through the deli. His gaze flashed over the space, landing on customers he knew or had waited on scores of times. Was the vandal one of his customers? His vision clouded, and he shook his head.

"I'm going out." He shot the words to his manager and left the deli before she responded.

Outside, the early morning air was brisk. It should have cooled him, but he was too wound up. He brushed past pedestrians on the sidewalk, ignored shopkeepers who nodded in greeting and narrowly avoided a honking car as he jaywalked across the street.

Someone grabbed his arm. "Aaron, are you okay?"

Sarah. He swallowed, absorbing her voice as it flooded through him. Her scent overwhelmed him. She stood in front of him, dressed in her standard black workout clothes, tormenting him with her presence. He'd wanted her with him yesterday, beside him while they cleaned the temple walls. Avoiding her gaze, he glared off into the distance and tried to tame his anger. Instead, it grew.

"Why do you care, Sarah?"

"Because you're my friend and you look like you're ready to murder someone. Not to mention, you almost got hit by a car. After what happened yesterday at the temple—"

"Why weren't you there with the rest of us?"

She gasped. "Why didn't you call me?"

"I never used to have to call you, Sarah. You were invested in the place as much or more than I was. We were always alerted to happenings at the temple. Now, you're a temporary visitor."

"Aaron, what—"

Rage boiled inside him, and he couldn't listen to her anymore. He needed space—from everyone, but especially from her. He escaped onto a side street. Away from the main thoroughfare, the streets were lined with trees and private houses. His steps didn't slow. His breath came in gasps, and still he continued. Eventually, he arrived at a park with paved walking trails crisscrossing the grass. Woods surrounded a duck pond. Off in the corner was a playground. He followed the paths aimlessly until his body tired and his mind slowed. He sank onto a nearby bench. He was finally able to think more clearly. Whoever defaced his synagogue would be caught and punished. Taking out his anger on others wouldn't help the situation.

His mind drifted to Sarah, and his heart thudded in his chest. Dammit. His words haunted him. He'd lashed out at the first person he'd run into and the one person he shouldn't have. Her life wasn't here. He shouldn't have expected her to be at the synagogue, no matter how much he wished she had been. He pulled his phone out of his pocket and tapped her contact on the screen, but the call went straight to voice mail. He texted instead.

can we talk

He stared at his screen, wondering if she would answer. Her read receipts were on, and the screen jumped, indicating she'd seen his message. Nothing happened. He waited. The dancing dots appeared. He waited some more.

why

He deserved that.

because I want to apologize

why

Oof.

sarah, please

There was a long moment before she answered. Sweat trickled down the back of his neck.

fine

He imagined the exasperation in her voice.

where are you

jogging over by the high school

don't suppose you want to meet me at the duck pond

Again, there was a long pause.

fine

Twenty minutes later, she appeared. Expression solemn, she stopped a few feet away from him, hands on hips, breathing hard and staring off into the distance.

He stood. She looked like she wanted to run away, but she remained where she was, as if she didn't want to give an inch of extra space to him. Silence stretched between them.

"I'm sorry," he said, breaking the silence first.

"For what?" She glared at him.

"For taking out my anger on you, for holding you to an impossible standard, for expecting you to magically appear somewhere and hating you for not being there. I was wrong."

She turned in a circle, still taking deep breaths. He waited, half expecting her to run away. "I can't keep doing this. *We* can't keep doing this."

He nodded. "I know. But the community pulled together and there was this hole where you were supposed to be."

"Aaron, I haven't been part of the synagogue for ten years."

"You slipped into place with such ease, and I guess… I don't know. We've never been attacked before, and I wanted you there."

She let out a breath and sat beside him on the bench. "If you'd called me, I'd have come. But you didn't, and I didn't know you wanted me there. I'm sorry."

"Me, too."

They sat in silence again. Ducks swam in the water, making circles and dipping their heads beneath the water. In the distance, children yelled on the playground. A few cyclists whizzed past on the paths.

She kneaded her hands into her thighs, drawing his attention to her well-toned legs. He wanted to touch her. He lifted his hand, before letting it rest again on the bench.

"I can't keep up with the mixed signals," she said.

He folded his arms across his chest and scowled. "What mixed signals?"

"First you ignore me, then you're mad at me and then you kiss me. Can't get more mixed than that."

"That's not mixed signals. That's a progression."

She rolled her eyes. "Oh please, Aaron. You've never been one to play games before. Why start now?"

"I'm not playing games."

"Oh really? Great. Then tell me what you were thinking."

"When?"

Sarah stood and paced away from the bench. "Come on, Aaron! Stop this. You know what I'm asking, come out with it and be honest."

"Honest? You want honest, Sarah?" His head pounded. "Fine. Here's honest. I hated you for asking me to wait, leaving and getting with another guy. But—"

"What other guy? There was only ever you, until you ghosted me. And then Matthew."

"Ghosted you?" He ran a hand through his hair. Any minute now, he was sure his head would explode. "I didn't ghost you. I came after you. But you were kissing another guy."

Her mouth dropped. "When? When did you ever see me kissing another guy?"

They were shouting at each other, and he looked around, wondering who could overhear. Part of him didn't care.

"Two months after you left. I decided to surprise you in DC, to see if we could figure out a way to make things work. Maybe figure out a way I could move down there. But I pulled up to your building and you were in the arms of another man. I saw you through the window."

She threw her hands up in the air. Venom poured from her mouth. "There was never anyone other than you, Aaron. I don't know what you're talking about."

"Are you saying I'm lying? I saw you with a guy—thin, blond hair."

"Blond hair?" Her jaw dropped, the brown eyes he could drown in got huge, and she stared at him. "The only blond guy I was friends with was Jared…"

Dawning flashed across her face, and he folded his arms across his chest.

"Oh. My. God." Her hands fluttered at her side. She stomped in circles and shook her head. "Let me get this straight." She ticked off items on her fingers. "You decided to come to DC without telling me, saw me with a man, assumed I was cheating on you and said nothing. For ten years?"

Put like that, he sounded childish.

"Well, I hope you've enjoyed yourself, you idiot." She paused, nodded and continued. "That man was my friend— my *gay* friend. If you saw me with him, in his arms, he was either comforting me when I missed you, or I was comforting him after a breakup. If you'd bothered to ask me, you would have known. But no. Not only didn't you tell me you were coming to DC to talk about our future—a future you'd said wasn't possible when I left, by the way—but you stopped calling me, never initiated phone or text conversations and said we couldn't work. You didn't bother to ask about him. So, you didn't get the answer to your suspicions. Suspicions I've never deserved."

His stomach dropped. He opened his mouth to speak but closed it before saying anything.

"Smart man," she said. "Tell me something—did anything in our history ever suggest I'd cheat on you, or move on from you so quickly?"

"No."

"Did I ever lie to you or not answer your questions when asked?"

"No."

Her voice wobbled. "Then why the hell did you drop me like you did?"

He rested his elbows on his knees and dropped his head into his hands. He'd caused her so much hurt. "I was young and immature, which is a lousy excuse. You had this fantastic opportunity, and I couldn't ask you to sacrifice your future for me. I loved you too much. You'd made a life for yourself. One that fit you so well. I heard it in your voice every time we spoke on the phone. So I spent a month or two trying to figure out what to do, thinking I could continue with the distance and realizing I couldn't. I came up with this plan for me to move to DC, go to grad school, and we could be together. I should have told you, but I wanted it to be a surprise. I imagined the look on your face and, I don't know, I guess I wanted reality to match my fantasy. When I saw what I thought was you with another guy, I broke. I ran away. And then my dad got sick and the responsibility of the deli, which was going to fall to me someday anyway, fell on me right then. How could I possibly ask you to come back when everything you'd dreamed of was in DC?"

"I wish you'd said something." She leaned away from him, and his last chance slipped away.

"I wish I did, too. I'm sorry." He clasped his hands together. "I tried to move on. I even fell for someone else a while back." She raised one eyebrow, and he shook his head. "It didn't work out. But I'm okay now. Except for the times when I'm…not. Do I like being with you? Sure. Am I attracted to you? Always. But I won't repeat my old mistakes."

"I guess it doesn't matter whether I think you're giving me mixed signals or not."

"Why?" His stomach clenched. *Please don't let her give up on us.*

"Obviously we're not meant to be together. Neither one of us tried to fight for us. You've got your life here and I've got mine there."

He closed the distance between them and cupped her arm. "I'm sorry, Sarah. I wish I'd done things differently." *I wish there was a way to fix this.*

"Me, too." Hurt pooled in her eyes.

"Maybe we can start over now, though."

"How?" she asked, her tone dejected. "Our lives are in different places."

He clenched and unclenched his jaw. He had to get this right, to man up and fight for her. For them. "Distance shouldn't stop us from being together if we want. You were right. You were getting mixed signals from me, because despite my anger, I'm still attracted to you."

She blinked. "I'm with someone else, Aaron."

"Who couldn't bother to come here with you?"

She paled. "That's not fair, Aaron. Matthew works in a senator's office and doesn't get the time off I do. He's asked me to marry him."

His chest tightened. It couldn't be too late. He closed and opened his eyes, before looking at her hand. There was no engagement ring. Some of the pressure eased. "Do you love him? Did you say yes?"

She stared out over the pond. "I'm supposed to consider his proposal while I'm here."

Relief washed over him. "I won't give up on you, Sarah. Not this time."

"There's nothing 'to give up.'" She shrugged, her voice exhausted. "You and I aren't together. And we can't be."

She spun around and jogged away. He thought about stopping her, but he let her go. He had a week to change her mind.

Sarah pushed away from the dining table that afternoon and helped her mother clear the dishes. It was the second day of Rosh Hashanah, and her mother always hosted a meal in celebration, with the Isaacsons usually joining the family. Instead of enjoying her time with her family, she'd turned over in her head her last conversation with

Aaron—and all of the miscommunications that had led to ten years' worth of hurt. Thank goodness the Isaacsons hadn't joined them this year. The last thing she wanted to deal with was another awkward conversation.

"That was delicious brisket, Shoshana." Her Aunt Ruth rose from the table. "It practically melted in my mouth."

"It's Rose's mother's recipe," Sarah's mom said. "Works every time."

"Well, I knew it couldn't be Mom's." Her aunt laughed. "She couldn't boil water."

"Come on, Aunt Ruth," Sarah said. "She wasn't that bad. I remember a few dinners—"

"—that I cooked, honey," her mom said. "I had her tell me what she was making, and I substituted mine for hers."

"How in the world were you able to do that?" Aunt Ruth asked.

"I made sure to distract her with something, usually one of the kids." Her mom scraped the plates and loaded them into the dishwasher.

"Is that why Grandma always asked to see my room?" Sarah asked.

"Guilty."

Her aunt turned to her. "Sarah, your mom is one sneaky woman."

"Another reason I wished I had siblings." Sarah laughed. "I could never get anything by her."

"And you think siblings would have helped you?" her mother asked.

"They might have worn you out."

The doorbell rang as the three women laughed.

"Oh, honey, can you answer that?" Sarah's mom asked. "The Isaacsons are coming over for dessert."

Sarah's stomach lurched, the delicious meal she'd eaten threatening to come right back up. "Speaking of sneaky."

"Go on, quickly. It's rude to keep them waiting."

Sarah approached the front door, her steps slow, her feet like lead weights. Dessert was going to be a nightmare. Straightening her posture, she pasted on a smile, and reached for the door handle. *Best to get this over with.*

"Hi, come on in! *Shanah Tovah!*" She ushered the Isaacsons inside. Aaron's dad and two brothers walked in first, and hugged Sarah before heading into the living room.

"It's nice to see you again, Sarah. I'll go put this in the kitchen." Aaron's mother nodded to the large pie plate she carried and bussed her on the cheek before following the men.

Sarah eyed Aaron as he stepped over the threshold, his body taking up the entire doorway as he loomed over her.

"Hi," she said.

"Hi again." He winked.

Her flush deepened. If seeing her didn't bother him, why did it bother her? Sweat popped on the nape of her neck. *Shake it off.*

"Did you know about this?" she asked him as they walked toward the dining room.

He nodded. "Yeah, didn't you?"

She shook her head.

Why hadn't he said anything this morning? She was about to ask but stopped as they stepped into the kitchen and took in the stares on everyone's faces. Her face burned as she walked to her customary seat, then stopped short as Aaron held it out for her. She stared at him. He waited.

"Sarah, sit already," her mother said. "We're waiting for you."

Great.

Aaron winked again.

Does he have something in his eye?

Collecting herself, she took her seat and let the voices swirl around her as she adjusted to the new guests.

Aaron's two brothers—Jordan and Gabriel—were twins and three years younger than Aaron. His older brother, Zachary, was already married with a child, and Sarah assumed he was spending the holidays with his in-laws.

Jordan and Gabriel helped themselves to her mother's Jewish apple cake, a heavy, moist cake filled with huge chunks of apple. It was one of Sarah's favorites. The last time she'd seen Aaron's brothers, they'd been in college, one studying business, the other studying something in the sciences. Now, in between stuffing bites of cake in their mouths, they talked football with her uncle, a huge Commanders fan.

Her aunt and mother spoke with Aaron's mother, who'd brought a plum pie. Sarah remembered loving her pies, and she'd accepted a piece despite her reservations. The idea of eating so much food made her stomach roil. But she ran this morning. She could spare some calories. Plus, it was a holiday.

Aaron elbowed her. "Not eating?"

His low voice did delicious things to her insides, things it had no right to do. In defiance, she took a bite of her pie. Sweet plum, tangy brandy and cinnamon combined in her mouth, and she swallowed a groan of delight. She'd missed this. Her stomach cooperated and settled.

"I'd never miss your mom's pie," she said.

"Good. It's nice to celebrate together again. Remember high school?"

"I remember your dad turning the Passover seder into a Star Wars-themed event," Sarah said, laughter bubbling as she remembered the choreographed chaos.

"Hey, don't forget when we all tried to sleep outside in the *sukkah*," Jordan said.

"Yeah, whoever had the bright idea to sleep outside in the backyard in the middle of October didn't take into consideration how cold it got at night," Sarah said, shivering at the memory.

"I walked downstairs the next morning to see all of you huddled on the sofa under blankets." Her mom laughed.

"Do you all still celebrate together now?" Sarah asked.

"Of course." Aaron nodded. "Different people cycle through, but our core remains the same."

He stared at her, as if saying "except you" without words. But she got the message loud and clear, and a twinge of regret reverberated through her.

Aaron's dad cleared his throat. "What happened at the synagogue was terrible. I hope it was only a couple of idiot kids."

Aaron stiffened.

"With the way the world is today, we shouldn't be surprised," her father added.

"The rabbi and cantor were a lot calmer about it than I was," Aaron said, clenching his hands into fists.

Sympathy washed over Sarah, and she folded her hands in her lap before she forgot herself and grabbed one of Aaron's hands to soothe him.

Her mother shook her head. "Well, let's hope they find whoever did it and it's an isolated incident."

"Amen," Aaron's mom agreed.

A pall settled around them as everyone reflected upon the morning's events.

"Something happened at our synagogue last year," her aunt said. "It was the beginning of several anti-Semitic events in the town."

Sarah's mom and Mrs. Isaacson exchanged shocked expressions, while the men's faces hardened. *So much for a relaxing lunch.*

"My office deals with things like this frequently," Sarah said. "You should speak up if it continues. Don't stay silent about it."

"Oh no, it won't spread here," her mother said. "We're such a diverse community, and we've always had a wonderful relationship with everyone. I'm sure it was foolish kids who didn't realize."

"Didn't realize?" Aaron's voice dripped with rage. "What kind of an idiot doesn't realize what will happen if you spray that on a synagogue?"

This time, Sarah reached beneath the table and touched his hand. As angry as he was, and justifiably so, shouting at everyone wouldn't get him anywhere. As if startled out of a trance, Aaron looked at her and his features lightened.

"Sorry. I didn't mean to yell, Mrs. Abrams," Aaron said. "Our diverse community is great. Hopefully, it will rally and help us out."

Sarah's mom gave a sympathetic smile. "No apology is necessary. It's upsetting. But we'll get through this."

Sarah nodded. "I hope so." She'd seen actions like this because of her job, and she hoped her mom's faith was justified.

"Sarah, maybe you can help out the rabbi with finding out who did this," her mother said.

She whipped around. "Mom, I'm not a private investigator."

Aaron coughed.

"I know, dear. But that doesn't mean you don't have valuable information and experience you can share."

Her father nodded. "You make quite a difference in the work you do, Sarah. We're proud of you."

Sarah wiped her mouth on her napkin and gave herself a chance to think. Her parents' unending pride in her work was flattering, but this was the first time she'd taken it as anything more than typical "daughter pride." Maybe she did have something to share with the temple. Pushing away her empty dessert plate, she looked at her mom. "If they want my help, I'm happy to do whatever I can. But I'm not here long."

Next to her, Aaron stiffened again. She looked at him and found him staring at her, his eyes pleading. He knew she wasn't here for long. Whatever she did here was temporary, and she'd better remember that.

Chapter Nine

Aaron pulled up to Sarah's house as the sun rose the next morning and gave a light tap on the door. She answered, dressed in black workout clothes, her gaze still unfocused. He handed her a coffee, made the way she'd liked it in high school—extra cream and sugar.

"Aaron, it's six thirty! These early mornings are starting to become a habit with you." She took a sip of the coffee and made a face. "God, that's sweet." She swallowed, licked her lips and drank some more.

"I had to catch you before you left for your jog. Come to the deli with me and help me open."

She stared at him. "Are you kidding?"

"Come on. You used to help me every Sunday morning. Don't tell me you forgot."

"But... I... It's Monday."

"Just like old times, like your coffee, almost."

He knew he had her when she took another long sip of her drink. Something inside him settled. He'd taken a chance, coming here without telling her. But after spending last night with her, he yearned for old times and wanted to remind her what she'd been missing.

"I was going to run." She followed him to his car.

"You can run later." He opened the passenger door and waited for her to get in before going around the front and climbing into the driver's side.

"This is really sweet." She raised her coffee cup.

"You used to love it that way."

She bit her lip. "Don't tell anyone, but I still do."

His grin stretched so wide his cheeks hurt. "Your secret's safe with me."

He drove the rest of the way to the deli in silence, the coffee aroma filling the enclosed space of his vehicle. Once inside, the two of them worked in tandem. He was pleased to see that Sarah still remembered how to open the store and working with her was like stepping back in time. By the time seven o'clock and the first customer arrived, they were ready.

"Mind helping me until the counter staff arrives?" he asked as he took bagel orders.

"Like I have a choice?" She smiled.

"You've always had one," he said under his breath.

Out of the corner of his eye, she hesitated before ringing up her next customer. Good, she needed to be knocked off balance a little, to be forced to take notice of what was right in front of her.

An hour later, his counter help arrived, and he turned over the running of the shop to his assistant manager. Untying the apron from his waist, he motioned for Sarah to follow him, then led the way into the office, where he'd left a brown bag. He closed the door before pulling an extra seat around and then motioned for her to sit.

"Here, eat." He handed her an everything bagel with

lox and cream cheese, then unwrapped the same for himself. "I made these before I picked you up."

"Oh, yum." Sinking into the chair, she bit into the bagel, and squished the cream cheese out the sides. "I've missed this."

He leaned over and wiped the corner of her mouth with his finger, before popping it into his mouth and sucking. His jeans tightened at the unplanned erotic movement. Clearing his throat, he returned to his breakfast. He needed to go slow so he wouldn't spook her. But God, slow was hard.

They ate in silence, broken finally when Sarah spoke.

"I shouldn't eat the rest of this." She wrapped the second half in the wax paper.

"Why not?"

"It's fattening."

He frowned at her, reached over and unwrapped her half of bagel. "You have nothing to worry about. Eat."

"No, I shouldn't." She pushed it away. "I didn't run this morning."

"Yes. You should." He pushed it toward her and waited.

After a few seconds dragged by, she reached for it. The tips of their fingers touched, and heat shot from his hand to his shoulder. He inhaled. He wanted to grab her hand, pull her onto his lap and kiss her, but he couldn't. Or rather, he shouldn't. Not yet. This time around, she would initiate whatever happened between them—if anything.

However, he wasn't against a little temptation.

He lifted his fingers and stroked hers. Once. Twice. Her chest rose and fell as if she had trouble breathing.

He knew the feeling.

Before he could go for three, she lifted the bagel to her mouth. Her hand shook a little. She took a bite and licked the excess cream cheese from her lips. Thank God he wasn't skimpy with his portions. Her jaw moved as she chewed, and her throat worked as she swallowed.

He pulled at the collar of his shirt.

God, it was hot in here.

"Are you going to join me?"

He blinked.

A small smile lifted the corners of her mouth, and she pointed to his bagel.

Oh. Right. Food. Two could play this game. He squeezed the bagel in his hand until the cream cheese oozed out, catching it with his tongue. She bit her lower lip.

Shifting in his chair, he let his leg bump into hers. He finished his breakfast, staring at her the entire time, imagining he was licking her. By the time he finished, he couldn't remember what he ate. Just the movements of her mouth and hands, and a raging desire to have sex with her on his desk.

A knock at the door doused his craving. She jumped.

"Come in," he called out.

Amanda, a local college student who worked on Mondays, stood in the doorway. Her puzzled gaze shifted between the two of them.

"Yes?" he asked.

"The Cramers want to place a catering order. Do you have the forms?"

He rummaged in his desk and handed her a stack of forms. "Here you go."

"Thanks." She backed out of the office.

Sarah grinned. "I think we scarred her for life."

Aaron ran a hand over his face. "I've seen her with her boyfriend, and let's just say I wish I hadn't."

She laughed. He wished he could record the sound and listen to it when she left. The thought sobered him, and he pushed away from the desk.

"There's an emergency temple meeting to discuss how to handle the vandalism," Aaron said. "Want to come?"

Sarah crumpled her garbage and handed it to him. "I'm only here for a few days. Will they want me there?"

"With all the work you do in DC? Sarah, you're smart and you know what you're talking about. Besides, you're still a member—you're welcome at everything, and you told your mom you'd help out for as long as you were here."

He wondered if she'd agree. He'd been angry at her for not helping remove the graffiti, and as she'd pointed out, she hadn't known about it. But this was different. If she was told about a meeting and refused to attend, that was an entirely different situation.

She nodded.

Relief flooded through him. "Let's go."

Excitement surged through Sarah as she left Aaron downstairs talking to her parents while she raced upstairs to change. The idea of helping guide her temple through this difficult time, providing them with tangible suggestions of what to do and how, was the silver lining in a horrible situation. Her work in DC filled her with satisfaction but had always taken a second seat to Matthew's. Here at home though, with her family's support and pride in her expertise—and Aaron thinking highly of her accomplishments—she experienced exhilaration in a new way.

She scanned the contents of her closet, searching for something to wear. A temple meeting wasn't as formal as services in the sanctuary, but she didn't want to show up wearing leggings and a sweaty athletic shirt. Her cheeks burned as she remembered what she'd done with a bagel. She'd never be able to eat one again. Sure, it was fun and mutual—in fact, Aaron had done more than she had. Little shivers of desire still ran through her. But she couldn't flirt with him any longer.

Her knees gave out and she sank hard on the edge of her bed. Any longer? How about at all?

Her stomach jumped every time he was in her presence. Her senses went on high alert, sounds were magnified and his scent drew her in. His hands on her face were rougher than Matthew's—

Ugh! There she went, comparing the two. But she couldn't help it. Aaron's skin was tougher, his muscles more pronounced, his presence more commanding. Matthew was more polished, his skin softer and less physically assertive. Both men possessed confidence, but Aaron's was quieter. Which man did she prefer?

She shook her head. Sure, her body reacted to Aaron— it always had—but he wasn't right for her. His dreams and lifestyle were different from what she wanted. How could she possibly trust that her interest in him was anything more than hormones and memories?

Regardless of what her mind might suggest, this was not a competition. There was no contest. None. She was not deciding between Matthew and Aaron. The only decision was whether to accept Matthew's proposal.

"Sarah, you ready?"

Aaron's voice called up the stairs, reverberating through her. She clenched her fingers into fists and stood.

"I'll be right there."

This time, she hurried, tossing items of clothing onto the bed until she settled on black pants with a black silk blouse. The people here liked her in color, but she needed her armor to withstand Aaron's assault, because although he wasn't declaring war, her insides were whispering *surrender*.

Jogging downstairs, she ignored Aaron's perusal, pretending she didn't notice his expression tighten. It didn't matter.

She grabbed her purse and kissed her mom's cheek. "I don't know how long I'll be…"

"It's okay, sweetheart. You're with Aaron and you're doing a *mitzvah*. However long it takes is fine."

Before she could react, Aaron ushered her out of the house and into his car. She fumed as he pulled out of her driveway.

"What's wrong?" He pulled onto the street.

"My mother's a traitor," she said, staring out the window as the burgeoning fall colors passed by in swaths of abstract shapes. She folded her arms across her middle and tried to convince herself she didn't look like a petulant teenager, but Aaron's quiet chuckle didn't help.

After a few minutes of silence passed—silence she'd spent reliving breakfast—she licked her lips and stifled a groan. "We can't do that again."

"Do what?"

She closed her eyes. "The bagels."

"We can't eat together? You know I own a deli, right? Food is kind of my thing."

She reached across the console and smacked his shoulder.

"Ow! What was that for?"

"Oh, come on, you big baby. It didn't hurt. You deserved it."

He pulled into the temple parking lot and shut off the engine. Frowning, he turned toward her. "First you hit me, then you call me a baby?"

She searched for the telltale glint of humor. His blue eyes were laser focused, but there was a lightness to them, a small crinkle in the corners.

"Like I said, you deserved it."

He rested his arm across the top of the steering wheel. His large hand dangled, the light dusting of hair on its back reflecting off the sun. His square nails were clean and short. She'd missed his hand.

"Why did I deserve it?" he asked.

It took her a moment to remember what they'd been talking about. "Because you're being purposely obtuse."

"About?"

"See!" She threw her hands up, frustrated. "You're doing it again!"

He stared at her like he could see deep into her soul. She refused to blink or look away, although the effort made her tremble.

"Seems like you enjoyed your bagel as much as I did. It'd be a shame not to eat one again." He released his seat belt and exited the truck. She sat in shock, until he opened her door. "Are you coming?"

He looked perfectly unaffected, until his nostrils flared a tiny bit. Two could play this game. Jumping from the cab, she brushed against him as she passed by, then called over her shoulder as she led the way into the temple, "Are you?"

His face reddening, he followed her inside.

Inside the temple, Aaron led Sarah into the conference room where monthly board meetings were held. This time, the large table was filled with board members and temple leaders. He nodded to several people and walked over to the rabbi.

"I hope you don't mind, but I thought Sarah might be able to help us."

The rabbi nodded. "I think she'd be a great asset today. Mike?" She turned toward the temple president who nodded in agreement, then pointed to two chairs. "Great. Please sit, both of you."

For the next half hour, people around the table spoke about how best to increase security at the temple without making their members feel uncomfortable or straining the budget. Aaron listened, his chest aching at the necessity for such measures. This was not the way he'd grown up.

Sarah cleared her throat. "If you don't mind, I also have a suggestion." Everyone turned to her. "I think you need to strengthen your connection to the community outside, in addition to the internal security measures you're discussing."

The rabbi tapped her hand on the table. "What do you mean?"

Sarah leaned forward. "Look, unfortunately the state-of-the-art security is a necessity, but it will only keep you physically safe. Now you need to address the relationship you have with the outside community. People are less inclined to harm you if they know you."

The rabbi nodded, as did several board members. Aaron leaned forward, captivated by a side of Sarah he'd never seen before.

"Let your neighbors know what's going on here," Sarah continued. "Ask them to help you keep an eye on the place. Invite them to activities that are more connection-based than religion-based."

"Such as?" Rhonda, one of the older women on the board, asked.

"Well, when you have a picnic and bonfire to celebrate *L'ag B'Omer*, invite your neighbors. Everyone likes to eat." Several people laughed. Aaron caught her eye and nodded.

"Or send them Happy New Year cards in January," she continued. "If you do an outdoor menorah lighting at Chanukah, invite their children to join in the lighting and the singing. Let people see us as people, just like them. You could also do a workshop or group event with local churches, mosques or Hindu temples. Look for activities that bring everyone together."

The rabbi steepled her fingers in front of her. "These are terrific ideas. Can you help us further develop them?"

Color rose in Sarah's cheeks. God, she was beautiful, Aaron thought.

"I'm only here for a few more days…"

She was here for a week. Not a few days—seven days. Aaron gripped the arms of his chair.

"For however long you're here, we could use your help," the rabbi said.

No one could refuse a rabbi. There was a long line of committee heads and volunteers to prove it, including half of the people in this room. Sarah was no exception, and Aaron withheld a smile of relief.

"If you'd like, I could draft a proposal and some sample letters for you to adapt as you see fit."

"Terrific. Our next board meeting isn't until after the High Holidays are over, thank goodness. We can present your information to the rest of the board then. With their approval, we should be able to start implementation for Chanukah, if not before."

When the meeting ended, Aaron held out her chair and walked Sarah out the door. Countless times, Sarah was stopped and thanked for her suggestions and willingness to help. Aaron couldn't stop the smile on his face, and the feeling of satisfaction was a nice relief after all his anger.

"Sarah, can I speak to you a minute?"

The rabbi's voice made Aaron pause.

"Yes, Rabbi, what can I do for you?" she asked.

"Would you mind coming into my office? Aaron, I assume you're her ride. Would you wait out here?"

* * *

Sarah stared at the book-filled shelves lining the walls of the rabbi's office, wondering what this was about.

The rabbi leaned forward. "It's so nice you're home to spend some time with everyone."

Sarah smiled. "It's been a long time. I like being back."

"Do you mind if I ask if you've thought of coming back here to stay?"

Sarah reared back. "My life is in DC. My job…"

"I know." The rabbi nodded. "But I also know of some employment opportunities that might be just your thing. I've seen how well you've fit in with your friends and family and now with our temple lay leaders. I just thought I'd mention it to you in case you want to give it some thought."

"I appreciate the thought. I really do," Sarah said. "But my life is in DC. Even if…"

"Even if…?" The rabbi let the words hang, prompting Sarah to continue.

Sarah stared out the window at the colorful autumn leaves. "I'm supposed to be considering my boyfriend's marriage proposal. He gave it out of the blue, and I told him I needed time to think about it. And then I came home, and…" She paused, unwilling to tell her about Aaron. "…and everything was so different."

The rabbi leaned forward. "And now?"

"I always thought we were perfect together and wanted the same things. But lately, while I've been here, I'm realizing there are things we don't agree on and it's just making me more confused, not less."

Sarah squeezed her hands together until they ached.

"You have to listen to your inner voice, regardless of what it's telling you. In my experience, a relationship with someone means not being able to picture living without them. It means accepting the good and the bad. It means being stronger together than you are apart."

Sarah's neck heated. "What if I'm never certain?"

The rabbi leaned back in her chair. "What if the thing you're actually afraid of is starting over?"

Sarah stilled. Could she be right?

"Trust yourself. You'll know." The rabbi rose and placed her arm around Sarah as they walked out of her office. "And just remember you have plenty of options."

Outside the rabbi's office, they caught up with Aaron and the three of them headed toward the lobby.

"Did the police find anything on the surveillance video?" Aaron asked as they walked to the door.

The rabbi shook her head. "Whomever did it kept their faces averted from the cameras, but from their size and the way they carried themselves, they appear to be teens or young adults."

"If they made sure to turn their faces away from the cameras, they knew we had them," Aaron said. "Which means they knew they were doing something wrong."

The rabbi nodded. "I mentioned that to the police chief. He knows a group of troubled kids he wants to talk to and said he'd let me know what happened. In the meantime, Sarah's suggestions are more important than ever. Maintaining our current relationships and creating new ones are essential. I want to nip this in the bud."

After saying their goodbyes, Aaron walked with Sarah to their car.

"You made a lot of good points to the rabbi."

"I'm glad I could help." Sarah smiled. "It felt good to offer advice."

He stuffed his hands in his pockets. "I have a friend who teaches at the middle school. He's noticed a spike in some troubling behavior. Any chance you want to talk to him with me?"

"What do you mean 'troubling behavior'?"

"He mentioned inappropriate jokes, whispering, things like that."

"It's a big leap to anti-Semitic graffiti."

"True, but maybe you'll notice something that I wouldn't."

She gave him a long look. Did he really need her help or was he making an excuse to keep her with him longer? Or maybe, she was just reading into things. "Okay."

He flashed her a smile. "Great. Thank you."

Chapter Ten

Sarah searched for Aaron in the dim lighting of the Gold Bar that evening. Spotting him across the room, she headed toward him as he rose and waved her over. She swallowed. He stood beneath the light, his hair bright like flames. The play of shadows and light accentuated his powerful build, making him resemble a god come to earth. She shook her head. It was no good thinking those kinds of thoughts. Nothing would come of them. Nothing *could* come of them.

As she approached the table, the other man stood, and Aaron held her chair.

"Hi, I'm Sarah." She met the man's outstretched hand. His smile was open and his appeared younger, more boyish, than Aaron, despite his bald head. She immediately liked him.

"Dave. Nice to meet you. Aaron's told me all about you." She shot a glance at Aaron. "I hope good things."

"Of course," Aaron confirmed, and Dave nodded.

As they sat, Aaron passed a glass of wine to Sarah. "I ordered you a chardonnay, but if you'd prefer something else, I can flag down the waitress."

Sarah took a sip, relishing the fruity flavor. "No, this is great. I don't remember this place."

"Probably three years old?" Dave said.

Aaron nodded. "Did you hear about the vandalism at the temple?"

"Yeah," Dave said. "It's a shame. I'm glad it was easily repaired, but I'm sure it shook you all up. I know how I would feel."

"It did," Aaron said. "You never think something like this will happen to you. And then it does."

"Do you know who did it?"

Aaron shook his head. "No, it's why I wanted to talk with you. Remember the conversation you and I had last week?"

Dave nodded.

"Well, I was wondering if you thought any of your students could have done it or know who did."

Sarah winced at Aaron's directness.

Dave fisted his hands on the table. "Whoa, it's a big leap from making inappropriate jokes to vandalizing a synagogue."

"You're right," Sarah interjected. "But in my experience, actions like these don't start in a vacuum. They need an opening."

Dave's jaw tightened, so she gentled her voice. "From the security video footage, the police think it was a group of kids. Kids talk. You're well positioned to hear something. If not, one of your students might."

"And since you have such a great rapport with them, maybe it will bother one of them enough, and they will come talk to you," Aaron added.

Dave's jaw relaxed, and he took a sip of his beer. "I can

put out some feelers tomorrow and see if I hear anything."
He turned to Sarah. "Any suggestions as to how I get my
students to understand why this behavior is wrong and to
feel free to come talk to me?"

Sarah nodded. "Absolutely. Give me your email, and
I can send you some links to resources and materials."

"I'd appreciate it," Dave said. "Thanks."

With the hard part of the conversation over, the guys
relaxed. Sarah studied them as they chatted about football.
Both men included Sarah, teasing her for being a Ravens
fan in Giants territory. While their friendship wasn't as
old as hers and Aaron's, she could see it ran deep.

Aaron sat back in his chair and stretched his arm along
the edge of hers, not making a move on her, but sending
the signal he would if she gave him any encouragement.
Something about the posture made her wish she could sink
into the crook of his arm.

She was practically engaged to Matthew—off-limits to
other men, and more importantly, flirting was off-limits
for her. Even if the nape of her neck tingled at Aaron's
proximity.

She focused on Dave's open expression. *He* didn't con-
fuse her. *His* voice didn't send shivers along her spine. *His*
brown eyes didn't focus on her like laser beams, making
her shift in her seat. He was just Dave, in his plain, boring jeans and green-and-blue-striped shirt.

Aaron's arm slipped off the back of her chair and rested
against her shoulder blades. Warmth spread through her.
She leaned forward a hair and his arm followed her.

"When's the last time you were home?" Dave asked.

She stared at him. What did he say? She blinked. Oh,
right!

She cleared her throat. "I'm not sure. It's been a while.

Mostly my parents come visit me. Or I've come in for a day here or there. But for a visit this long? I can't remember."

Aaron stiffened next to her. Home was filled with memories she hadn't wanted to face at first. Later, she'd been busy setting up her own life in DC. She'd joined a synagogue and invited her parents to come to her. Memories of home faded over time, and with them, the importance of the people and places she'd grown up with. She shouldn't have stayed away so long, but she hadn't known how to handle the emotions this place brought out in her. Aaron's presence here never strayed from her mind. After this visit, she doubted he ever would.

"Are you glad to be home?" Dave asked.

"I am." She nodded. "I didn't realize how much I'd missed it."

"But your life is still there," Aaron said.

She met his gaze. "Yes. It is."

Aaron grunted before bringing his beer to his lips and drinking. He was attracted to her. But attraction was different than wanting to make a life with her.

"Well, it's great to have you here." Dave's glance shifted between them, and he rose, pulled his wallet from his pocket and dropped a fifty on the table. "I've got to run. My treat."

Aaron opened his mouth as though he might refuse, but Dave shot him a stern glare. Aaron threw his hands up in surrender and grinned. "Thanks, man. I'll get you next time."

"I suppose it would be useless for me to offer," Sarah said.

"You found yourself a smart woman," Dave said to Aaron.

Aaron winked. Sarah wanted to protest, to say she wasn't Aaron's anything, but she didn't want to draw more attention to a situation of which she was already losing control. The three of them left the bar, and after saying goodbye to Dave, Aaron walked Sarah to her car.

"Thanks for including me tonight," she said. "Dave is a nice guy."

Beneath the streetlight, Aaron's shoulders rose, a look of uncertainty crossing his face.

Sarah's heart squeezed. "It'll be okay, Aaron. The community is pulling together, and the vandals will be caught."

His features smoothed out, and Sarah fisted her hands at her sides to keep from reaching out and touching his cheek. It would be rough with end-of-day stubble, but warm like him—and inappropriate in every way.

"I hope you're right." He stuffed his hands in his pockets and swallowed before continuing. "I work tomorrow until four. Can I interest you in axe throwing afterward?"

"Axe throwing?"

"Yeah, it's awesome."

"I don't think I've ever held an axe, much less thrown one."

He folded his arms across his chest. "Are you chicken?"

"Of dying, yes."

He laughed. "They give you lessons, and I promise you won't die."

"I don't want to get maimed, either. I like all my parts where they are."

His eyes roamed over her. "I like all your parts, too."

Sarah's face heated, but a shiver of awareness shot through her.

Aaron waggled his eyebrows. "Come on. It'll be fun. I promise."

"I can't believe I'm considering this."

"I'll pick you up after work. Wear sneakers and clothes you can move in."

"Are you sure about this?"

Aaron leaned against her car, his stare intense. "I'd never let anything happen to you."

Of all the activities Aaron could have suggested, axe throwing was one of his more brilliant ones. Especially when Sarah walked toward his car, and he noticed her outfit.

Her fitted gray athletic shirt and black leggings left little to the imagination. His mouth dried when he thought about the "moves" she could make in them. Her natural soap-and-shampoo scent filled his truck's cab, and he envisioned removing her ponytail from its band and running his fingers through her long brown hair while his mouth explored every inch of her body.

Now that they'd arrived and her nerves were coming to the fore, she stood as close to him as possible.

He was a genius.

As he signed the waiver, he vowed he'd work harder at being humble tomorrow. Today, he'd appreciate every ounce of his brilliance while admiring every inch of her body.

The instructor brought them to an area resembling a batting cage, with a wooden target on one end and a tree stump in the middle. He pulled a variety of axes and tomahawks from the stump, and he fitted each of them with one that was the correct size and weight for their arms. After a few instructional rounds, they were left on their own to practice.

"That's it?" Sarah's voice squeaked as the instructor left.

Aaron suppressed a laugh. "What else do you need?" Raising his arms high over his head, he aimed for the target and threw the axe. It tumbled end over end and landed inside the outer ring. Not bad, but he could do better.

"Oh, I don't know, more than a toss or two before being considered capable." She eyed the tools warily. "These are deadly weapons, and we could kill someone."

"Not unless we block the target." He stood behind her in the "safe zone."

She raised an eyebrow. "I know someone who went golfing once, swung at the ball and sent it backward— right through a Mercedes's window."

Aaron choked. "It was you, wasn't it?"

"Of course not!" Annoyance flashed in her eyes, lightening them to an amber color.

"Well then, I have nothing to worry about over here." He jerked his chin toward the target. "Go for it."

She gripped her axe in her right hand, turned toward the target and drew in a deep breath. Her shoulders rose and fell, trepidation palpable from where he stood. She raised both arms over her head and tossed the axe. It sailed through the air, bounced off the target and landed on the ground.

"Come here." He moved toward her.

"Planning to gloat?"

"Nope." He turned her toward the target and stood behind her, taking each of her wrists in his hands. Raising her arms over her head, he positioned them correctly for her. The warmth of her body seeped into him, and his heartbeat increased. His mouth close to her ear, he said, "Try this next time."

"Okay."

Her voice was breathless. He wondered if she was afraid of him or if she was as affected by their bodies pressed against each other as he was. She was warm and supple. Her rounded backside pressed against his groin. Her silky hair tickled his jaw. Her smooth skin sent heat up his arms straight to his heart, which beat faster every second she remained in his arms.

Axes were weapons all right. But not of war.

"You two got it under control over there?" the instructor called.

With a last squeeze, Aaron stepped away. "Yeah, we're good." His voice rasped and he cleared his throat. "Thanks."

After a few rounds, Sarah's confidence grew and, with it, the force of her throw. Soon, she hit the target as well.

"See, you can do it, and no one gets hurt." He put his arm around her shoulder, and something settled as she fit into his space. She belonged there.

God, he was in so much trouble.

She grinned. "Maybe I've found my new calling."

"I'd say don't quit your day job, but I like having you here, so…" He watched her while he voiced his opinion. Would she become uncomfortable again or say something flippant? He kind of enjoyed keeping her off balance.

"I like being here, too," she said softly.

The room tilted. Did she mean what he thought she might mean?

"But axe throwing doesn't pay enough to support me." She winked and his insides went into overdrive.

"We'll have to work on that one." He tried to maintain his equilibrium. It wouldn't do to spook her. He wanted her to stay, not send her running for the hills.

"You guys ready for a game?" the instructor asked as he returned to them.

It was all Aaron could do to concentrate on Sarah. A game requiring strategy? He wasn't sure he could manage. "Sure," he said.

When Sarah nodded, the instructor showed them how to play a version of tic-tac-toe.

"Wait, you mean I have to aim?" Sarah asked.

"It's fun," the instructor said. "And you might surprise yourself."

Aaron didn't think he could handle any more surprises.

A tic-tac-toe board? Sarah shook her head. Xs and Os she could handle. Three in a row—no problem. But add in the axe part, and she was toast. The instructor correlated certain squares with certain areas of the target. By looking at the board, you determined where you needed your axe to land. All you had to do was throw for that spot. Easy peasy.

Except it wasn't. Not in the slightest. She could throw the axe. She could hit the target three out of four times. But hit a specific area of the target on purpose and win at tic-tac-toe?

This was their fourth game and Aaron had won the previous three with ease. He was on track to win this one, too. She sighed.

"Hey, don't worry." He removed his axe from the target and returned to the ready position. "This is your first time. You're doing great."

"You're saying that because the loser has to buy the winner dinner."

He turned his broad grin on her, and she retreated a step. His smiles were blinding, especially when they were directed at her.

"There is that."

She aimed and threw the axe. It bounced and landed on the ground. "You know, for someone who works with food every day, you'd think going out to eat wouldn't be exciting."

"It isn't."

She frowned. "Why did you make the bet?"

"You weren't listening." He shook his head.

"Of course I was."

The muscles in his forearms rippled as he placed the axe on the stump before turning to her. "What did I say?"

She swallowed. "You said loser buys winner dinner."

"Pitiful."

"You're the one who suggested betting on tic-tac-toe."

He stepped closer, and she resisted the urge to step away. "I said the loser *provides* dinner. Big difference." He took another step toward her, reminding her of a tiger stalking its prey.

"It's the same thing."

He laughed. The rumble of his voice traveled along her spine. "No, it's very different."

"How so?"

One last step and he stood toe-to-toe with her. His breath was minty. His body heat wrapped around her like a warm blanket. His blue irises glowed, specks of darker and lighter blue winking like light shining on a diamond. "Winner gets to choose."

"Choose…?"

He glanced at the tic-tac-toe board. "I won. I choose a meal…that you cook."

His words doused the heat consuming her. "You want me to cook for you?"

"I do." He puffed out his chest and smiled at her.

"I don't cook."

"Right. Everyone cooks, Sarah, even if it's not a gourmet meal. Pasta, eggs—"

"No, seriously, I don't cook."

He retreated a step and finally, she could breathe.

"How do you eat if you don't cook?" He quirked a brow.

"Takeout, business dinners, Matthew…"

Aaron circled her, his eyes roving over her slight frame. "I guess it's why you stay thin. He must not take you to good restaurants."

When Matthew mentioned how thin she was, he meant it as a compliment. Coming from Aaron, however, it was definitely *not* a compliment.

Resentment built inside of her. "I'm sorry if I think it's important to watch how I look."

He held up his hands in surrender. "I didn't say anything."

She narrowed her eyes. He didn't have to say anything—judgment oozed out from his pores. "I meet with important people, and I need to be taken seriously. And unfortunately, some of them still judge on first impressions."

"I find it hard to believe someone would think you're less capable with a few extra pounds on you. Or any poundage, for that matter. Your brains are important, not your body mass index."

He was right and she knew it—had known it even when she'd opened her mouth and defended her body. But he'd caught her off guard. And no matter how she explained it, telling Aaron that her looks were important to Matthew would make her almost fiancé look bad. As maybe he should.

Sarah swallowed as Aaron continued staring at her, examining her with the same appreciation a farmer might look over a prize heifer he was about to purchase. In moments like this, asinine things tended to pop out of her mouth. Retorts like, "Thank you for noticing."

Heat flooded Sarah's cheeks as she realized her imagined words had tumbled out of her mouth without her permission.

Aaron stopped. A look flashed across his face, almost like he might make a snide comment or tease her for admitting he was right. But it disappeared as fast as she processed it and a slow, lazy, sexy grin appeared in its place. "You're welcome. And for the record, out of all the things

I notice about you—and the list is extensive—your intelligence is the most important."

Her heart squeezed. It was the loveliest thing he could've said to her. She nodded, then turned away to compose herself. When she could speak without her voice wobbling, she turned toward him. "My intelligence helps me pick great restaurants."

He chuckled. "I'm not letting you off that easy, Sarah. Didn't your mom show you how to cook?"

"Sure, years ago. And I haven't touched an oven since."

"Stove?"

She shook her head.

"Slow cooker?"

"I don't know what that is."

He groaned. "You have a lot to learn."

"Why, because I'm a woman who doesn't cook? Sexist, much?"

Once again, he stood too close to her. "You needing to learn to cook has nothing to do with your gender, but rather with independence. A person cannot live on microwaves alone or something like that. Not to mention, you might learn to enjoy it." His face brightened. "In fact, I have the perfect idea."

"Why do I think I won't like this?"

He put his arm around her shoulders, and she wished she could curl into him.

"I'm going to teach you to cook, starting with our dinner, right now."

Chapter Eleven

Aaron busied himself with pulling pans from drawers and ingredients from the fridge. Anything to keep from noticing how Sarah's presence in his apartment, in his kitchen, made it feel like home.

"I can't believe you don't know how to cook." He pulled out a bowl while Sarah tied her hair into a ponytail. He paused, admiring the delicate bone structure of her face.

She shrugged. "It isn't part of my daily routine."

"I think you might be the only Jewish girl I know who can't."

She bristled, and he withheld a laugh. He loved teasing her.

"First of all, I'm a Jewish *woman*, not *girl*. Second, stereotype much? And third, how many do you know?"

He focused on lathering his hands with dish soap, his back to her so she couldn't see his smile. "Enough to know you're in the minority."

"Humph. Too chicken to name a number?"

"Not chicken," he said. "Wise."

She nudged him with her hip, and he moved over, making room for her at the sink.

"Where's your hand soap?" she asked.

"Hand soap? What hand soap? Use the dish soap."

"You may know lots of Jewish women, but none of them wash their hands here." She tore off a square of paper towel. "Because if they did, you'd have hand soap."

He grunted. He couldn't remember Melissa asking for hand soap, not to mention her fitting in so well here. "Or maybe I don't want my hands to smell like flowers."

She raised an eyebrow at him, and he relaxed. Attraction to Sarah aside, he loved that they still could banter with each other.

"I'm going to teach you how to make an omelet. They're easy and can be breakfast, lunch or dinner, so you're getting a three-in-one meal lesson."

"Wow. Lucky me."

"Careful, or I'll make you do the dishes, too."

"Make me." She made air quotes. "That's funny."

He wanted to grab her, throw her over his shoulder and make her pay for her sass. With a deep breath, he handed her an egg. "Can I assume you know how to crack this?"

"In the bowl or over your head?" She grabbed it out of his hand and slapped it against the edge of her bowl. The shell shattered, piercing the yolk and resulting in an eggy mess in the bowl.

Without saying a word, he cracked an egg into his own bowl, splitting the shell two and dropping a perfect raw egg into the center of his bowl.

"Show off." She stuck her tongue out and picked the eggshell pieces out with well-manicured, pale pink nails.

At least she didn't paint her nails black, too. He cleared his throat and broke three more eggs.

She looked at him for direction when she'd finished.

"Is that all?" he asked. "One egg?"

"How many do I need?"

"For an omelet, at least two, although three would be better."

She sighed and cracked two more, doing only a little better with the eggshells. Huffing, she blew an errant strand of hair out of her face.

He restrained himself from tucking it behind her ear. Doing so would cross the line, as would most of his thoughts about what he'd like to do with her.

When she finished, he splashed a little milk in his bowl and handed it to her. "Just a little," he said. "Better to have to add more than to make it milky."

He closed one eye and waited while she added milk to her own bowl, sure she would pour in half a gallon.

"Very good." He grinned at the tiny splash she'd managed.

She stuck her nose in the air. "See, I'm not totally useless." She peeked down at her bowl. "Except when it comes to eggs."

"Well, in the future, you'll know to crack them into a separate bowl before adding them to whatever recipe you're making."

"I think I remember my grandma doing that," she said.

Grabbing a whisk, he showed her how to beat the eggs until they were light and frothy. "If she kept kosher, she probably did. From a strict Jewish law point of view, you're supposed to inspect the egg before you add it to the other ingredients. That way if there's something wrong with it, you don't *treif* the entire dish."

"She did," Sarah said. "And I remember learning that in Hebrew school, but only now that you mention it."

He nodded, then pointed to the counter, where he'd laid

out cheeses and vegetables. "What do you want in your omelet?"

Sarah looked over her options. "Provolone, spinach and mushrooms."

He handed her a small frying pan. "Melt a pat or two of butter."

Sarah tossed two pats of butter into the pan, set it on the stove and watched it melt from a yellow square to a liquid.

"Now add a handful of mushrooms and spinach and stir."

Again, she followed his instructions, tossing in the vegetables and stirring so they didn't burn. When he was sure she had it under control, he did the same.

"Wait," she said. "I thought I was making dinner for you."

"You are."

"How? I'm cooking my own omelet."

"Just wait." He turned off the heat and Sarah did the same. He grabbed two more frying pans and handed one to Sarah. "Add another pat or two of butter to this one."

When the butter melted, he pointed to her bowl of eggs. "Pour the eggs into the new pan and let them cook a little."

Under Aaron's tutelage and close watch, she cooked the eggs—adding the cheese and sautéed vegetables, too—to near perfection before it was time for the last step: folding the omelet.

"I don't think I can do this," she said.

"Sure, you can." He demonstrated with his own.

Sarah bit her lip and closed one eye. Then, with a quick movement, she flipped one half of the egg over onto its other half. "It worked!"

Her smile was so wide, he was momentarily transfixed. "I knew you could do it. Now, flip it over."

When the omelets were finished and plated, they carried

them to the table. As they sat, he handed her the omelet he'd made. It took only a second before a look of understanding crossed her face. Her eyes glittered with suppressed laughter as she handed him her plate. "I think I'm getting the better part of this deal."

Aaron watched as she stabbed a bite of egg and lifted it to her lips before chewing slowly. All coherent thought fled, leaving him unable to manage a response.

"This is delicious," she said. "You should sell this at the deli."

He shook his head, both to clear it and to respond. "I like having food I make because I enjoy it, not because I have to make it for others." He cut into the omelet she'd made him and took a bite. It wasn't as aesthetically pleasing as the one he'd prepared for her—and the edges were crispier than he preferred—but, overall, it tasted good. "Nice job."

"Really? Or are you saying that? Because yours looks much better than mine."

He swallowed and drank a gulp of water. "Practice will improve how it looks. But the taste and the texture are great. Now you can cook for your boyfriend."

He cursed at himself for ruining the moment. Why did he bring the guy up?

Sarah pushed a lock of hair behind her ear, then took a long drink of her iced tea. She placed the glass on the table but kept her hand clenched around it. He couldn't help wondering if she regretted his mention of her boyfriend, too.

Sarah glanced down at her plate and pushed a piece of egg around. "Matthew's not big on home-cooked meals."

There was more to it. The tone of her voice gave her away, like she was keeping secrets. But Aaron still knew her better than most and she'd never completely fool him.

While he didn't know what those secrets were, he knew she had them.

Aaron was torn. He wanted to know more, but he knew she didn't want to be pushed. Part of him wanted to respect her wishes and keep their time together comfortable, like it had been before he mentioned the boyfriend. The other part of him wanted more information. He grappled with the decision a long moment, finally deciding he respected her too much to go against her wishes.

"Well, it's always good to increase your repertoire," he said, opting for a neutral response.

When their dinner was finished, they rose to clear the table in a slightly awkward silence.

"I'll wash. You dry." Aaron piled the dishes on the counter.

"But I lost the bet."

"And you cooked."

"So did you."

He handed her the dish towel. "Shush."

She paused mid reach. "Did you 'shush' me?"

A memory from their high school days flashed in his mind, and he hung his head.

There'd been about twenty of them in the brightly colored youth lounge in the temple basement. Officers sat on a cherry red sofa, while the rest of them sprawled on multicolored beanbags, ramshackle hand-me-down sofas and the indoor-outdoor carpeted floor. Sarah, as president, led the meeting. Aaron didn't remember what she was saying, only that he believed she'd been talking too long. So, he'd said "shush," loud enough for the rest of the room to hear. Gasps and "oohs" echoed. Sarah shut her mouth and dumped her water bottle over his head. As he sputtered, the rabbi chose that moment to walk in.

"What did you do to deserve that?" she'd asked Aaron.

Wiping his face, he'd answered.

The rabbi winked at Sarah. The next time she saw Aaron, she called him into her office, told him a short story about how relationships should be mutually respectful and handed him a towel, personalized with his name. "I think you're going to need this."

The memory seared his brain for a long time. How could he have slipped now?

"Sorry," he mumbled.

The water turned on, and he jerked his attention to her, his eyes wide. "Don't you dare."

Her lips quivered. "I don't know how to wash dishes without turning on the water."

Shaking his head, he grabbed the dish soap and a sponge and scrubbed the pot. Her quiet laughter next to him filled him with warmth. He could get used to this. She flicked him with the towel, and he arched his brow. "Really? You sure about this?"

She bit her lip, nodded and ran out of the room. After turning off the water, he raced after her, her squeals echoing through the hallway. He caught her in his living room and tackled her on the sofa.

Lying on top of her—their noses millimeters apart, her breath fanning his face—his body roared to life. The scent of her shampoo, something fruity, filled his nostrils. When they were younger, she'd always smelled like strawberries and cream. Now? He wasn't sure what the scent was. He inhaled, wanting her to fill his soul. He ran his fingers through her hair. It was silkier than he remembered. Wrapped around his wrists, her hair acted like a binding, connecting him to her, and he hated to pull away. Her eyes dilated, turning a molten brown. Her lashes were thick and long and fluttered as he massaged her scalp. And her lips? They trembled, and he wanted more than anything to taste them.

Last time wasn't enough.

Last time.

When he'd stolen a kiss.

Stolen because she wasn't his.

She was someone else's.

He wasn't a thief.

Taking a deep breath, he pulled away from her. "I'm sorry, I shouldn't have done that."

Sarah moved away from him. "No, I shouldn't have, either."

He tried to catch his breath and rein in his libido. "Nothing happened."

"And nothing can." She wrapped her arms around her middle and drew her knees up, as far away from him as possible on the couch. "I should go."

He didn't want his time with her to end. "Please stay, Sarah."

She stared at him for a second, then buried her head in her knees. "I can't. We can't."

"Are you sure?" His vision tunneled. She was here, but still far away.

Jerking her head up, she flashed daggers at him with her gaze. "What does that mean?"

"It means you're here, and he's not." A tiny flame of hope, like the eternal flame above the ark in the synagogue, formed inside him. He'd wanted to bring this discussion out in the open, make her see he was here and the boyfriend wasn't. That he was the man for her.

Her face paled, masking all expression and preventing him from reading her at all. The "new" Sarah was back.

"So what?" she challenged. "Do you spend every waking moment with your girlfriends?"

I don't care about them—I want to spend all my time with you. "I try to. I want to."

"Well, we don't like to smother each other."

He raised an eyebrow at her. *Does she believe that or is that what she tells herself?*

"What, you think there's only one way to have a relationship?" She folded her arms across her chest. "Since we're practically engaged, obviously you're wrong."

"Maybe not since you need time to think about it. You used to say you'd know the minute you met the man you wanted to spend the rest of your life with." His gaze bore into her.

"We both said a lot of things we didn't mean when we were younger."

The flame of hope inside him flickered. Moving toward her, he stood and stared down at her stony figure on the sofa. With her knees pulled tightly to her chest and her chin high in the air, she appeared both defiant and fragile at the same time. As usual, she tied him in knots. "I meant everything I said," he said, his voice low. "Everything."

She blanched and blinked up at him multiple times. Finally, she rose and pushed him away from her. "I have to get out of here. This discussion is over." She glared at him. "*We* are over."

Sarah's feet pounded the pavement.

"No, no, no." Her breath came in spurts and seemed to shout *Tease!*

Images of Aaron's body, taut with desire, filled her mind. She ran until her side ached, desperately wishing she could escape what had almost happened with Aaron. Sweat poured off her face and she picked up speed, but no matter how fast she ran, she couldn't outrun the memory of how close she'd come to cheating on Matthew. She had led Aaron on. She hated people like herself.

How could she consider Matthew's proposal if she was tempted—oh so tempted—by Aaron? She might've changed her mind about knowing who she'd marry—after all, she'd been a child when she'd made that declaration to Aaron—but her opinion *about* marriage hadn't changed. Marriage was sacred. For that matter, so were relationships. She'd never been a serial dater, and she'd never been a cheater. Until today, when she'd nearly thrown away the commitment she'd made to Matthew. How could she do something like that? What kind of person did that? A terrible one—one who didn't deserve the love of another human being. It didn't matter that she hadn't completed the act of cheating. She'd *almost* cheated. And she'd certainly been more than tempted. Despite her mother's teasing and saying, "almost doesn't count," it did.

And Aaron? There was no doubt he was attracted to her. Heck, she could practically smell the pheromones whenever he was near her. In the space of a few days, he'd somehow gone from resenting her to wanting her. And even if it was unintentional on her part, leading him on was unfair to him. Besides, she wasn't the same person he'd known ten years ago. She'd changed.

Truce be damned, it was time to regain control. For both their sakes, she'd have to keep her distance.

By the time she reached her parents' house, she was sweaty, exhausted and resolute. She tiptoed inside, not wanting to deal with the questions her parents were sure to ask if they saw her looking like this. In the kitchen, however, was a note stating they'd gone out with friends. With a sigh of relief, she pulled off her clothes and headed to the shower. As she turned off the water and wrapped herself in a towel, she straightened her shoulders. It was time to get this over with. She pulled in a deep breath and, with shaking hands, dialed the phone. It rang three times before he answered.

"Hey, Sarah." Matthew's voice was bright. "I was thinking of you."

Her throat clogged at the sound of his voice. She closed her eyes and dug deep for strength.

"I can't do this anymore, Matthew."

"What do you mean?" A rustling noise accompanied his voice.

"Us. Marriage. Any of it." She took a deep breath. "I'm sorry, Matthew."

There was a muffled sound through the phone. "Hold on a sec, Sarah." After a brief moment, she heard a click. "I'm back," he said, his voice echoing. "I thought we said we weren't going to make any rash decisions."

Her stomach tightened. Matthew used the word *we* as if he was somehow part of her decision. Which he was, but not in the way he meant. No one could tell her who to marry, not even the man she was considering marrying.

"I'm not making a rash decision," she said. Through the phone, she heard knocking. "Where are you?"

"I'm in the bathroom. Hold on!"

She pulled the phone away from her ear. She'd assumed he was talking to her, but then a female voice laughed in the background.

"Matthew, what's going on?"

"Nothing, Sarah, just give me a second." The phone grew muffled again, like he was covering it with his hand.

The woman laughed again, and Sarah's heart sank to her stomach. Her hands grew cold, and her body went numb.

"Matthew, are you alone?"

"Of course I am, Sarah." His voice was calm, but it held

an underlying streak of anxiety that only someone who knew him well would notice.

He was lying. How could she consider marrying him? The future she'd imagined, the one she'd discussed with Matthew, mocked her. His looks, the reputation he was so proud of and their plans—all of it dissolved right in front of her. The benefits of having a politician for a husband flitted away.

Matthew was the wrong man for her.

"Do you want to reconsider that answer?" She waited and wondered how he would explain this away. She knew he'd try to spin it. Her vision tunneled, making the furniture in her bedroom seem very far away. A high-pitched sound rang in her ears.

Matthew groaned. "It's no big deal," he said in the same way he did when commenting about a vote that didn't go as planned. "The other day, I had a work dinner with a colleague. She's flirted with me before. I told you about Leanne, didn't I? She leaned over to kiss me goodnight, and it got a little more involved than I'd planned."

"The other day? So, tonight isn't the first time."

The colorful walls of her bedroom, the scent of the fresh-baked cookies her mom had made earlier in the day and the photos on her dresser of her parents laughing, magnified as if in a fun house. They stared at her as if mocking the difference between what she thought she wanted and what she'd end up with if she married Matthew.

In that moment, all the guilt she'd held regarding her reactions to Aaron slipped away.

"No, but it was nothing. Come on, Sarah. You can't argue about it when you did the same thing."

The same thing?

Sarah held back a gasp. Aaron had kissed her, and she'd

confessed as much to Matthew. "How is this even remotely the same?"

There's no way she could marry Matthew now, not after what she'd discovered.

"The important thing is we told each other," Matthew said. "A mistake every now and then isn't a big deal."

Every now and then? She couldn't subject herself to a life with a man who cheated on her. She'd made mistakes, of course—who didn't? But she'd agonized over every one of them, then confessed them to Matthew and begged his forgiveness. But what good was his forgiveness if the only reason he'd given it was so he could give himself permission for his future transgressions?

"You're kidding, right?" This time she did gasp out loud. "Do you think I'd be okay with something like this? With you kissing other women?"

"Sarah, come on. We're not engaged yet. And if we're discreet, mistakes are forgivable. We're human, after all."

She might be a different woman than the girl who left here ten years ago, but she still had her dignity, her self-worth and her pride—and no man who stomped on those three things was worth her time.

"You've got to be joking, Matthew! Is this repayment for what happened with Aaron?" Sarah's temples pounded. "While we might not officially be engaged, *you* asked me to marry you. Did that change because I didn't say yes right away?"

"Sarah, what's gotten into you?"

She closed her eyes. "We're done, Matthew." She hung up the phone and tossed it onto the bed.

It rang immediately, and Matthew's number flashed on the screen. She turned off the phone and left the room.

The walls around her shook as the door slammed behind her. Sarah smiled. *Damn, that felt good!*

* * *

Aaron stood behind the deli counter, taking up space. He'd stepped back and was watching Michael—one of the teens who worked part time for him on weekends—slice tomatoes and rolls for sandwiches. He'd been in a bear of a mood since the previous night with Sarah, and he'd growled at more people than he'd served. When two tiny old ladies turned tail and scuttled out the door, presumably in fear of being the next target of his temper, Michael offered to make the rest of the sandwiches. Since then, everyone had tiptoed around him—quite a feat given how busy the deli was that afternoon.

"Excuse me," a customer called to him.

"What!" He turned a fierce glare on the older man with the black glasses.

From across the room, his father excused himself from the conversation he'd been having with someone on the floor and marched toward him. Reaching Aaron's side, he grabbed his elbow in a not-so-gentle grip and pushed him toward the office. Behind the counter, his staff apologized to the bewildered customer and rushed to help.

"I don't know what's going on with you, son, but until you can be civil, you need to stick to paperwork." With a gentle shove, Aaron found himself seated behind his desk. Then, without a backward glance, his father left and closed the door behind him.

He stared at the door. He wouldn't be shocked to find he'd been locked in. He'd probably deserve it. He dropped his head into his hands.

He'd tossed and turned all night, unable to stop thinking about Sarah. She was attracted to him. He knew she was—every bit as much as he was to her. Could she throw everything they'd had, everything they still had, away? Time was running out. Soon she'd leave and give that other guy an answer and she'd be lost to Aaron forever. He'd vowed to convince her they deserved a chance, but so far, she hadn't relented.

His leg bounced beneath his desk and the walls closed in around him. He needed to burn off some steam and quiet the rising fear of losing her. He pushed away from his desk, grabbed his jacket and walked out of his office and through the deli, leaving a mostly full store filled with customers and employees gaping after him.

Aaron's first stop was the school to see if Dave was free. As he pulled into the parking lot, the police chief's cruiser pulled up next to him.

"Hey, Aaron." Chief Forsyth smiled. "Going back to school?"

"Funny, I could ask you the same thing. I'm sure our football team could use your help."

"Ha, pretty sure my joints would creak louder than the play calls."

"I hear that." Aaron grinned. "Any progress on who vandalized the temple?"

A pair of lines formed between the chief's brows and his body stiffened. "We're getting there. Still running down leads."

"Keep me in the loop, and let me know if I can help out, will you?"

"Will do." With a nod, he rolled up his window and pulled away.

Aaron frowned, wishing there was more progress. The lot was nearly vacant now that most of the staff, teachers and students left for the day. Dave's car was still there, so he climbed out of his own and headed toward the front entrance. Once inside, he walked toward Dave's classroom and arrived as his friend was putting on his jacket.

"Hey." Dave turned at the knock on his door and smiled at Aaron. "What are you doing here?"

"I needed to get out of the deli and clear my head."

Dave smirked. "You wouldn't have a pretty brunette on your mind, would you?"

Aaron's fists tightened at the sudden desire to slug his friend. "Want to hit the batting cages?"

His face lit up. "Great idea. Meet you there."

Fifteen minutes later, Aaron pulled into the local athletic center. Impatient, he tapped the steering wheel until Dave's black sports car pulled into the empty spot next to him. They walked into the building together, signed for a batting cage and grabbed helmets.

Aaron was up at bat first. Dave said nothing as Aaron missed the first two balls, but when the third ball blew right past his left ear, Dave let out a quiet rumble of laughter.

Aaron shot him a glare. "What?"

"You're off your game."

He nodded but didn't engage. "Did Chief Forsyth interview any students at school today?"

"Not that I'm aware of." Dave stepped up to the plate and swung his bat, hitting the ball with a resounding crack. "Why?"

"I saw him in the parking lot when I arrived."

"Probably patrolling the area, as usual."

"Could be."

"You telling me you're this wound up over the chief being at the school?"

Aaron growled.

"I knew it was Sarah." Dave laughed, but his gaze quickly turned serious. "Don't tie yourself in knots. She's leaving soon."

Aaron took Dave's place at the plate, swung his bat and

connected with the ball. It clanged against the fence on the far wall. "I know."

"Focus on finding a way to coexist. Get your friendship on solid footing."

The pitching machine threw the next ball and Aaron slammed the bat against it, breaking the outside covering. The ball went one way and the leather cover flew the other. The ripple up his arms satisfied him. "Don't know if I can do that. I thought I might be able to change her mind and get her to stay. But I'm not sure it's possible. It's killing me. I feel like I'm in high school again."

"It's tough, man." Dave placed a hand on his shoulder. "I get it. Maybe instead of forcing your way into her life, you need a break."

Maybe he was right. When he'd first seen Sarah, he'd vowed to avoid her. Then they'd agreed on a truce. Since then, he'd been pursuing her. Perhaps the best thing for his sanity was to let things settle. She'd be gone soon, and his family's business took priority. No matter how dissatisfied he was with the deli now, he had a responsibility to his parents. They counted on him, and he couldn't continue taking time off for her—or because of her.

"You might be right," he said. "I'll keep my distance."

"Sounds like a wise plan, Aaron."

Except late that night, his phone buzzed with a text. He read it and swore to himself. So much for his plans to keep his distance.

Chapter Twelve

"Emily!" Sarah raised her voice over the din of the bar as her friend approached the empty stool next to her. When Emily was seated, Sarah caught the bartender's attention, raised her martini glass and grinned. "Another one for me and one for my friend, here."

"Shh, you're loud," Emily said. "And she'll have club soda while I catch up."

"Club soda, why?" Sarah asked. "And since when did you become this bossy?"

"Since you started getting drunk without me. What's going on?"

Although they'd been out of touch for years, Emily clearly had no trouble sizing up Sarah's mood in one glance. The concerned crinkle in Emily's brown eyes brought all of Sarah's emotions to the surface.

"The asshole cheated on me." She gulped her club soda and grimaced at the lack of alcohol. Bubbles alone wouldn't help her drown her sorrows. "And he tried to make it seem like I should do it, too."

"What? Who? Aaron?"

"No, Matthew." Sarah frowned. "Keep up. I mean, just because I kissed Aaron doesn't mean he's got a license to cheat on me, right?"

"You kissed Aaron?"

Sarah shook her head. "No—*he* kissed *me*. Anyway, that's not the point. Taking time to consider a marriage proposal is not the same thing as sampling other sexy goods, although—oh, man—Aaron has them." She closed her eyes, her body tingling at the memory.

Emily placed a cool hand on Sarah's arm. In the dim light of the bar, the difference in skin tone reminded Sarah of an old sepia-colored photo. "You have a lot of explaining to do."

Sarah's eyes opened and filled with tears. She reached for a napkin. "I am not crying over that asshole. Especially since I told him no."

"Okay, let's get you sober and you can explain everything to me."

"I don't want to be sober. I want Aaron. I mean—oh hell, I don't know what I mean." She dropped her head onto the bar. Out of the corner of her eye, she saw Emily's curly hair fall forward as she texted someone.

"Who are you texting?" Sarah asked. "I thought we were hanging out together."

"We are. Although I thought you'd be a bit more sober to start out with." She slipped her phone into her purse.

"You don't know, Em. You don't know what happened." She tried moving off the stool, but it wobbled.

Emily reached for her. "Hey, easy there. Let's sit here for a little bit, okay?"

"For what? Another drink?" Sarah brightened. "That would be great. Bartender!"

The bartender glanced her way, then turned and, ignoring her, moved to the other end of the bar.

"That's rude," Sarah said. "Isn't he supposed to serve me?"

"Not when you're this sloshed." Emily glanced at her phone. "Tell me what happened. Why did you kiss Aaron?"

"Because he kissed me! And I didn't kiss him. I didn't pull away as fast as I should have. But then we flirted. And I liked it."

"And now you're trying to decide what to do?"

"No," Sarah said. "I told Matthew what happened. And it turns out he's been cheating on me. So, I told him I couldn't marry him. And I came here, to get away from my phone."

"You don't have your phone with you?" Emily stared at her. "Sarah, that's dangerous. What if something happened to you?"

She gripped the bar, then moved her head from left to right. When she didn't lose her balance, she grinned. "Nothing's going to happen to me. You're here."

"I'm sorry about your breakup. Were you together long?"

"Almost three years." Sarah shrugged. "He asked him to marry me. I mean, he asked me to marry him right before I came to visit. I was supposed to give him an answer when I got back."

"And instead, you broke up with him when you found out he cheated on you?"

Sarah nodded and the room spun. "Yes."

"You're right. He sounds like an asshole. You're better off without him."

"What am I going to do with all my black clothes?" she wailed.

Emily shook her head, her curls bouncing. "You could burn them."

"I can't burn them! You of all people should know you don't burn Givenchy! Even if I did get them on sale."

"Good point."

The bartender raised his hand and a shadow crossed Sarah's vision.

"Oh, thank God you're here." Emily breathed out a relieved sigh.

Sarah squinted. "Here? Of course I'm here."

"Not you. Aaron."

"Aaron?" Sarah squeaked. "Why is he here?"

"Because I texted him," Emily said.

"Hey, Em." Aaron's deep voice penetrated Sarah's drunken haze.

"Aren't you going to say hello to me?" Sarah asked.

"Looks like you two are enjoying yourselves," he said instead.

"Ha," Sarah said. "Just because we're in a bar drinking, doesn't mean we're having fun."

"Hey." Emily gently pushed her shoulder. "I thought you *wanted* to hang out with me."

"Sorry, Em," Sarah said. "I like you."

Aaron laughed.

Anger shot through Sarah. "Don't laugh at me."

"Would you rather I yelled at you?" he asked.

"Maybe calling you wasn't the best idea." Emily glanced between the two of them.

Sarah tried to spin around in her seat but swayed. Hands grabbed her. Whose, she didn't know. "Wait, I didn't invite him to our party. I thought we were going to have a girls' night together."

"We were, but not with the way you are now," Emily

said. "Having a girl's night out is different from drowning your sorrows. You need to talk to Aaron."

"I don't want to talk to him. He got me into this mess in the first place. Well, maybe not." Sarah frowned. "Matthew did. I don't know. Men did. Men are jerks."

Emily pulled her into a hug and whispered in her ear. "This one isn't a jerk. Deep inside, you know that."

Emily gave her one last squeeze and then turned to Aaron. Their whispered voices floated next to her, but she couldn't focus to make out their words. Maybe three martinis on an empty stomach were a bad idea.

"Okay, sweetie, this was delicious," Emily said. "Matthew's an ass, and I'm leaving. Aaron will help you get home. Call me tomorrow when you're awake and functioning so we can reschedule."

With Aaron beside her, all her senses rose to the forefront. He leaned toward her, and his scent mixed with the smell of alcohol. His arm brushed against hers, and goose bumps rose along her flesh. His voice rumbled in her ear.

"Are you ready to leave or would you like to sit here for a little longer?"

Her pulse quickened and she swallowed hard. "Why do you care? I told you we were done."

"I've always cared about you, Sarah. You need help. I'm here. I figure forcing you to do something will make this hard on both of us. When you're ready to leave, you let me know. In the meantime, I'll sit here and make sure Charles doesn't serve you any more alcohol."

"You're no fun." She pouted.

"Probably not, but you'll thank me later."

"Now you sound like Matthew." She lowered her voice and screwed her face into a stern and patriarchal imitation of her cheating, ex-almost-fiancé. "'You can't argue when you've done the same thing.'" She straightened her face and resumed her normal voice. "For the record, I can argue about anything, and it's not the same thing. Not at all."

"I know you can." Aaron's lips twitched in what suspiciously resembled a suppressed smirk. "As for what's the same thing, I have no idea, but I'm sure you're right."

"See, that's the first smart thing you've said," Sarah said.

Aaron cleared his throat. "Thanks."

"Sorry. I might not have meant that. Or I might. Right now, I'm too drunk to figure it out. But at least you never cheated on me."

Aaron stilled next to her. "Who cheated on you?"

"Matthew." Her throat thickened. Dammit, she needed another drink. She took a sip of club soda, but it didn't help. Tears clouded her vision.

"When?"

"While I've been here. He was working late with some chick who's into him. He swears it didn't mean anything. And the worst of it is, he doesn't think I should be mad at him since you kissed me. But it's not the same thing. At all." It wasn't, was it? She was sure it wasn't, but her brain still couldn't wrap itself around that part.

"No, it's not." His voice was gentle.

Her head pounded and her stomach sloshed. "I think I need to go now."

Strong arms helped her off the stool and held her in place while she adjusted to the new position. "I'll drive you home."

"No, I can't be with you." She knew this was true, but her brain was too fuzzy to figure out why not.

"You still need a ride home."

"But—"

"Come on."

She let him guide her to his car, because no matter how

much she shouldn't be with him, she couldn't stop herself from following his lead. She'd explain to Matthew later.

Wait, you don't have to explain anything to him. You broke up with him.

She smiled at Aaron. "Let's do something."

He helped her into his truck and steadied her when she wobbled. "You're not in any shape to do anything, Sarah. I'm taking you home."

"Spoilsport."

He climbed inside and started the engine. "Yup."

"When did you become no fun?"

"When I had to become the responsible one." His voice held an edge, like he'd erected a wall between them.

She leaned against the headrest and drifted to sleep during the short drive to her house, only opening her eyes as Aaron pulled into her driveway.

Her parents' house loomed in front of her and she swallowed hard. "I haven't been drunk around my parents in a long time."

He chuckled. "At least you're legal this time."

"Thanks for the ride."

"I'll walk you inside."

"No, I'm good." She stumbled getting out of the truck but righted herself.

"You sure you're okay?" he asked through the rolled down window.

She waved without looking at him. Because if she did, she might beg him to come inside.

Early the next morning, Aaron stared at his phone the whole time he prepped the deli for opening, unable to stop thinking about Sarah.

What was he supposed to do?

Sarah—the new one, or the old one he'd grown up

with—didn't get drunk unless she was upset. Devastated, to be precise. Which meant she'd need time to recover, and not just from drinking too much. The best thing he could do for her was keep his distance. Unfortunately, his body and his heart disagreed, both screaming *No!* He'd spent ten years keeping his distance. How much longer was he supposed to wait? For ten years, he'd left her alone because he'd thought she cheated on him. He'd been wrong, and he didn't want to make the same mistake again.

Had the alcohol made her ill? He swore under his breath. Responsibility was as much ingrained in him as the color of his hair or the size of his feet. He was proud of the man it helped him to be. Sometimes, though, it sucked.

When he couldn't take it another minute, he dialed Sarah's number, tapping his foot and waiting for her to pick up. Instead, his call went straight to voice mail.

"Hey, Sarah, it's Aaron. I wanted to check in on you— make sure you're feeling okay. Let me know."

Some of the tension left his shoulders. He'd done his duty, and he could get on with his day. Movement outside the large front window caught his attention. The sun hadn't risen yet, but the sky had lightened from navy to light purple. Outside the deli stood three kids—waiting for the high school bus, he supposed. It came early, and he thought maybe they were hoping he was open for breakfast. He walked to the front door and turned the lock before swinging it wide open.

The boys froze, their eyes wide, as if surprised to see him.

"Hey!" Aaron smiled in greeting. "I'm not open yet, but if you want breakfast, I can make you some bagels."

The boys looked at each other. Aaron glanced at them, one at a time, and waited. They were just boys—one was almost a man, at least in height and stature, but in the light, it was hard to tell.

The smallest one cleared his throat. "No, it's okay, but thanks."

"Okay. If you change your mind, I open at seven."

The boys nodded and walked away.

Aaron stared after them. Nostalgia thickened his throat. Man, he missed being a teenager, when everything seemed important but was really a blip on the radar. He'd had a girlfriend, a great family, parents who took care of him and the future was wide open.

Now? Other than the girlfriend part, he still had those things. But somewhere along the line, the responsibility had become a weight on his shoulders. When his dad had gotten sick, it had scared the crap out of him, but it made him realize the importance of stepping up and helping them. He wanted to help his parents—hell, he needed to. But lately, every time he walked into the deli, he wondered what he was missing. His future suddenly seemed too narrow and stifling. He wondered whether it was time to investigate other options. And if he decided to do that, where would he even start?

The girlfriend part didn't look promising, either. What was the point of upending his entire life if Sarah wasn't part of it?

Recently, he'd started poking around on his computer and looking into commercial real estate properties, potential deli locations and customer trends in and around the DC area. Just for kicks, he'd fired off a few emails to Realtors, asking preliminary questions. The idea of opening another deli in DC was new—the idea hit him one night as he swung the bat against the ball in the batting cage. It had scared the hell out of him, but he'd pursued it before he completely lost his nerve. Now what?

The door opened again, and this time, it was Jordan. Aaron frowned. "What are you doing here?"

"I thought I'd see if you needed any help. Dad mentioned—"

His chest squeezed. Was his father worried about him? Was he losing faith in him? Was he stressing over his decision to let Aaron run the place? Aaron's worry must have shown on his face, because his brother reached over and grabbed his arm.

Jordan eyed him, wary. "Hey—Dad's fine. You're doing amazing things to this place. No one has any doubts about your ability."

"I know." Aaron breathed a quiet sigh of relief. It was good to hear, but he didn't want his brother knowing he'd been worried.

"Just because you run the deli, doesn't mean I can't pitch in or help you out. I know you're Superman, but even he had the Superfriends. And my business degree could be useful. Think about it."

Aaron's tension eased and he cracked a smile. When they were little, they'd all been obsessed with superheroes. Aaron had always insisted on being the one in charge. The one who saved the day. He shook his head. Some things never changed.

"I appreciate it, Jordan," he said. "I do. I have a lot on my mind."

"I know. And I'm here if you need me."

It was weird having his little brother offer support. Weird, but nice. He handed him a broom and together, they finished cleaning the place.

Sarah's head pounded, her throat was dry and gross tasting and the sun had no right to shine as brightly as it did on Tuesday morning when she awoke. She hadn't drunk that much in… She couldn't remember how long. If this is how she felt after a single night of drinking, she'd never drink another sip of alcohol again. With a groan, she sank into her pillow as memories from the night before came flashing back. *Oh my God, how could I have done that when Emily and I were supposed to have a "catch up/apologize for abandoning you" night?*

She reached for her phone to call Emily and noticed she'd missed several calls. When she played her voice mail—ignoring the three from Matthew—she groaned again. *Aaron.* She'd humiliated herself in front of him. Her temperature spiked and sweat popped on her brow. She'd never live this down. She'd have to avoid him the rest of her time here. Which, when she thought about it, was a good idea. Men weren't high on her list right now. Perhaps a solid chunk of time away from all of them would be wise.

Her phone buzzed with another text from Matthew, and she turned it off. She couldn't deal with him now, either. No, right now she needed to get herself up and functioning so she could meet with the rabbi for their scheduled appointment. Later—much later—she'd deal with Matthew.

She eased herself out of bed, washed up and got dressed, then tiptoed downstairs. She thought she was safe until her mom's voice sliced like a knife.

"Sarah, darling, I didn't hear you come in last night."

She squinted, both at the bright kitchen light and her mom's chipper voice. "I got in late." She brought one hand to her forehead to keep her brain from spilling out of her head.

Her mom looked her up and down, then turned to the cabinet without saying a word and handed her the head-ache medicine, a large glass of water and a big chunk of bread. "Sit, eat and drink."

"I have a meeting with the rabbi and Chief Forsyth."

Her mom's eyes widened. "You can't go to any meeting—but especially one with the rabbi of the temple where

I have to show my face after you leave—looking like you do." Without waiting for Sarah to answer, she turned to the stove and started preparing breakfast.

"There's no way I'll be able to eat whatever you're preparing." Sarah lowered herself onto the seat, swallowed the pain meds and sipped at her water.

"It'll help. Trust me."

Trust her? If Sarah hadn't hurt so bad, she might've laughed. How many hangovers had her mother endured? No, on second thought, she didn't want to know. She nibbled at the bread and her stomach slowly settled. By the time her mother placed a plate of greasy eggs in front of her, she thought she might be able to swallow a bite or two.

"You and Emily have a little too much fun last night?" her mother asked.

Sarah lifted one shoulder. "Emily was fine. I got carried away."

"What happened?"

She squeezed a hand around the water glass, not wanting to share the details with her mom.

"Does this have anything to do with Matthew or Aaron?" her mom asked.

Sarah blew out a breath. Of course her mom was psychic when it came to men. Instead of answering the question, however, she stood. "I have to go to my meeting."

Her mom followed her. "I know. But I'd like to discuss this with you."

"We'll talk later, Mom," she said, knowing she wouldn't avoid the topic forever, but hoping she could at least put it off for a while.

Sarah arrived at the temple with five minutes to spare. She gripped the folder of materials she'd prepared and entered the building.

"Hello, Sarah. I can't wait to see what you came up with."

The rabbi greeted Sarah and led her into her office where the police chief was waiting. "Sarah, you remember Chief Forsyth?"

"I do," she said, shaking his hand when he stood. "It's nice to see you again."

"Likewise." The police chief nodded.

They took seats at a small table in the corner of the rabbi's office.

Sarah opened her folder and laid out her documents. "I went through my files and pulled some examples other temples and institutions have used. I adapted them for you, but you can make any changes you want." She handed the rabbi an introductory letter and then turned to the police chief. "Would you like a copy?"

He waved off her question. "I'm here to listen to what you suggest. Don't worry about me."

The rabbi's face glowed as she read. "This is fantastic. It's warm and approachable, and I love the idea of inviting them to meet us for dessert in the *sukkah*. I'll show this to the board and get these sent out right away."

She passed the letter to the chief, who nodded in agreement.

Next, Sarah handed her three sample invitations. "These are suggestions I have to invite the neighbors to an outdoor Chanukah lighting, a *L'ag B'Omer* picnic and a summer BBQ."

The rabbi nodded, jotting notes on her phone. "These are also great for congregant engagement."

"And finally, this is an example of a Happy New Year card. A secular one. Which is self-evident, but as I mentioned to you the other day, it might be a nice touch."

"I can't wait to use them."

Sarah smiled. "Great. And here's a thumb drive, so you don't have to re-create everything."

The rabbi beamed. "You are a godsend."

"Connecting with the community is the best way to show people you're not different from each other," Chief Forsyth said. "I'm glad to see you're doing this. Rabbi, I'll update you on our progress as soon as I can." He shook hands with Sarah. "It was nice to meet you, Sarah."

The rabbi walked the chief out. When she returned, she sat in her chair and looked at Sarah. "Now, how are you doing?"

Sarah laughed. She assumed starting with "you mean my hangover?" was in no one's best interest. "I broke up with my boyfriend. It's surprisingly freeing."

The rabbi nodded. "I often counsel people that the fear of making a decision is worse than the actual decision, and once it's made, you feel better. Even if the result isn't a joyful one."

"Well, he cheated on me, and while I can make allowances for a lot of things, I draw my line at spreading the wealth."

The rabbi covered her mouth, her eyes sparkling. "I'm sorry. What he did was awful. I'm not laughing at *that*. I'm laughing at your description." She cleared her throat. "A betrayal isn't a laughing matter, though. What can I do to help?"

Sarah shrugged. "I'm not as upset about losing him as I thought I would be. The cheating bothers me more than losing him. I mean, we were great together at one point, but somehow, things changed, and being home pointed those changes out to me."

"So, what will you do now?"

She shifted in her seat. "That's what I'm not sure about. He keeps calling and texting me, and I keep avoiding him. I don't know what else there is to say."

"Maybe there's nothing else that needs to be said." The rabbi crossed her legs.

Sarah had to remind herself she was talking to a rabbi. Something about this woman's presence made her feel like she was talking to a friend. Maybe it's why confiding in her was so easy...

"Unless, of course, you're afraid if you talk to him, you'll change your mind," the rabbi added.

Sarah bit her lip. "No, I won't. I'd never marry someone because it's easier than standing up for myself. I just... So much of my life in DC is tied to him. Not just our jobs, but the future I saw for myself."

"What do you mean?"

"I've always wanted a job where I could make a difference, and I have that in DC. But I also had it with Matthew. He's a politician, and he'll do great things. I guess a part of me wonders if I can still make a difference without being connected to him."

"There are many ways to make a difference, Sarah. As I told you before, I'm happy to refer you to some job opportunities."

Sarah pushed her hair away from her neck and sighed. "It's like I had this path, with each brick a different step that led to a goal. Because of the types of work Matthew did, a lot of those bricks overlapped with my personal life. Once I separate everything out, I need to figure out how best to continue my goal."

The rabbi nodded. "What does Aaron say about all this?"

"We haven't discussed it." She vaguely recollected telling Aaron in the midst of her drunken stupor that Matthew had cheated on her, but beyond that? Her cheeks heated.

The rabbi smiled. "Maybe you should."

Chapter Thirteen

"Aaron, you're taking Grandma to bingo at the temple today, right?" his mother asked as she refilled his coffee cup.

He'd stopped by his parents' house this morning after the deli was up and running to apologize for his behavior yesterday and reassure them it wouldn't happen again.

As his mother poured the hot liquid, he considered strategies for keeping his feelings in check. He knew he couldn't continue letting the way he felt affect the business his parents had built. They'd put him on family duty today and called in his brothers Jordan and Gabriel for reinforcement. That's why Jordan had shown up when he had, and Gabriel followed soon after. This solution was temporary, and he needed a permanent one.

"Of course, Mom. And anywhere else she wants to go."

His mom sipped from her own cup. "Well, not anywhere. You know how she can be."

"She's wily. I know. I'll keep an eye on her and won't let her get into trouble."

"Don't let her get *either* of you into trouble." His mother laughed.

Most days, Aaron would laugh, too, but today, he couldn't find it in him. Sarah still hadn't answered his message from earlier, and as much as he wanted to forget about her, he couldn't. Even the emails he'd received from commercial Realtors about DC prospects hadn't helped.

Pushing away from the table, he hugged his mom and left for the assisted living facility to pick up his grandmother. She, not Sarah, was his responsibility. When he arrived, his grandmother stood waiting for him on the porch.

"It's about time, sonny boy! I was getting ready to Uber," she called out while toddling down the stairs toward him.

"Hi, *Bubbe*." He pulled her into a hug and kissed her cheek. "Since when do you know how to Uber?"

"Morty's grandson visited a few weeks ago and helped me load the app."

God help him. He shuddered as he imagined how much trouble she'd get into with a ride service at her disposal.

"Terrific. Wait for me to sign you out. And I'm not late." He looked at his watch. "I'm five minutes early."

"Humph. What am I, a prisoner?" she muttered. "Sign me out."

He quickly signed her out, then walked her to his car. She was barely seated before she began fiddling with the radio. He closed his eyes and groaned when she found her favorite rap song from Eminem and jacked up the volume.

"This is more like it!" She bobbed her head in time with the music as she rapped along.

"Do you play this garbage in there?" He pulled away from the brick structure.

"Nah, the old fogies don't like it."

He glanced at her out of the corner of his eye. She sported a fresh haircut since he'd seen her last week. Her white hair was cropped close to her head. She was maybe five feet tall and so full of wrinkles that he wondered if she'd gain any height if you stretched them out.

The music was too loud for conversation, which was better for him, so he drove the short distance to the weekly bingo game in silence. When they arrived, he helped her out of the truck and into the social hall where she greeted her friends.

"Oh no, I'm not talking to Sally," she whispered and busied herself straightening her board.

"Why not?" He sat next to her as they waited for the tables to fill.

"All she does is complain about her joints and talk about who died. It's like reading the obituaries—the badly written ones."

"Too late." He eyed an old woman leaning on a cane decorated with bright colored fake flowers as she toddled across the room. "She's coming over."

"Dammit." She breathed out a frustrated sigh while pasting a bright smile on her face. "Hi, Sally. How are you today?"

"*Oy*, hello, Sadie."

His grandmother's nostrils flared as she sat through the litany of complaints. When she'd had enough, she interrupted the other woman midsentence. "I'm sorry to cut you off, dear, but I need to help my grandson with something."

Sally pulled a chair out from an empty place at the table. "Oh, well then. I'll just—"

"Oh, I'm afraid these seats are taken." His grandmother cut her off again. "Next time!"

"Well!" Sally huffed and scooted away as fast as her cane would allow her.

His grandmother grinned like the wolf posing as Red Riding Hood's grandmother, but her smile faded when she turned to look at him. "What's wrong, sonny boy? You haven't looked happy at all today."

He was about to make an excuse when her friend Terri sat next to her. She wore a velour tracksuit in bright pink with matching lipstick and thick, rhinestone glasses. "Hi, Sadie. Hello, Aaron. What's wrong?"

"Wrong?" An older man with thinning hair, whose name Aaron couldn't remember, joined them. "What's wrong with who?"

"Whom," Terri corrected. "I used to be an editor." She tapped her glasses as if they signaled a Pulitzer.

"Aaron looks upset." Sadie patted Aaron's hand.

"Aaron? Who's Aaron?" the older man asked.

His grandmother rolled her eyes. "My grandson, you fool!"

The man turned to Aaron, then back to Sadie as if Aaron were invisible. "You're right, he does. Maybe he needs some prunes."

"He's too young for prunes," Terri said.

"June?" Another woman, this one with hair a very unnatural shade of burgundy, sat at their table and pulled out a dinner roll, wrapped in a paper napkin, from her oversize purse. "My birthday is in June. My kids want to throw me a party, but at my age all I want is good food." She studied Aaron, her eyes slowly roving over him from the top of his head down to his toes. She grinned and offered him a cheeky wink before continuing. "And maybe a sexy young man. Or another vibrator."

Heat rose to Aaron's cheeks. He needed to leave before the conversation got more out of hand, but his grandmother placed a hand on his arm, gripping it like she could read his mind.

She stood and rapped on the table. "Listen, everyone. My grandson is upset. He doesn't need prunes, his birthday isn't in June and, Ruth, he's not your type. We are going to help him!"

Three sets of eyes ogled him, and he wished he'd refused his mother's request to bring his grandmother today. He scowled.

"Oh wow, he really is upset!" The burgundy-haired woman commented. "Darren, what's wrong?"

"His name is Aaron, not Darren," his grandmother corrected, then turned toward him. "Now, tell us what's going on."

"Yeah but be quick. I don't want to miss the bingo game," the old man said, spreading five cards in front of him with his gnarled hands and positioning each one just so.

"My grandson is more important than a stupid bingo game, Bob. And besides, you lose every week." She squeezed Aaron's arm. "Come on, now. Don't be shy."

The last thing he needed was a bunch of strangers in his business. But apparently, rather than bingo winnings, he was getting a gaggle of *yentas*.

"It's a female problem." He sighed.

His grandmother arched her painted-on eyebrow. "Are you transitioning?"

He reared back in his chair. "Of course not! Why would you think I was transitioning?"

"You said it was a female problem, so…" She winked.

"*Bubbe*, I didn't know you knew what that was."

She frowned at him. "Of course I do. I read the internets."

He took a deep breath, noticing the rapt attention of everyone at the table. "I'm having a problem *with* females."

"Ohhh, he's a player!" Terri whispered so loud that people at the next table craned their necks and stared at Aaron.

"I'm not a player," he said through clenched teeth. "I'm having a problem with one female. Just one."

Bob leaned over and pulled a prescription bottle out of his brown vest pocket. Opening the bottle, he shook out a little blue pill and held it out for Aaron in his open palm. "Want one of these?"

Aaron stared in disbelief. "No, Bob, I don't."

Bob shrugged and dropped the pill back into the bottle. "Suit yourself, then."

"Thank you, Bob. That was very sweet." His grandmother beamed at Bob. "Now, Aaron, tell me what's going on with you and Sarah."

He jerked at his grandmother's use of her name and looked around. "How'd you know I meant Sarah?"

"Who else could you mean? I know your mom and aunt want to set you up with Stephanie, but it's been you and Sarah for as long as I can remember. Besides, when you brought her here last week, you two fit together like my favorite girdle used to fit me." She sighed and stared off into the distance. "Those were the good days. Anyway, what happened between then and now, and what are you going to do about it?"

"I'm not sure this is the best place to discuss it."

"Not to worry, sonny boy. Half of them won't hear it, and the other half won't remember."

"What did you say? I missed that," the burgundy-haired woman said.

"See?" His grandmother grinned.

Even still, Aaron leaned toward his grandmother and spoke in hushed tones, explaining his predicament. Around them, her friends complained, wanting all the details of his woman troubles and an opportunity to give their sage advice, but she waved them off.

"Go back to your business. This is between a boy and

his grandmother. "I'll let you know if we need help from the peanut gallery." She turned back to her grandson and patted his cheek. "Go ahead, dear."

Groans rose around them, but neither Aaron nor his grandmother cared or paid any attention. When he finished, Aaron leaned back in his chair and waited while his grandmother pondered his dilemma.

She fluttered her fingers together and thought in silence a few moments. "When you say you have female problems, you aren't kidding."

He nodded.

"You know I love Sarah," she said. "I think the two of you belong together. But her almost-fiancé sounds like a *schmuck*. Anyone who cheats on someone is. It's time you got off that cute ass of yours and made your move."

"Grandma!" His cheeks burned.

"Don't 'grandma' me, *boychik*. There's a difference between a *mensch* and a *nebbish*. A *mensch* is honorable, which you've been while you thought she was engaged."

"She is. Or she was. Or she might be." He ran a hand through his hair. "At this point, I'm not sure what she is."

"But a *nebbish* twiddles his thumbs and waits for things to happen. Nobody likes a *nebbish*. You want her, you go after her. Especially now you know her fiancé is a *schmuck*. Don't wait around all namby-pambies."

"I'm not waiting around, Grandma." The old people around the table scooted closer. He glared at them, and three gazes dropped to their bingo boards, although the game hadn't yet started. "But she's not the same Sarah as before. I'm not sure I like the new one. And I'm trying to give her space."

His grandmother made a sound like she'd swallowed a dry piece of overcooked brisket. "Space, shmace. You're not the same, either, *boychik*. At least I hope you're not.

Because the boy you used to be was rigid and uncompromising. I would hope you've matured."

He pondered her words for a second and realized he had been rigid and uncompromising in his youth. It was weird having his grandmother call him out. "I think I have."

"So, maybe she has too. Or maybe she's still figuring herself out. Either way, you need to go after her."

"Listen to your grandmother, sonny boy. You need to woo her." Bob raised his bushy eyebrows until they were inches away from the strands of white hair he'd plastered across his sun-spotted head.

The other ladies at the table nodded.

"A girl likes to be wooed," Ruth said.

"Flowers, poetry, maybe a serenade." The burgundy-haired woman got a dreamy look in her eye.

He cleared his throat. "I don't think Sarah would like the pressure."

His grandmother patted his hand. "You keep making excuses, Aaron. How do you know unless you try?"

He had responsibilities. Whereas Sarah… He didn't know what to make of her. Could she marry a guy who hadn't remained faithful to her while she visited her family for a holiday? The Sarah he used to know wouldn't have, but he wasn't sure of the new version.

He groaned. She was tying him in knots. He wanted to scream at her at the same time he wanted to defend her and kiss her. But he couldn't do anything when she wouldn't even return his phone calls.

His grandmother handed him a bingo card, "You need to go after her. But until then, let's beat the pants off these *alta-kakas*!"

"So, when are you and Matthew getting married?" Sarah's mother asked at lunch that day.

Sarah choked on the water she'd been drinking, and people at the next table in the cute restaurant looked on in concern. Her eyes watered, and her mother rushed around to her side of the table and pounded her back. When Sarah could breathe again, she wiped her face, nodded at the other patrons and swallowed.

She cleared her throat. "I'm fine." Her voice was scratchy. Her heart ached. And the rabbi's advice confused her. But sure, she was fine.

"And you and Matthew?"

"Matthew and I broke up." Her phone buzzed again, and knowing it was probably Matthew again, she quieted it. One of these days she'd have to talk to him. But not now.

Surprise, confusion, sympathy and hurt crossed her mother's face. Sarah had seen those looks directed at her throughout her entire life—when her mother wanted to understand a test grade, when she'd come home later than expected from a party, when she'd bought an outfit her mother thought showed too much skin. But the hurt? It was new, and it pierced Sarah to the core. She wished she could slide under the table and hide like a five-year-old.

"I'm sorry to spring the news on you, Mom. It just happened."

Her mother was silent, so Sarah picked up her menu and stared blindly at it. She'd already decided what to order—a kale, quinoa and avocado salad with lemon Dijon vinaigrette dressing. But while the menu offered a physical barrier between her and her mother, it didn't lessen the guilt consuming her. She'd stopped talking to everyone, including her mother, and her actions were hurting people.

"You used to tell me things," her mother prodded.

"I know, and I'm sorry. I'm an adult now. I have a right to my privacy, but I think I took it too far, especially with

you. I never meant to shut you out of my life. I promise—
the breakup just happened."

Her mother nodded. "Are you as okay as you seem?"

Sarah shrugged. "I'm relieved I made a decision. What
he did hurt me, but I think we'd grown apart and coming
home helped me see that. I thought I'd be a lot more upset
than I am, though."

If she was honest with herself, Matthew's cheating was
only part of the problem. He was always busy and rarely
had time for her. At one point, she'd thought that meant
he was important. But now she wasn't so sure. An image
of Aaron, taking the day off from his deli to entertain her,
flashed through her mind. She shook her head, dispers-
ing the image.

"I'm sorry he hurt you and that I couldn't help you
more. But I'm glad you made the right decision. I'm proud
of you."

"Why? I kept making excuses. That's nothing to be
proud of."

"Any time you decide what's right for yourself deep
down—no matter how hard or easy, no matter how long
it takes—that's brave. And I'm proud of you. I mean, I always am, but especially now."

Sarah's throat clogged with unshed tears. When the
waitress took their orders and menus, she dropped her
hands in her lap. She needed to change the subject before
she turned into a puddle at the table.

"I'm glad you have the time to spend with us," her
mother said. "It's been a long time, and it's a rare treat.
I'm always here to talk if you want."

Her mother's smile sent shards of guilt straight to her
stomach. She shouldn't have avoided coming home for so
long. She'd do better from now on.

Sarah placed her hand over her mother's across the table. "I'm glad to be here, too."

"You know, there are plenty of opportunities in this Jewish community for you. You could move here and work in New York, even."

"We've talked about this, Mom. I'm happy where I am. I love my job, and now without Matthew, I'll have more time to devote to it." She swallowed the lump in her throat "But I'll admit I shouldn't have stayed away for so long. I'll do better, I promise."

Her mom gave her a wistful smile. "I'm glad you and Aaron have repaired things. It's been nice seeing the two of you together. Like old times."

"I've got to do better keeping in touch with a lot of people. I didn't realize how much I missed Caroline until I went jogging with her the other day."

"Are you able to jog in DC? It's always been so crowded when we've visited you."

Sarah nodded her head. "There are plenty of jogging paths and parks. It's not much different from jogging here or anywhere else. Except there, I get to see the monuments."

"Those photos you sent me of the Jefferson Memorial during cherry blossom season were beautiful. Did you see Dad framed them and hung them in the bathroom?"

"I did. It was nice of him. Next time, the two of you will have to come in the spring, and I'll take you there."

The waitress served their food and Sarah looked at hers with dismay. For some reason, she had a sudden craving for carbs. Or anything that wasn't as healthy as this. She had to remind herself next time that she was no longer tied to someone who complained about her diet.

Her mom leaned across the table and winked. "I wouldn't

want to eat that, either. Want to split this?" She pulled half of her chicken salad sandwich apart and handed it to Sarah.

Growing up, Sarah loved her mom's chicken salad. Now, looking at the restaurant's version of her old favorite filled her with a desire to crawl back in time to when she was young, and everything could be solved with a kiss.

She pushed her plate away. "Yeah, I don't know what I was thinking."

"You were thinking about your waistline." She pointed a red painted fingernail at her. "There's more to life than work, and there's more to eating than counting calories."

As Sarah's teeth sunk into the sandwich and she tasted the almonds, chicken, grapes and cucumbers, the comfort food worked its magic and her stomach unknotted. "You're right."

Her mother arched an eyebrow. "About more than you give me credit for."

Aaron observed his grandmother for the fourth time on their short drive to her assisted living facility. She looked pale to him, and he'd thought so ever since the bingo game ended and conversation started up about the temple vandalism. She'd insisted nothing was wrong, but now she was rubbing her arm and fidgeting in her seat.

"Grandma, you don't look good. How about we call the doctor?"

"It's nothing, sonny boy. Just part of getting old."

"I don't think so. I'm worried about you."

"Nonsense. You don't need to worry about me. I'm fine. I'm annoyed you didn't bring me more luck. I usually win more games when you join me."

If she'd felt better, he would've argued with her—joked around, or something. But she didn't look good. He pulled into the parking lot of her building and dialed his mother.

"Mom, I'm with grandma and she doesn't look good. She says she's fine, but I'm not convinced. She looks pale, almost sweaty to me."

"Stop, Aaron!" His grandmother's voice wasn't as strong as usual, and she panted in between each word. "Don't worry your mother for nothing."

"Don't listen to her," his mother said over the phone. "Take her right to the hospital. Dad and I will meet you."

The call disconnected and Aaron threw his truck into reverse to pull out of the parking space.

"Where are we going?" His grandmother's voice was feeble now.

"Nowhere, Grandma. Just rest. I'll take care of everything."

He sped toward the hospital emergency room, pulled up to the entrance and raced inside. "I need some help, please!"

Two orderlies followed him out and gently helped his grandmother into a wheelchair. Aaron's heart thudded painfully in his chest as they wheeled her into the emergency room.

"Sir, can you give us information about her?" the receptionist asked.

He was about to explain he was her grandson when his parents swooped in and took over. With nothing else to do, he went back outside and parked his car. Now alone and with the active emergency behind him, his hands shook and his heart continued beating hard and fast in his chest. He had no idea what was wrong with his grandmother, but his head hurt with the stress and concern.

"Aaron! Is she all right?"

He turned at the sound of his name.

His brothers raced toward him.

He shook his head. "I don't know. I'm sure there's nothing you need to worry about."

Gabriel grabbed his elbow. "Stop! We're not little kids anymore."

Jordan nodded. "She's our grandmother, too. We're here to help."

He looked at both of his younger brothers—their strong broad shoulders, their expressions calm, despite the worry in their eyes. They were so much like him, not only in looks and stature, but in the way they carried themselves. He realized they'd grown up, and they no longer needed his protection. They hadn't for a long time.

"Sorry. Thanks." He shook his head again. "I don't know. I brought her here, and mom and dad showed up."

Gabriel slung an arm over his shoulder. "Let's go see what we can find out."

With a deep breath, he walked inside with his brothers on each side of him. His parents were nowhere in sight.

"Excuse me." Aaron cleared his throat, hoping to get the receptionist's attention. "Do you know where they took the elderly woman I brought in? Sadie Isaacson?"

The woman nodded. "Your parents followed them into the emergency room. If you wait out here, someone will fill you in when they know something."

He thanked the receptionist and walked toward the waiting room, but he couldn't sit still. Instead, he paced, gripping his scalp, and tried to forget the vulnerable sound of his grandmother's voice as she argued with him.

He needed to talk to someone, to distract himself. His brothers were equally worried but talking to them wouldn't help. Reaching for his phone, he called Dave, but the call went straight to voice mail. He blew out a frustrated breath and glanced at his watch. Of course, Dave didn't answer—it was still the middle of the school day.

He called the deli and checked in but was quickly reassured they had everything under control. He disconnected the call and stalked the floor, pacing once again.

Behind him, the doors swished open and a fruity scent permeated the sanitized smell of the hospital waiting room. He paused and his heart flipped over in his chest.

"Aaron?"

At Sarah's voice, he turned toward her and a burst of relief flowed through him. "You're here?"

She stood with her mother only a few feet away from him. She looked much better than the last time he'd seen her. She'd sobered up since then, but she hadn't returned any of his calls. He stared at her, unsure whether he wanted to pull her close or run away.

"Your mom called mine to tell her about your grandmother. We were on our way home from lunch, so we thought we'd see if you needed anything." She turned her attention to her brothers and lifted her hand in a tiny wave. "Hey, Jordan, Gabriel. I'm sorry your grandmother is unwell."

His brothers rose and greeted her with a hug.

Aaron's mind reeled. She wanted to know if he needed anything? What he needed was to vent his frustrations about her and his grandmother and life in general. But there were people in the waiting room, so what he needed would have to wait.

"Hi, Mrs. Abrams." He nodded at her mother. "Thanks for coming."

Sarah's dark eyes filled with sympathy, and he wanted to reach out and pull her into his arms. Instead, he made fists at his sides.

"Want to go for a walk?" she asked.

A walk? With her?

Woo her, his grandmother had said.

He stared at her a beat too long as her question and his grandmother's advice swirled in his head. At the moment, he couldn't handle thinking, much less *wooing* her.

"I can let you know if there's any news," her mother offered.

"One of us will come get you," Gabriel added.

Aaron had always been the responsible one, and right now his grandmother was ill and his family needed him. But the thought of staying cooped up indoors made him claustrophobic, despite the large windows and soothing decor. Almost on autopilot, he followed her out of the building.

"I don't want to go far." He paused outside the sliding glass doors. "I need to be available—"

"We'll walk along that grassy area across the lot." She pointed to a small space with a few trees and a bench. "It's close enough to the entrance. They'll see us, and we'll hear them if they need you."

Gabriel *had* promised he'd let him know if anything changed. Once again, he was depending on his brothers. The feeling was so alien to him that he didn't even know how he'd describe it to himself. At the moment, it was too much for his brain to consider—the only thing he could think about was his grandmother's pale face in the car.

He followed Sarah. They walked in silence around the area, making a rectangle. Her presence calmed him.

"Do you remember baking *hamentaschen* with your grandma for Purim?" Sarah's question startled him out of the silence.

He smiled at the childhood memory. "I remember you, covered head to toe in flour."

Sarah smiled. "I might've gotten a bit carried away rolling out the cookie dough. But in my defense, she wasn't specific about how much flour to use, and I didn't want the dough to stick when I made the circle cutouts."

He looked at her. She was trying to defend herself, but even she saw the humor in the situation.

"So, what was your excuse for getting the apricot jelly everywhere?" Aaron smiled, remembering how his grandmother had substituted the recipe's traditional prune filling with apricot jelly because Sarah wouldn't touch anything made with prunes.

Like the flour, she'd used too much and gotten the sticky jelly all over herself and his grandmother's kitchen.

Sarah bit back a smile, her cheeks flushing red. "I couldn't help taste-testing to make sure it was turning out right."

"Or adding double what the recipe called for of the apricot jelly?"

"Hey. I told you I'm not a cook. Or a baker."

Visions of their omelet making flashed in his head. "You've gotten better at cooking. We'll have to work on your baking." The words had slipped out, and he wasn't sure what made him say it. He'd expected her to remind him she was leaving soon, like she always did.

She took a deep breath. "I'd like that."

He wanted to push her, to find out if she meant it. He wanted to ask her about the other evening when she'd been drunk—to find out how she could consider marrying someone who cheated on her. But he was afraid if he opened his mouth, his fears about his grandmother would come pouring out, and he'd take his fear and anger out on her. Before he could decide what to do, his phone buzzed.

He jumped. "Hello?"

"She's okay," his father said. "Come inside."

"Thank God." He pocketed his phone and then grabbed Sarah's hand and raced toward the door. "She's going to be okay."

His father and Gabriel were waiting for him in the waiting room. "Hi, Sarah," his father said. "Your mom and my wife went for a cup of coffee."

"Hi, Mr. Isaacson. How's Grandma Sadie?"

Aaron's heart ached as he remembered how his grandmother always loved when Sarah called her by that name. *Please let her be okay.*

"She's dehydrated," his father said. "They have her on fluids and will keep her overnight, but she's going to be fine."

"That's it?" Aaron asked. "She needed to drink more?"

His father nodded. "Apparently. You can go in and see her now. Both of you."

This time, Aaron took off, leaving Sarah to follow behind him. He stopped in the doorway of his grandmother's room and studied her a long moment before going in. She was so tiny in her hospital bed, with IV lines attached to her wrinkled and mottled arm. She was still too pale, but her color was better than earlier. He slumped against the wall as relief crashed into him.

As he stared at the floor, the toes of Sarah's tennis sneakers touched his.

"I need a minute." He said the words under his breath without looking up at her. For some reason, talking to her was easier if he didn't have to look at her.

Sarah grabbed his hand and leaned against the wall next to him. "Take as long as you need."

Her voice soothed him. If he let himself, he could forget about all his frustrations. His stomach was so tied up in knots—first about Sarah and then about his grandmother— that it would be a relief to walk away and let off some steam. But he didn't want to leave his grandmother alone for however long it might take him to pull himself together. So, he said nothing and pushed off the wall, pull-

ing his hand away from Sarah's and entering his grandmother's room.

Her eyelids fluttered open.

"Some people will do anything for attention," he said
to his grandmother.

She smiled and struggled to sit up.

"No, lie down." He pulled a chair over to her bedside
and sat next to her.

Sarah approached from his other side. "Hi, Grandma
Sadie."

"Sarah, *bubbelah*!" his grandmother exclaimed. "Aaron,
why aren't you letting her sit?"

Aaron moved to stand, but Sarah motioned him to stay
seated.

"I don't want to sit," she said quickly. "I'm glad to see
you're all right."

His grandmother shook her head. "Everyone made a big
deal out of nothing. If I'd taken another drink of water, I
wouldn't have to be here."

"Better to be cautious," Aaron said. "I'm glad it wasn't
serious this time, but you have to take better care of yourself, Grandma. It's more than a drink of water."

She patted his arm with bony fingers. "I will, sonny boy.
I'm sorry I scared you."

She had no idea. "No worries. But I'm going to get you
a water bottle to carry around."

"Then you'd better get me a porta-potty, too." She snorted.
"Do you have any idea how often a woman my age has to
pee?"

Sarah laughed.

Aaron allowed himself a small smile as he pushed down
all the emotions struggling toward the surface. He listened passively as his grandmother complained about all
the fussing the nurses were doing. Sarah commiserated

with her, and the two women chatted like longtime confidants until he grew so uncomfortable, he suddenly felt like an outsider.

He stood abruptly. "Grandma, I'm going to get a soda."

Without giving either woman a chance to respond, he strode out of the room. By the time he reached the vending machine, he was breathing in short gasps. Spots floated in front of his eyes and his temples pounded.

Breathe. She's going to be fine.

He pulled in a breath, as deep as his constricted lungs allowed, then exhaled slowly. He closed his eyes, allowing the spots in his vision time to disperse. If he wasn't careful, the hospital would admit him.

An image of Sarah fussing over him flitted through his mind. It morphed into her wearing a skimpy nurse's outfit, complete with a white hat and not much else. He opened his eyes and blinked.

Pulling out his wallet, he removed a dollar bill. The room swayed and he gripped one side of the vending machine before ramming the bill into the slot with his other hand. He punched the button, then stuffed his hand into the drawer below when the can fell. Opening it, he swallowed nearly half the contents in only a few gulps. The fizzy liquid burned his throat, but he ignored the discomfort. Swallowing the last drop, he leaned back against the wall and closed his eyes for several long moments. When he felt sufficiently composed, he dropped the can into the recycling bin and returned to his grandmother's room.

As he approached her room, his heart lifted at the sound of his grandmother and Sarah's quiet laughter. He paused in the doorway, watching the two women reconnect after so many years.

His grandmother wiped away a tear with a corner of her bedsheet. "Now, Sarah, tell me what's new with you."

"I'm reinventing myself." She laughed again, but this time something in her tone made Aaron think she didn't find it funny.

"I hope that includes finding a new boyfriend and moving back home."

He stepped into the room. "Sarah, you can't move home!"

His grandmother and Sarah turned surprised expressions his direction.

Aaron cringed internally. He hadn't meant to shout, but his emotions had overcome his reason when he'd heard her words. Her dreams were too big for this place—always had been—and just because she broke up with a lying, two-timing boyfriend, didn't mean she should give up her career aspirations. He clenched his hands into fists before he said something he'd really regret.

"I don't recall asking your permission." Sarah's eyes blazed, but her voice remained quiet.

"Your job—"

"Stop." She held up a hand and glared at Aaron a moment before turning to his grandma. "I'm so glad you're feeling better. It's been good to see you, but I have to go now." She squeezed the old woman's hand and stalked out of the room without even a passing glance at him.

Aaron watched Sarah walk away and pinched the bridge of his nose. He'd swear the temperature dropped ten degrees as she swept past him. Without thought, he turned to go after her but his grandmother stopped him.

"Hold up, sonny boy." The words were a demand, not a request. "Let her go. And next time, maybe don't order her around."

"You did." He tapped his foot, torn between his grandmother and Sarah.

Sarah's footsteps receded until they disappeared entirely. He returned his attention to his grandmother.

"She'll make allowances for me since I'm old. When she cools down, you can have a conversation with her."

He sat in the vacated chair next to her bed and took her bony hand in his. "I don't think she's going to want to talk to me."

His grandmother smiled. "Probably not. But sometimes, you must force the issue. The ball's in your court, *boychik*."

Chapter Fourteen

Sarah's phone pinged for what seemed like the one hundredth time as she and her mother climbed into the car outside the hospital. Another text from Matthew, to go with his four voice mails and twenty-six other texts.

"Are you ever going to answer him?" Her mother nodded toward the phone.

"I don't know what else to say to him. I told him we were through."

Her mother gasped. "Sarah Abrams, I am so proud of the woman you've become, but I did not raise you to be rude and dismissive to someone you have, or had, feelings for."

Sarah gaped at her. "I didn't mean I was going to ignore him. Of course we have to talk. I'd never be so rude to someone I cared about, even if my feelings for him have changed. I don't know what to say to him and need time to think."

"Okay. Good." She nodded. "I'm sorry I blew up at you. I guess being at the hospital upset me more than I realized."

Sarah looked at her mother. "I know I've been terrible at coming home, but you know if you or Daddy ever got sick, I'd drop everything to be with you, right?"

Her mother nodded. "I love you, sweetheart. And we support everything you do. But it's clear to both me and your father your independence has included pulling away from both of us. And we were fine with it. We *are* fine with it. But this—" her mom's voice shook with emotion "—this threw me. I'm sorry."

"Oh Mom, I'm sorry." She reached across the console and hugged her mother. "I hate what I've done. I hate what I've become, but I'm lost. I don't know how to find me again, and if I can't figure it out myself, how in the world am I supposed to explain how I've changed to Matthew?"

Her mother held her, and for the first time in years, Sarah recognized her old self. She was independent and capable and had the power to make everything right. She inhaled her mom's perfume and listened to her mom's heartbeat, letting it soothe her.

Everything around her stopped. Sarah thought about her parents' marriage—how they laughed and loved each other, how respectful they were to each other. She couldn't picture either of them with someone else. That's what she wanted. She wanted a partner who gave and accepted support in equal measure. Someone who believed in who she was and who she could become, without making her into some variation of his perfect woman. She wanted to be someone's whole world, just as that person would be hers. She could adapt, change and compromise, but she deserved better. She wanted better. And she expected better. Peace settled around her.

She pulled away and looked at her mother. "I think I might be falling for Aaron."

Her mother grasped her hand. "I know. But first, you

need to tell Matthew why the two of you aren't right for each other. As much as the thought of him cheating on you kills me, it's also about how he makes you feel. Your feelings for Aaron are irrelevant to your decision, and Matthew needs to understand that if he's to accept your decision. You owe him the truth, but more than that, you owe yourself the truth. Everything will become clear after that."

She leaned over and hugged her mother again. "You're right. I'm going to drive back to DC after I drop you at home so I can talk to Matthew in person. We'll have a face-to-face conversation once and for all and be finished."

Her mom cradled her face. "Then you can decide what to do with the rest of your life."

She nodded. "Right."

After dropping her mom at the house and grabbing an overnight bag, she guided the car onto the highway.

Four hours later, after running through multiple potential conversations in her head, she approached the outskirts of the city. Stop and go traffic took up another thirty minutes, adding to the queasiness already in her belly, but finally she reached her apartment. The place was quiet, frozen in time. Was it only a week since she'd been home? She turned on lights as she meandered through the space. What she once found soothing, she now found boring. Why did she think decorating in neutral, monochromatic colors was a good idea? There was no life, no vibrancy, here. Not like home.

She pulled up short. *This* was home. Except it wasn't. Not any longer. How could that be? She'd lived here ten years, but gone home for one week and all her roots were tossed?

Or maybe her roots were more firmly planted where they were supposed to be—where her family was. Where Aaron was...

She dropped her purse, grabbed her MetroCard and took off for Matthew's office in the heart of downtown Washington. It was late, but she knew he'd be there. He always worked late.

"Hey, Sherry." She greeted Matthew's secretary as she entered his office.

"Sarah! I thought you went home for the holidays."

"I did. Is he in?" She paused outside the door of his private office,

Sherry nodded. "Go on in."

The office door creaked as she opened it, and she poked her head around the corner.

"Sarah, thank God!" Matthew rose from behind his desk and rushed over to her, grabbed her in a hug and squeezed hard.

She noted the way his brown hair was slicked back off his high forehead and knew he'd pull away if she ran her fingers through it. His lean body was hard but didn't feel like home. He didn't smell like home, either. Instead, he smelled of expensive cologne purchased from a high-end, luxury store where reputation was everything. Towering above her, he made her feel small—not in a delicate way, but in a powerless one.

He pulled away and stared into her face. "Why haven't you answered any of my calls or texts?"

She stiffened. "We need to talk."

"I know." He sighed and pointed to the sofa in his office.

Her stomach lurched, suddenly wondering what else had happened on that sofa. Shaking her head, she chose a seat on one of the upholstered chairs at his desk.

He joined her by taking the opposite chair and reached for her hands. "I was an ass, and what I did was unforgivable. I'm sorry."

"I know. I listened to your voice mails in the car." She'd

also read his texts and found nothing but apologies, but not nearly enough to change her mind.

His face lit up. "So, you'll marry me? I promise you won't regret it, Sarah. We're perfect for each other. And I'll never betray you like that again."

"My answer is still no." Her voice was strong.

"Come on, Sarah. We're perfect for each other. Look, I admit I made a terrible mistake, but was it so different from yours?"

Her chest burned with suppressed anger, but she tamped it down. "You slept with another woman, Matthew, and when I confronted you about it, you claimed it was no big deal. It's true I didn't stop Aaron's kiss right away, but I came to you and confessed what happened, and promised to never let it happen again. It's completely different!"

He raked a hand through the immaculate hair she'd once admired. One of many things she'd admired about him.

"But it meant nothing." His eyes widened, pleading.

"Why did you do it?"

He stood and paced the office. "I've been kicking myself and asking myself the same question since you called."

"And have you come to an answer?"

"Other than loneliness and stupidity, you mean? No."

A strangled sob escaped her lips, and she looked away. Somewhere deep inside, the little girl part of her had hoped for an answer that would ease the hurt of his betrayal, though the adult side of her had known all along she'd likely never get it. She should've realized sooner that they never would've worked out.

"Don't you think we could get past this?" he asked. "We were so good together. Our marriage made sense."

"Made sense?" She gaped at him. "Matthew, marriage should be for love, not because it 'makes sense.'"

"It can be for both."

She shook her head. "If you loved me, you never would have slept with Leanne."

"Maybe you and I have different definitions of love."

Perhaps he was right—they had different definitions of love. If she'd never returned home, she might not have even realized or even objected to his definition of the emotion. But she had returned home, and she'd seen what her parents still had after all these years. It's what she wanted. No—it's what she *needed*.

"I deserve better, Matthew. I deserve someone who loves me the way I love them—someone who treats me with loyalty and respect."

His gaze narrowed. "Like Aaron?"

Her heart fluttered at the mention of his name. "I don't know. But I do know Aaron would never cheat on someone he loved."

A range of emotions flickered across Matthew's face—disappointment, anger, disbelief. "You're a grown woman, Sarah, and if you think about us—really think about us—you'll realize our relationship is an adult one. It's not a fairy tale."

"I want the fairy tale." She shrugged. "My parents have it, and I want what they have."

"You told me our relationship was everything you've ever wanted." His tone was contemplative, his expression unsure.

For a moment, he reminded her of the man she'd first fallen in love with, when they'd met three years ago. They'd both changed. She'd almost lost the Sarah she used to be, and she was determined to rescue her before she disappeared forever.

"I thought it was," she said. "But I need honesty and trust, and you never gave me that."

"I told you I was sorry."

"I know. But sorry isn't enough."

"So, you can't forgive me?"

"It not about forgiveness, Matthew. It's about honesty and trust. It's about who I am and the way I need to be loved for my own dignity and fulfillment. You need me to be someone I'm not, and I can't be the woman you need, Matthew. We just aren't compatible in the ways that are most important."

"What do you mean 'honesty'?" Out of everything she'd said, he focused on that one word, looking at her like she'd spoken a foreign language.

"Would you have told me about Leanne if I hadn't caught you?"

"It wasn't necessary, Sarah, because like I keep saying, it didn't mean anything."

Sarah blew out a breath. "And that's the crux of the problem and why we're too different."

"Do you want to give all this up?" Matthew pounded his fist on his desk, then flung his arms wide, motioning toward the window with its view of the Capitol Building. "For a small-town, average, powerless life?"

Sarah let loose her anger. "This life you describe isn't worth it."

"I helped you develop into the person you are." He paused and his eyes flashed over her, his face screwing up in malicious sneer. "Well, the person you're supposed to be."

"Don't you dare say you created me." She advanced on him, her temper flaring. "You're not God! I'm my own person, and I like who I am. If you loved me enough, you would like the person I am, too."

"You're right. I'm sorry." He lowered his head and paced the room, his hands at his waist. "It's just… I don't understand. I thought we were good together. I thought you liked who you were with me." He turned back to her, his brow creased with a hurt expression.

"I'm sorry, too, Matthew," she said softly. "I made the mistake of letting you convince me I wasn't good enough the way I was. But I like who I used to be better. I can't marry you. Even if I could get past your cheating, which I can't, I know I'd never be happy the way I *need* to be happy."

Color rose high in his face and his gaze flit over every surface of his office, never once landing on her, "I wish you came home to tell me something different, but I can't fault you for your logic."

Logic? She swallowed. *Logic has nothing to do with it.*

"You're making a mistake—huge. We would have been great together. But I'll let you go. Not that I have much of a choice." His voice caught, like he was laughing at himself. His eyes rose to hers and, for the first time, he focused on her as he ushered her toward the door. "Good luck, Sarah."

Sarah let out a huge breath as he shut the door behind her. The anger, hurt, frustration and insecurity that had consumed her disappeared. She was scared—of her next move and the rest of her life—but she was free.

Chapter Fifteen

Aaron jerked awake. The 2:45 a.m. glowed bright on his phone next to the bed. He looked around, dazed from being woken from a sound sleep. Something wasn't right.

After climbing out of bed, he stepped into a pair of jeans and sneakers and stashed his phone in his back pocket. He rubbed his hand along his face and squinted in the shadowy room. Moonlight glanced off the dresser and splashed onto the floor. He padded out of his bedroom and took a quick look around his apartment. A noise stopped him.

The deli.

He tiptoed downstairs and opened the door leading into the rear of the deli. The storage room was messy, as usual. Moving to the kitchen, he found everything there in place there as well. He walked into the public part of the deli and stopped. Grabbing his phone, he dialed 911.

"I need the police. Someone vandalized my deli."

Shards of glass littered the floor surrounding what had

once been the front window. Lying in the midst of the destruction were several rocks the size of his hand. He turned on the lights and winced at both the glare and the damaged storefront. The refrigerator was dented on both sides and smashed across the front, and sticky, fizzing liquid sprayed from soda cans onto the floor. Display cases were cracked and broken into pieces, and shelves were overturned with their food packages spread over a six-foot area. Aaron's shoes stuck to the floor as he made his way to the cash register. Although it was emptied every night, the vandals wouldn't have known. But when he looked, it sat untouched.

He ran a hand through his hair, massaging his scalp. The food waste bothered him and the property destruction hurt him, but the cash register confused him. Why hadn't they messed with the cash register?

Red and blue lights flashed outside, and he rushed forward to meet the police. He winced as the cool air hit his bare chest, reminding him he'd come downstairs without a shirt.

"Officer, I'm Aaron Isaacson. This is my store. I called you." Although he knew several members of the police force, played against their softball team on occasion, he didn't recognize the ones who responded.

The cop shook his hand and shined his flashlight around the space. "Anyone else here?"

"No, it was empty when I arrived."

"Okay, let us look around. My partner, Officer Delgado, will take your statement."

For the next two hours, Aaron reported what he'd heard and found and watched as the police investigated. The inside wasn't the worst—outside, the vandals had spray painted swastikas on the beige brick. The ugly red paint dripped like blood down the facade of the building.

Aaron's stomach clenched. Burglary wasn't the motive. Hatred was.

Chief Forsyth arrived but didn't greet Aaron. Instead, he conferred with the other officers and left before Aaron had a chance to talk to him. By the time the rest of the police left, the sun was rising. Normally, he'd be in the deli's kitchen, preparing breakfast for his customers. But yellow police tape cordoned off the area, and the customers who showed up gawked, offered to help with cleanup later and left. The deli wouldn't open today. Probably not the rest of the week, or as long as it took to clean and restock. He'd texted his employees, telling them they would be closed. After he called the insurance company, he would call his parents. He didn't look forward to sharing this news with them, and his body sagged with exhaustion and despair.

This time, the violence was directed at his business, at his family. At him, personally. Rage filled him, but it had nowhere to go. The police were gone. The vandals hadn't yet been found. And for the moment, he was alone, with no one he could vent to. Sarah's image flitted through his brain. He shook his head—this was his problem.

He wandered around inside, picking his way around the mess. This business was his family. They'd all put their love and loyalty into it, building it into a successful venture that was respected and valued around town. Yet, someone tried to destroy it. Who would do such a thing? Would he have to be suspicious of his customers? His neighbors? His friends? Was it the same person who'd vandalized the temple? His deli wasn't the only Jewish business in town. Had anyone else been targeted? He should have asked the police when they were here. His shoulders slumped. He'd call later and ask when he had more energy.

He was supposed to spend the time between Rosh Hashanah and Yom Kippur thinking about being a better person and repenting for his sins, not cleaning up after others.

Aaron cleared glass off a stool, sat and put his head in his hands. He knew he needed to call his parents, but his heart sank at having to tell them. With a sigh, he grabbed his phone and dialed. His father answered on the second ring, but Aaron's throat closed before he could get the words out. He cleared it and tried again.

"Dad, I need you and Mom to come to the store. It's been vandalized."

When they arrived forty-five minutes later, his parents' faces mirrored his own shock. In silence, they walked around in circles, touching a broken case, stepping over a rock, straightening a crooked blind. After about ten minutes, his mother straightened her shoulders and turned to him.

"We'll clean this place up, restock and be back in business." She gave him a single, brisk nod. "You did the right thing, calling the insurance company. Now call your brothers to help. We'll need brooms and lots of cleaning supplies."

"We don't need to bother Jordan and Gabriel."

His mother marched over to him and grabbed his arm. "You have got to stop assuming you alone are responsible for this store. It is a family business, and we are all family. Now call them."

He froze. When had he become so fixated on responsibility that he'd ignored the rest of his family's need and ability to help? No wonder the stress of taking care of this place was getting to him.

"I've never wanted to disappoint you." His voice was hoarse.

His mother took his face in her hands. "Nothing you ever do will disappoint us. You are our life. You're beyond our wildest expectations, and we love you." Her eyes were shiny with tears, and his throat burned with his own suppressed tears.

He nodded, unable to speak. Ideas and misconceptions and realizations flitted through his head, but this wasn't the time to examine them. His mother's determination was unexpected and contagious. With her words echoing and filling his heart, and a direction to follow, he called his brothers. Twenty minutes later, Jordan and Gabriel arrived. By nine in the morning, the insurance adjuster had arrived and was already photographing the destruction and cross-checking their policy. By ten, the police returned, removed the yellow tape and cleared the scene for cleanup. As customers stopped in that morning and learned of the destruction, his mother passed out coupons for use after Yom Kippur, encouraging them to return when the store was cleaned and restocked. Local business owners offered to help sandblast the graffiti.

At eleven, Sarah showed up. His heart pounded in his chest as she crossed the doorway. She was here—again—when he needed her the most.

"Oh my God, Aaron, are you all right?"

It surprised him in that moment to realize no one had asked him that question—not his parents or brothers, not the police, nor any of his customers. Of course, Sarah would.

Was he all right? Not even close. So many emotions struggled inside of him that he couldn't name them all. He was afraid of what might happen if he even tried.

He opened and closed his mouth, struggling for the right words. Finally, he settled for, "I'm fine."

She looked him up and down as if she didn't believe him then took a step forward as if she might touch him. He retreated a step. He wanted her, but too many contradictory thoughts circulated through his head.

Why was she here?

Where had she gone after she left the hospital?

Was she still angry with him?

What did that look on her face mean?

He couldn't form the words to ask her any of those questions. Not when they had so much to discuss and when her touch might break him.

She froze and her face flushed. Glancing down at her watch, she shook her head. "Listen, I just returned from DC, and I have to go home and change. But I'm coming back."

She'd gone to DC. His stomach dropped. After his grandmother confronted her in the hospital, she'd returned to Matthew.

He shook his head. "It's okay, Sarah. We've got it under control."

"I know you do, but you need me." She reached for his arm and squeezed his elbow gently. "We can talk about it later. In fact, we're going to."

The touch of her palm on his elbow sent shivers along his arm. He clenched his fist, not sure if he wanted to catch that electric feeling or stop himself from pushing her away. He wasn't sure who he was anymore, let alone why she was here with him. He was too tired to analyze anything. He needed to keep moving and get his store back in order.

Instead of saying anything, he watched her go. It seemed like all he did was watch her leave. But this time, she was coming back. And when she did, he wouldn't let her leave again. Not without a long-overdue conversation.

Sarah was barely gone a full hour when she returned, ready to work. She found Aaron cleaning an unknown substance off his hands with a yellow rag.

"What do you need me to do?"

Her quiet question sent him into a tailspin. Such a loaded set of words. There were many ways to answer the question,

none of which he could say in front of the mass of people
who showed up on his doorstep to help clean the store. As
he stared at her, everyone else faded into the background
and all he could see was her. Her dark, glossy hair. Her
warm skin. Her lips. He tried to clear his thoughts.

"You can help Annabelle clean out the bagel shelves."
The words slipped from him like poppy seeds in a bread-
basket. Unstoppable.

With a nod, she walked over to Annabelle and grabbed
a rag. Her lithe body moved in ways that made his body
ache. He clenched his hands at his sides as he thought about
what it would be like to cup her ass.

"We'll have this place up and running in no time." He
jumped at his father's voice behind him.

His father was right. With so many people helping, what
had seemed an insurmountable task was now manage-
able. In other circumstances, with everyone pitching in
on a project together, it would be fun. Annabelle, who
owned the dry-cleaning business across the street, had arrived with her husband, Jai, as soon as they'd opened that
morning. Last year, they'd been robbed, and Aaron loaned
them money to get back on their feet. They'd repaid him
with interest and brought pot stickers to his parents every
week for three months.

Kesha, the clothing boutique owner down the street,
brought her wife, Kim, and the two women swept out the
storeroom. Aaron had defended them from some rowdy
teenagers a couple of months ago.

Mr. and Mrs. Paul, loyal customers since his parents
ran the place, sorted through the paperwork scattered on
the floor, bickering as usual. But he'd caught Mr. Paul
lovingly stroking his wife's hand. There were others, too,
who'd moved in and out as the day went on.

Now, Sarah. She wasn't his, and she wasn't staying, but

she was here. His heart kicked into high gear at her presence, and for a moment, Aaron enjoyed letting his dreams carry him away with her. He imagined the two of them working together, laughing together, loving together.

Loving?

He paused a long moment, pondering the word. Did he love her? He nodded to himself. Yes, he did love her. Always had, always would. He couldn't imagine a full life without her, as much as he'd tried while she was gone. Now that she was back, though, he knew better. She was his life.

Reality returned soon enough, though, and sometimes, love wasn't enough. Sarah was leaving—she *needed* to leave, and he knew that. In fact, he supported her leaving. After all, what kind of a *schmuck* would he be if he forced her to stay?

His father nodded toward her. "She's a good girl."

He cringed at the term "girl," but nodded and headed outside where they were sandblasting graffiti off the side of the building.

He was relieved to find the offensive mark was almost gone, but his stomach still clenched when he looked at the place it had been. Would he ever be able to look at the outside of this store—his livelihood, his heritage—and *not* see it? The noise from the sandblaster made his head pound, so he returned inside and entered his office.

Deciding he'd work on paperwork, he filled out every insurance form and double-checked each one before hitting send on the computer. The good news was that they were covered for the damage. If only that could make what happened okay. It couldn't. Nothing could.

A light tap sounded on his office door. He looked up and found Sarah standing in his doorway.

He took a deep breath. "Are you leaving?"

"Of course not. You need me." She waved at the destruction behind her. "You know, whoever vandalized the temple probably did this too, right?"

His body temperature dropped, and he couldn't breathe. His heart refused to connect the two incidents, no matter how logical the connection appeared. Buying time, he focused on her. How could she stand there and talk to him as if they were two normal people, as if this were a normal day? How could she focus when there were so many details vying for attention, not the least of which was that cheating bastard, Matthew, her job in DC and, right now, the deli?

He gripped the edge of his desk. "Until we catch whoever did this, I can't know for sure and I'm not willing to make the connection. Besides, a temple is different from a deli." Even as he said the words, he knew he was wrong.

Sarah ventured into the office. Her nearness made him dizzy. Her fruity scent filled his senses. All he could do was inhale.

"Not to whoever did this," she said. "You might want to consider contacting the local Jewish Federation. Although with their sources, they've probably already heard by now."

"Why?"

"They're good with advocacy. You know, helping when someone in the community has a problem like this."

He spread his hands. "Most of the local community is here, helping to clean up."

Sarah nodded. "And that's great. But there's more to it. They can help with making sure everyone knows, maybe head something like this off in the future. Trust me, Aaron, there is a lot more everyone can do."

"Why do you care?" He studied her. "It's not your problem."

Her expression focused in a way he hadn't seen in so long. "It's everyone's problem. This is my home, Aaron. Anything that hurts you hurts me, too."

He couldn't let himself believe her, no matter how much he wanted to. No matter how much he wanted her to stay. No matter how much he loved her, she had to chase her dreams in DC. If she stayed here for him, she'd eventually resent him. And he'd feel guilty for the rest of his life. He needed to make her leave, for her own good, no matter how much it killed him.

"How fortunate something like this could happen while you're here. It's right in your wheelhouse, isn't it? Gives you something to feel a connection to, and you get to leave once you've done your thing. Thanks, Sarah, but you can go back to Washington with a clear conscience. We've got this."

The shock on Sarah's face pierced his armor anyway. He wanted to take back his words, redo the last five minutes. But he couldn't. His body trembled with want and fear and disappointment.

Sarah's face whitened and her voice shook. "You have no idea what you're talking about, Aaron. About anything."

Sarah shoved her way past Dave as he entered the cramped office, nearly knocking him off balance in her race to exit Aaron's office.

"Whoa, what was that about?" Dave turned to Aaron and lifted an eyebrow.

"I don't think you want to be around me right now." Aaron ran his hands through his hair.

"You need a beer."

He looked at Dave, askance. "It's barely noon."

"Then you need lunch along with a beer." He glanced around. "Somewhere else. Come on."

Aaron's stomach growled and he realized he hadn't eaten anything today. With reluctance, he followed Dave out into the main part of the deli. His gaze scanned the area, searching, but he didn't see Sarah anywhere. Sadness filled him, even though he'd practically forced her to leave.

"Hey guys, thanks for all your help today," he said. "Take some time off for lunch, please. We'll be here around three if anyone else wants to help."

After ensuring his parents were going home to rest, Aaron followed Dave around the block to a gastropub. They slid into a booth with soft, well-worn seats.

Bill, the owner, approached them and nodded to Aaron. "Whatever you two want, it's on the house."

Too weary to argue, Aaron thanked him and studied the menu in front of him. The words swam on the page.

"So, you want to talk about what happened to your deli, or about Sarah?" Dave slid his menu to the edge of the table.

"Why are those my only two options? What if I want to talk about the Red Sox?"

"You hate the Red Sox."

"Exactly," said Aaron. "There are a million ways to hate on them. It could occupy me for hours."

"Sorry, I'm a good friend, but not that good a friend."

The waitress arrived and took their order before leaving them alone once again.

Aaron shook his head. "I would say I want my life to return to normal. But then this happens, and I realize normal won't happen for a long time."

"Sarah's leaving in a few more days, right? After Yom Kippur?"

Aaron shrugged. "That's her plan."

Dave studied him. "She's gotten awfully involved for someone who's leaving in a few days."

"She went to DC overnight." He rubbed his forehead. "And that's the problem. No matter how much I might want her to stay, she has to leave. Everything she needs is in DC." *Except me.*

"Yet she keeps returning to you. When I walked in on you two, the sparks between you two—"

Aaron interrupted. "Don't tell me you're going all woo-woo on me."

Dave laughed. "The pheromones were off the charts in there. Someone as clueless as I could smell them. That woman is into you."

Aaron grabbed the silverware and squeezed, the cool metal digging into his palms. "I thought I could make it work between us. But now that the deli was vandalized, I have too much on my plate to think about anything else. My responsibilities are here. Hers aren't."

"You sure?"

Aaron leaned forward. "I'd give anything if I could make it work between us. But what kind of *putz* would I be if I forced her to choose?"

Sarah scrubbed the floor of the deli as if she could erase the mistakes of her past with soap, water and elbow grease. On her hands and knees, she surveyed her progress. Everyone else left when Aaron dismissed them for lunch, but she'd taken a lap around the block to cool her anger and returned to an empty deli. The solitude was a welcome balm. Alone, she'd gotten a lot done, although her stomach growled while she worked. She had one third of the floor left to scrub, and with renewed determination, she set to work.

Aaron was pigheaded. She scrubbed harder, pushing the scrub brush into the floor, making sure to hit every groove.

She couldn't believe *this* was the man she loved. He was wrong about everything. He actually thought she used the vandalism for her own purposes. She moved to a new area and scrubbed even harder.

What an ass. He wasn't the only one with deep connections. Well, in truth, she hadn't appreciated them properly before now. She scrubbed until she thought her arms would fall off, then wiped over the cleaned area with a damp cloth.

Better.

Sarah sat on her haunches and surveyed the clean floor. It looked so much better, and the bonus was that it had worked out some of her anger. Her gaze darted around the deli. It was almost fixed, unlike her life, which was still up in the air. With time to think, the import of her conversation with Matthew slammed into her. She'd devoted the past three years to *him—Matthew*. That cheating bastard. She'd let him shape who she was, how she thought and how she dressed.

With a bitter laugh, she looked at the clothes she was wearing—the clothes Matthew had scorned. They were wet and dirty, not the clothes he thought she should wear. A weight lifted from her. Her clothes didn't matter. Whatever Matthew thought about them, or anything else about her, didn't matter. Truth was, it should never have mattered. But she'd convinced herself he could help her get ahead in her goals, and she'd let it go too far. And now she was free to be herself.

Since she'd been home, she was more like herself than she'd ever been in DC. It was a start. And if she was lucky, when she returned to her job in DC, maybe she could bring some of this Jersey-Sarah back with her.

As for Aaron, well, the more she thought about him, the more she realized she loved him. Despite his stubbornness and bossiness, deep down he had a streak of honor and kindness that she admired. He brought out the best, and worst, in her. She couldn't rush headlong into a relationship with him, even if he wanted one with her, which, by every indication, he didn't.

"What are you doing here?" Aaron's voice boomed in the quiet deli, jolting her out of her reverie.

"I never left."

Despite his exhaustion and her annoyance, she had never been more attracted to him.

He frowned. "I told everyone to leave. Where were you?"

She rose, wiped her hands on her thighs and shrugged. "You must have missed me. Once everyone left, I decided to finish what I was doing. There's still so much to be done…" Her voice trailed off.

Aaron walked in a circle and stopped when he was so close to her that she could kiss him—or slap him. At the moment, she wasn't sure which urge might win out.

"Missed you," he repeated. He stepped closer, boxing her in.

His scent filled her nostrils. His gaze burned holes into her until she'd swear he could see inside her. See her desire for him, despite everything.

The air around them thickened. He raised his hand and trailed his knuckles over her cheekbone and along her jawline, leaving a trail of goose bumps in their wake. Her pulse pounded in her ears and need built inside her.

"God, I've missed you." He crushed her mouth with his.

She moaned and pulled him close, arching against him, feeling his hardness at her core. Despite everything, she'd waited for this, for him.

His breath came fast and hot. She pulled on his belt loops, hands shaking. In a flurry of hands and fingers and half-uttered words and grunts, they tore off each other's clothes until she was naked beneath him.

"Condom," he sputtered, reaching blindly for his pants pocket.

"What?" Wonderment at his preparation flitted through

her mind before she grabbed the foil from him, tore it open and rolled it on.

He gritted his teeth at her touch, the cords in his neck popping. He shook above her, and another part of her mind loved the power she held over him. She gripped him, and he pulsed and throbbed in her hand.

"Sarah," he ground out. "No games. Not now."

He adjusted her beneath him, met her gaze and when she nodded, he thrust into her, long and deep. There was no foreplay, no sweet words, just pure physical need. Exactly what she needed at this moment. They rocked against each other as their lust built. His eyes glittered like diamonds. Sweat popped on his brow. The Jewish star pendant he wore around his neck swung back and forth between them, like a pendulum.

She buried her face in his neck, his warmth and strength satisfying something deep within her. He didn't hold her back or mold her or show her how to please him. He let her find her own rhythm and he followed, wrapping his arms around her and holding her tight as pleasure coursed through her, spiraling tighter and tighter until she peaked and screamed his name.

"Aaron!"

She wrapped her legs around his waist and soared over the edge. As she came down, he arched, shouted something incoherent and pumped into her fast and hard and deep.

Their breaths echoed in the silence around them. Sliding her hands up and down his back, she relished the smoothness of his skin beneath her fingertips. He hugged her tight as aftershocks rippled through her body.

When they'd both calmed, he pulled back, watching her, his expression intent. In silence, he rose, held out a hand and pulled her up. She put her clothes on, staring at his back muscles that rippled as he dressed.

He'd satisfied a primal need that had been building for a while. But there was still so much more. Maybe now they could get to what was growing between them.

"I don't get you, Sarah." His comment broke the charged silence, cooled the previously too-warm air and left her more exposed than when she'd been naked.

"It's been a long time since you tried."

"What's that mean?"

"It means you make assumptions and accusations without giving me a chance to explain," she said.

"It's hard not to when I haven't seen you for ten years."

He'd kept track. He'd also not moved on from her leaving in the first place, no matter how clear she'd been in the past.

"You made it damned uncomfortable for me to visit," she said. "All I heard from my parents was how essential and involved in the community you were. You hated me. How was I supposed to come home?"

"It was ten years ago. It doesn't matter. What matters is now." He looked around the store. "Why did you do this?"

"Why did I do what?"

"Stay? You could have left."

"I could have. But I needed to help here…in your deli."

"Why does my deli matter to you?"

Was he really asking her this? "I told you, Aaron. You and your deli are one. What happened here, in this place, happened to *you*. And you matter to me. How can you think I'd ignore you?"

"I don't know what you'd do anymore, Sarah."

Chapter Sixteen

Aaron climbed out of bed after a sleepless night and groaned. His entire body ached, from the extra physical activity he'd put it through yesterday, from tension and from sex on the hard floor. More than anything, he wanted to stay in bed, pull the sheets over his head and live in a blanket fort like he'd done when he was five.

But he wasn't five any longer.

And lying here would only make him think of Sarah and all he would miss without her. He'd already spent far too many hours reliving every minute detail of sex with her, questioning why they couldn't work and wracking his brain for a solution. He hadn't come to any conclusions.

He'd spent last night talking with his parents and siblings, finalizing things with the insurance company and checking in again with the police. With this new attack, the police had gone on high alert, and he hoped they'd have some leads soon. Yesterday, the store had been cleaned from top to bottom. Today, the last of the repairs would be done and the shelves would be restocked. Tomorrow, they'd open for business, and he'd still be able to complete the break fast orders for after Yom Kippur. He couldn't have done it without the assistance of his friends and neighbors.

Including Sarah.

He fell back onto his pillow and groaned. Sarah. When he'd been able to catch a few minutes of sleep, she'd invaded his dreams. Truth be told, she'd invaded his thoughts for this entire week. It was like walking around with Jiminy Cricket on his shoulder, if Jiminy Cricket was a hot babe with gorgeous hair, luscious lips and endless legs. His groin hardened. Damn. He couldn't believe he'd pushed her away. What had he done? Panic crept up his spine. He fisted the sheets in his hands and gulped air into his lungs. He'd done the only thing he could under the circumstances.

His phone buzzed and he grabbed it, happy for the distraction. It was a text from Dave.

Police are here questioning me about some of my students.

Aaron shook his head in sympathy, knowing anything that might hurt Dave's students would hurt his friend equally as much. That's rough. You okay?

I'll call you later.

Aaron sent a thumbs-up emoji and tossed the phone onto the bed. Glancing at his watch, he groaned again. He had things to do. With one quick stretch of his muscles, he showered and dressed for the day.

Normally, he'd grab breakfast at the deli. But he couldn't face the place on an empty stomach after having sex there with Sarah. Instead, he walked around the block to the coffee shop where Tricia, one of the baristas, greeted him and had a mug filled with steaming black brew ready for him by the time he reached the counter. He reached for his wallet, but she held up a hand and stopped him.

"Nope—this one's on the house."

"Not necessary."

She shooed him away. "Go, before I change my mind and charge you double for aggravating me."

He grinned and tipped his cup at her in a salute. "Yes, ma'am." He settled into a corner table to relax before starting his day.

Randi, a local banker, stopped on her way out the door with a latte. "I heard about your store. If there's anything the bank can do, let me know."

"I appreciate it," he said. "Pretty sure insurance covers everything, but I'll let you know."

She patted his shoulder. "If you need help later, call. I'm off at one."

He smiled at her as she walked out the door and felt touched by her thoughtfulness. Everyone had gone out of their way to reach out to him or his parents. Last night, the local insurance adjuster sent a catered dinner to his parents' home. They'd have to do something big to thank everyone. He wasn't sure what yet.

After finishing his coffee, he waved goodbye to Tricia and returned to the deli where he found the workmen waiting on him to open the doors. Most of the work had been completed yesterday, but the windows still needed repair, and the cracked and broken glass display cases needed to be replaced. He let them in, then moved to his office where he sat with his office door open and watched them work.

One of the workers stood exactly where Sarah had when she'd told him she'd changed. Another worker, this one maneuvering the old glass case, was standing on the exact spot of floor where he'd first noticed her cleaning after he returned from lunch yesterday. A few feet to his left was where they'd had sex. There were other areas of the deli she'd infused with her spirit and presence, but they weren't visible from this angle.

Was she everywhere? Was he destined to think of her constantly? Shaking his head, he tried focusing on ordering supplies, but the numbers swam on the page. The black lines reminded him of her hair, and his hand tingled as he remembered how he'd stroked the dark tresses while he climaxed. He pushed himself out of his chair and swallowed a curse.

Trying for a completely new line of thinking, he searched the listings the Realtors had sent him, plotting on a map where they were and, more importantly, where they weren't.

Gah! Was this just a pipe dream? He'd said one of them would always be miserable, and it looked like he was right. She couldn't stay here, but how could he leave his family? What if he left and this deli failed? Could he really abandon his home and responsibilities to chase her?

He pulled his phone from his pocket and dialed Jordan's number. "Hey, can you spot me at the deli for an hour? I need to run out, and the workmen are here."

"Sure. Everything okay?"

"Yeah. I just have some things I need to take care of."

"No problem. Give me twenty."

Aaron hung up, then paced the small hallway until his brother arrived.

When Jordan opened the door to the deli, he took in Aaron's appearance and his eyes clouded over with worry. "You sure everything's okay?"

He nodded. "I just need to clear my head."

"Too bad Sarah's not around," he said. "I'll bet she could distract you."

If he only knew. Aaron shook his head and clapped his brother on the back a little harder than necessary, then strode out the door. He climbed into his car and drove to Feldon Park. The ball fields were empty this early, but later they'd be filled with soccer players. The playground, however, was crowded with young children playing while their parents stood in groups talking or supervised their actions. Walking trails led from the parking lot toward the water, and he followed the path through the trees. He inhaled the crisp air that hinted of autumn. Muted colors of reds and oranges mixed with the deep greens of summer. In another week or two, the leaves would be brilliant.

Sarah would be back in DC in a few days. Would he still think about her during his every waking and sleeping moment? His boots cracked acorns beneath his feet. Scurrying in the bushes around him alerted him to squirrels and chipmunks storing food for the colder weather. Still, he built up a sweat with his fast pace. If only he could build a resistance to Sarah.

He sat on a bench and nodded to parents with strollers as they passed. If he were honest with himself, he shouldn't be surprised that he couldn't get his thoughts off Sarah. He had always focused on one thing at a time. It was his strategy for dealing with life. Focus on one thing, then the next, then the next. If he didn't like something—or if something didn't go his way—he ruminated on why, fixed the problem and moved on. He'd never been big on talking it over with people and rarely shared his feelings.

When Sarah left for DC, he'd thought there was no room in her life for him. Sure, he'd thought she'd cheated on him, but it was more than a misunderstanding about a random other guy. He should have realized it earlier, but throughout their relationship, he'd been singularly focused on her while she explored her career and her life. Her life changed, while his stayed the same. He'd returned home and assumed he'd get over her in his own time. And he did, on the surface, at least. He'd kept busy with the deli and dated other women, pushing all thoughts of Sarah into the farthest, darkest recesses of his mind.

But seeing her again brought it all to the surface. His stomach soured, including all the little dissatisfactions with his life he'd tried to ignore. For the first time, he resented being the one to always take care of the family.

His phone rang as he walked back toward his car. He glanced at the caller ID but didn't recognize the number. He slid his finger across the glass and brought the phone to his ear.

"Hello?"

"Mr. Isaacson? This is Officer Paul of the Browerville Police Department. I wanted to let you know we have three people in custody."

Aaron froze and the blood rushed from his head. He leaned against a car. "You do? That was fast."

"Can you come to the police station? We have some questions."

"I'm on my way."

The ten-minute drive felt like it lasted an hour, but he still pulled into the police parking lot before he was quite ready. Leaning his forehead against the steering wheel, he took several deep breaths. He was ready to put this incident behind him but knowing someone had been arrested made it more real, more serious, than he'd considered. He recalled Sarah's comment about how the deli and the temple vandalism were probably connected. Now he'd find out if she was right.

When he had his breathing under control, he climbed out of his truck, gave himself a mental shake and entered the precinct. After giving his name to the desk sergeant, he was led to another desk, this one belonging to the officer who called him. Beside him sat a woman wearing a dark blue windbreaker with large yellow letters reading "FBI" where the left breast pocket should be.

"Thanks for coming in quickly," Officer Paul said. "This is SSA Daniels with the FBI. Chief Forsyth has recused himself, so she'll be overseeing the case. Now, reviewing the report you filed, you never saw anyone in your deli, right?"

"Correct." Aaron eyed the agent, confused by Chief Forsyth's recusal, but not sure it was the time or place for his questions. "I heard noises, but by the time I got downstairs, no one was there."

"So, we don't need you as an eyewitness. However, do you recognize these people?" He pushed a piece of paper toward Aaron with three photos.

"Is that—"

The officer nodded and cut him off. "It's why the police chief recused himself."

"Jesus." Aaron rubbed a hand over his face. "The chief's son? I think he and the other two were outside my store a couple days before the incident. But I can't be positive."

Voices rose behind him. He turned and found the rabbi had arrived along with an ashy-faced Dave. The rabbi nodded, and she and Dave walked away with a group of officers and FBI agents. Aaron's heart thudded. All three vandals were teenagers.

"I'm sorry." Aaron shook his head. "I wish I could help you."

"It's okay. We're trying to figure out if they targeted you for personal reasons or not."

"I can't imagine they did. I'd remember."

"Reread your statement, please, and let me know if there's anything you need to add."

Aaron skimmed the paper, his mind hopping in a million different directions. "I think that's everything. What will happen to them?"

The officer sat in his chair. "Well, if the evidence points to them, which so far it does, they'll be charged with a hate crime. Though they're kids, they'll serve time. Where, I'm not sure. It's a shame, really, the hate these kids learn."

That's what bothered Aaron the most. They were kids. How would jail help dissolve the hate that consumed them? And did hatred motivate them, or was it a dare?

And what about the chief's son, Kevin? From everything he'd heard, Kevin was a good kid. How had this happened? Why was he involved?

Aaron shook hands with the two officers and walked across the precinct. Dave met him in the hallway.

"What are you doing here?" Aaron asked him.

"Kevin is my student. The other two used to be." Dave covered his face with his hands. "I'll admit, the two older ones don't surprise me as much. They always hung with a rough crowd. But Kevin? I can't believe he would do something like this."

Aaron put his hand on Dave's shoulder. He usually had no sympathy for vandals, but these were teenagers. It was more complicated than good guy versus bad guy. As he tried to think of something to say to his friend, the rabbi walked over.

"You two okay?" she asked.

Aaron shrugged. "I don't know how to feel when the perpetrators are kids—" he pointed at Dave "—and he's dealing with them being his students."

The rabbi nodded. "The police told me the same group

of people committed both crimes. It's a complicated and heartbreaking situation, made more so by the fact that one is the police chief's son. Why don't you two come talk to me later? Maybe tomorrow morning?"

"Sure. Say nine o'clock?" Aaron said.

"Yeah, okay." Dave nodded. "We'll see you then."

The rabbi headed out, and Aaron and Dave followed some distance behind. As they reached the parking lot, Dave stopped and turned to Aaron.

"We've gotta help Kevin, Aaron," Dave said. "We can't let him go to jail."

"I don't know, Dave." Aaron ran a hand over his jaw. "The three of them broke the law. They need to learn consequences. We can't make an exception for Kevin because his dad is the police chief."

Dave shook his head. "I know, but I've got to do something. I can't let him get sent away without at least trying."

Sarah hit Send, clicked out of her email and shut off her computer. It was the worst time of year to apply for a job at a Jewish organization, but the rabbi had forwarded her the job opportunity like a sign from God. If she waited until the timing was better, she'd chicken out. At least it gave her something other than Aaron to focus on.

"You'll come with us to break the fast, right?" her mother asked as Sarah walked into the kitchen. "You'll be okay with Aaron?"

Her body heated at the mention of his name, but dread left her chest aching. "Maybe he won't show up."

"To his mother's event?"

She straightened her shoulders. "I'll deal."

With any luck, she'd be too hungry to do anything but focus on the food. And with Caroline and Jessica there, she'd have friends to keep her occupied. She'd probably never notice him.

Right.

Images of Aaron's broad chest, his muscular arms, dimpled cheek and naked ass flashed through her mind.

Traitor.

"Do you think we should offer to bring food?" her mother asked. "I mean, it feels strange asking the owners of a deli, but with all the destruction, maybe we should?"

"I'm sure they'll be able to manage," Sarah said. "The sign said they would reopen tomorrow."

Her mom nodded. "Good, because their food is by far the best. A break-the-fast meal without the Isaacson's platters is like a Jewish mother who doesn't want her child to be a doctor. It doesn't work."

Sarah laughed. "You know I'm not a doctor, right?"

Her mom gave her a hug. "You are exactly who and what you need to be. I couldn't be prouder. As for where, well, I do wish you were closer."

Sarah swallowed the words on the tip of her tongue. No sense getting her mother's hopes up unless the job came through. "I promise I'll be much better at visiting."

Her mother studied her. "You were finding yourself and figuring out who you needed to be. Sometimes, it requires distance."

It was a very positive spin on a negative situation, and Sarah's chest swelled at her mom's unconditional love.

Her mom continued. "With Matthew out of the picture, maybe you'll find what—and who—you're looking for closer to home."

Oy. "Let me have a little time to myself before you start setting me up, please."

Her mom nodded. "You don't seem upset about Matthew. Is that true, or are you keeping it to yourself?"

"I miss the idea of Matthew more than the man himself, as awful as that sounds. He needs someone he can mold. It took me a long time to realize that about him, and longer to realize I can't be that person. I don't want to be."

"Does this mean I can put bright colors back on the Chanukah list?"

Sarah shuddered. "One step at a time, Mom. Aaron and I aren't going to work."

Her mother frowned. "Why not?"

"He's convinced my life is there and his is here, and one of us will always be miserable."

"And what do you think?"

Sarah focused on the place mat, afraid of what she'd see in her mom's glance.

"I think he's chickening out." A sudden surge of anger heated her cheeks. "I don't see why we can't figure out a way to make it work. He disagrees. So, he is either afraid or he doesn't want me."

Sarah deliberately left out the "as much as I want him." There were some things she wouldn't say to her mother.

"Oh honey, not everything is one or the other. You both have very strong dreams, and until a few days ago, neither of those dreams included the other. Maybe he needs time to figure out how to adapt. Just like you do."

A sliver of hope blunted some of her anger. "What do I do until then?"

"Give him time." Her mom placed a hand over hers. "Give him space to decide if he can change without you. And in the meantime, do what you do best."

The following morning, Aaron paced outside the temple while he waited for Dave to arrive. He'd spent much of yesterday trying to reconcile the Kevin he knew—the quiet kid who was always polite whenever he came into the deli—with the kind of kid he imagined would deface a synagogue and vandalize a deli. The two didn't mesh.

"Hey, you ready?" Dave walked over to Aaron.

"Yeah." Aaron held the door open, and the two men walked inside.

They found the rabbi in her office where she greeted them and offered them seats on comfortable blue uphol-stered chairs. Instead of sitting behind her desk, she joined them in the seating area of her office, and Aaron envi-sioned her counseling families in this spot.

"I thought it would be a good idea for the three of us to talk," she said. "Not only because an event like this is traumatic, but also because I think it would help if we were all on the same page going forward with what we choose to do."

When neither Dave nor Aaron spoke up, the rabbi con-tinued. "The three kids who were arrested will be brought up on charges of vandalism. But because they attacked two Jewish buildings, they are also accused of hate crimes, which carry far more serious punishments."

Dave groaned and Aaron glanced at him, taking in his bloodshot eyes. He realized, for the first time, not only how little sleep Dave must've had last night, but how con-cerned he was about the situation.

The rabbi turned her attention to Dave. "Yes?"

He was silent for several seconds, possibly finding the right words. "Kevin's life will be destroyed by this. I wish…"

He let the sentence hang and they sat in silence for several long moments, allowing him to finish whatever thought he'd begun.

"What do you wish?" the rabbi finally asked.

"I wish there was a way to intervene."

Aaron blew out a frustrated breath. "Dave, we talked

yesterday about this. He has to be punished for what he did."

"I know." Dave dropped his head in his hands. "But he's such a good kid. I'm not saying it because he's the police chief's son. He gets straight As and volunteers with Key Club. He sings in his church choir. He's literally the stereotypical wunderkind."

"It shouldn't give him a free pass, though." Aaron's voice rose and his pulse pounded in his ears. "There's no way we can condone letting him off scot-free."

"Maybe there's a compromise solution." The rabbi's voice was calm.

"How do you compromise?" Aaron asked. "You think we should turn the other cheek and let him go with a 'but next time'? How can you think that?"

The rabbi stared at him.

He swallowed hard. "I'm sorry, Rabbi."

She nodded. "I understand. Believe me, I understand exactly how angry and violated you feel. But there were three people who committed these crimes, and if you look at them, there are significant differences between two of them and Kevin."

"How do you know this?" Aaron asked.

"As a rabbi, I'm privy to information you aren't. Information was summarized for me, and Dave is right. Kevin is a good kid. From what the police told me, he was a bystander."

"The police? How do we know they're not sticking up for their own?"

"Because, Aaron, the police chief recused himself and handed his duties over to the deputy chief. And the FBI is overseeing the investigation."

"Bystanders are also guilty, Rabbi," Aaron argued.

"I'm not suggesting he get off without any punishment.

But compared to the other two, who have records and will be fully prosecuted to the extent allowed, I'm not sure jail time is the right move for Kevin. I think if we, as the victims, were to urge leniency, it would go a long way."

Aaron shook his head. "What do you mean by leniency?"

The rabbi pulled out a small stack of papers. "Sarah gave me this information. I think there's a possibility we could use what happened to us as a teaching moment, both for Kevin and the community at large." Aaron opened his mouth to interrupt, but she held up one hand and stopped him. "Please, Aaron. Look these over before you say anything."

Aaron took the papers from the rabbi, then pulled in a deep breath. His jaw loosened and his shoulders relaxed before focusing on the papers. What the Jewish Federation— a national nonprofit that provided services to local Jewish communities—did in cases like these was useful. They educated the community, ran programs for teens, worked with community leaders and counseled victims. And they were unbiased.

"I thought perhaps we could all work together to create an alternative plan and incorporate some of this information into Kevin's sentence. That way, instead of going to jail—which is deserved in some cases—we can make this a learning experience for Kevin, where he can get a better understanding for what a swastika means to the Jewish community and the emotional impact his actions have on those around him."

Aaron leaned forward and clasped his hands between his knees.

"Aaron, he wouldn't get off scot-free," the rabbi said. "He'll have to pay for what he did. But this way, he'll be less likely to do it again."

"And the other two?"

The rabbi leaned forward. "They go to trial. They have records, but Kevin doesn't. Think about it—the opportunity to help him learn from his mistakes is too great an opportunity to pass up." She leaned back in her chair. "However, we can't ask the prosecutor to consider it unless we're all on board."

"They attacked us because we're Jewish." Aaron couldn't keep the anguish out of his voice. "My synagogue, and my parents' business."

Sympathy welled in the rabbi's eyes. "I know. It scares me and infuriates me, too. But we have an opportunity to step in and make a difference. We have a chance with this one kid to break the bonds of hatred before they form further and, by doing so, can set an example for the entire community."

Aaron sat back in his chair and steepled his fingers together, thinking for a long moment before he finally responded. "Just Kevin?"

"Just Kevin." The rabbi nodded.

He stared out the window and watched the leaves as they fell from the trees in the yard beyond. The colors were changing from green to yellow and orange.

Change.

Everything changed. Even people.

"Okay," he said. "I'll go along with it."

Dave let out a huge breath. "Thank you, Aaron. You won't regret this."

Chapter Seventeen

Sarah walked into the temple later that day and knocked on the rabbi's open office door.

The rabbi rose and gestured to the seats in front of her desk. "Sarah, how nice to see you."

"I wanted to thank you for passing along the job opportunity. Your timing is impeccable."

The rabbi laughed. "I thought it might be an auspicious sign for you. You sent your résumé?"

"I did. I didn't expect to hear right away, since we're in the middle of the holidays."

The rabbi gestured around her office, at her white holiday robes hanging from a doorway, the books piled on her desk and the many papers and folders scattered around. "Believe me, I know. You'd think, knowing how crazy this time of year is, I'd finish my sermons earlier. But every year, it's down to the wire."

Sarah clutched her hands together. "I'm sure the vandalism didn't help."

The air thickened with the seriousness of the situation. "No, it didn't. It's difficult being the example for others, but sometimes it's necessary for the greater good. Thank you again for your help."

"I'm happy to help. If there's anything else you need, let me know."

"I'll do that." The rabbi stood and walked with Sarah outside, into the cool breeze with its hint of autumn temperatures. As they reached Sarah's car, the rabbi stopped and turned to her. "Please let me know what happens with the job."

Sarah wrapped her arms around her waist. "I have an interview on Tuesday."

"Good luck. I assume I'll see you with your family tonight?"

"We never miss *Kol Nidre* services."

"Good." The rabbi smiled.

Sarah opened her car door and dropped into the driver's seat. Satisfaction with the direction of her professional life left her feeling lighter than she had in a couple of days. The more time she spent here, the more opportunities she found for making a difference, and the less scary starting over was. She'd always assumed she needed to be at the heart of government, but she'd begun to wonder if her assumptions had been wrong. Perhaps, if this interview went well, she'd have other options to consider.

Driving into town, she stopped at Hard As Nails for a manicure. The salon was celebrating Pink Day with a half-off sale on pink manicures and pedicures. As she opened the main doors to the salon, the sound system played Pink's "Get the Party Started" and Sarah couldn't help smiling to herself. She loved this quirky place.

After having her name placed on the waiting list for the next chair, she took a seat in the front room and waited for her turn to be called. Her smile dimmed when she realized the topic of everyone's conversation was the vandalism at the temple and deli. Most of the salon's clients had helped in some way. Some had cleaned the mess alongside her and others had brought food or supplies. All were horrified.

"I hope they charge those kids," a woman her mother's age said.

"I think the police chief should resign," said another, this one a young mother waiting with her preteen daughter. "How can he continue working here?"

"And during the Jewish holidays," said another woman her mother's age.

Sarah's stomach clenched. The women echoed her own feelings, but education was an important component, too. She hoped the courts would agree.

Her name was called, and she sat at Irma's table while she painted her nails a pale pink.

"Sarah, I hear you have experience with this," Irma said. "What are your thoughts?"

Once again, surprise mixed with pride that so many people asked for her advice. The people here reminded her that her success had come from her own hard work. She chose her words with care before replying.

"I think you have to weigh intent with punishment." The women around them reacted with not-so-hushed voices raised at her response, so Sarah's voice rose. "I don't believe anyone should get off without consequences, but I think automatic punishment doesn't help anyone."

A woman sitting to her right glared at her.

She continued, speaking quickly before she lost them. "In my experience, forging relationships helps calm things."

There was silence after she finished speaking and Sarah averted her gaze, focusing on the sweep of the brush as

Irma applied the lacquer. So much for their good opinion of her.

"She's not wrong," Irma said. "When you talk out your differences, both sides understand each other better."

"But it doesn't mean the vandals shouldn't be punished," A woman Sarah remembered from high school—Madeline, she thought—responded.

"Of course not," Sarah said. "But it has to be just."

"Now see, Sarah," Irma said, moving Sarah's hands beneath the dryer. "If you lived in town again, you could offer great advice to us all the time. You know what you're talking about."

Sarah smiled and waited while her polish dried under the purple light. When it finished, she paid and said good-bye to everyone. If she got the job from Tuesday's inter-view, she could stay, start over, make a new life for herself here. She glanced down the street at Aaron's deli. Now if only he'd let them start over as well.

"Girlie, it is good to see you sober!" Emily exclaimed as Sarah walked around the sidelines of the soccer field.

Emily's younger brother Robert was a referee and the two women had agreed to meet at the soccer game and catch up so Emily could watch her brother in action.

Sarah gave Emily a hug. "Thanks for the other night."

"Did you get everything straightened out?"

Sarah bit her lip. "I applied for a job doing advocacy training with the Jewish Federation here. If all goes well, I'll be around a lot more."

Robert blew his whistle and the game started. Along the sidelines, parents cheered as their kids ran all over the field.

Emily squealed, her umber eyes sparkling. "Fantastic! You need a place to stay? A roommate? Furniture?"

Sarah laughed. "Whoa, one thing at a time. First, I need to pass the job interview."

"You will." Emily waved her hand as if it were a done deal.

"Well, it's not a sure thing. However, if I get the the job, I'll probably move in with my parents until I find a place to stay."

Sarah looked around at the parents sitting on the sidelines, wondering if she might be them in a few years—married with kids and running from sports games to other activities. She gulped.

Emily leaned forward. "You can room with me if you want. My apartment is next to the train station because I commute. It's big and airy, and my old roommate moved out last month. I mean, it won't be kosher, but if you don't mind grits, you know I love bagels!"

Sarah grinned, remembering how she and her youth group friends included Emily in their temple's social activities, despite her different religion and race, and how Emily's parents always treated her like their own daughter. They'd always been willing to share their experiences when Sarah wanted to learn about racial inequality. It was those conversations that made her realize how much she wanted to become involved and help people. She owed them a lot.

"That would be great, Em. Can I look at it and get all the information?"

One of the goalies stopped the ball and the other sideline cheered, nearly drowning out their conversation.

Emily leaned forward and raised her voice. "Of course. You want to take things slow. So, go slow, and I'll let you know before I sublet the other room. But you know we'd have fun."

"Definitely," Sarah said. "I don't want to make housing plans until I have a job."

Emily eyed her, her head tilting slightly to one side. "Everything okay? You seem a bit overwhelmed."

"That's an understatement." She filled her friend in about her quick trip to DC and her conversation with Matthew.

"I'm glad you stood up for yourself and realized your worth. I mean, I love how you try to put yourself in everyone's shoes, but you need to stay out of that man's loafers. I assume he wears loafers, right? He must wear loafers—Beltway men wear loafers. Anyway, my metaphor works. He asked you to marry him. If he didn't love you enough to stay faithful, he shouldn't have asked. You did the right thing."

Sarah nodded. "I deserve better. I wish I'd ended things with him before I kissed Aaron, though." She twisted a blade of grass between her fingers. "I think I might be in love with him."

"Woo-hoo! I knew it! Aaron is so much better than that jerk. He's a great guy, and if he loves you, he'll love you forever. Plus, he'll remain faithful and respect you."

"I know. But right now, he can't stand to look at me." She shook her head. "Enough about me. Tell me about you."

For the next half an hour, Emily regaled Sarah with stories from her job and dating history. When they parted, Sarah hugged her goodbye.

"I'm glad we had a chance to talk. I'll call you when I'm here to look at your apartment."

Tuesday morning, Aaron's stomach churned, and not from yesterday's Yom Kippur fasting or the overeating afterward at his parents' break-the-fast celebration. As his grandmother warned, Stephanie Cohen had attended, and her aunt hinted broadly about how great a couple the two of them would be. While he'd resisted the obvious setup, he'd been willing to talk to Stephanie. However, the more he and Stephanie talked, the more he desired Sarah. He couldn't stop thinking about her or tracking her whereabouts in the room. If only his heart would listen to his brain.

How one woman could tie him up tighter than the leather bands of the *tefillin* that religious men bound around their heads and arms was beyond him. Fear made his stomach clench. Was it too late for them? He didn't know how to get past the guilt of letting his family down if he moved to DC, not to mention the self-loathing if he made Sarah give up her dreams.

And now he had to attend today's pretrial hearing. His face burned and he gripped the steering wheel hard enough that his knuckles whitened as he maneuvered his car into the parking lot at the courthouse. The breakfast he'd eaten this morning threatened to reappear. He swallowed hard and leaned his head against the headrest, closing his eyes.

Somehow, he had to focus on the legal proceedings. He wasn't sure he could do it. His head swam with a million images. Sarah and the deli had become intertwined, and he couldn't think of one without the other. But he had to separate them.

He'd signed off on the request for leniency for Kevin. The police chief's voice had clogged with tears, and the proud man had looked stooped and haggard when he'd come over and thanked Aaron for doing so. It hadn't made Aaron feel better, but he'd read the materials from the Jewish Federation and he'd made a promise to Dave and the rabbi. He'd also read prison stats, and the logical part of him knew what they were requesting from the court was best for Kevin. The rest of him, though, felt he was disappointing his family.

With a deep sigh, he climbed out of the car, walked into the courthouse and made his way through security. Dave and the rabbi waited for him in the hallway, and they shook hands before entering the courtroom where the defendants were already seated next to their attorneys.

Once everyone was seated, the judge began proceedings and the lawyers spoke. Aaron didn't understand all the legal terms, and most of the early conversation was technical and administrative. Then the prosecutor motioned to Kevin, asking him to rise.

The prosecutor turned to the judge. "Your Honor, both sides have come to an agreement over the minor involved in this case, Mr. Kevin Forsyth. We would like to make a motion he be granted two years' probation, including mandatory education on discrimination and anti-Semitism, a minimum of five hundred hours of volunteer work, and a ten-thousand dollar fine for his part in the damages."

With that announcement, the judge called both lawyers into his chambers. Aaron once again sat alone with his thoughts, which skittered around his brain like a pinball. Hearing the list of requirements made him realize Kevin wasn't getting off easy. He'd agreed to let the kid do some of his volunteer hours at his deli, but he was conflicted and wondered if he'd made a mistake. How in the world could he trust him after what he'd done?

"You're doing the right thing," Jordan whispered.

Aaron jumped. "What are you doing here?"

"Supporting you and our family. I know you think you're the only one who can handle the responsibility of the deli—"

"That's not true, Jordan!"

His brother held up a hand. "We can discuss that part later. You're not letting us down by agreeing to the deal."

Aaron's jaw dropped and his pulse pounded in his ears. "How do you know?"

"Which part?"

Aaron rolled his eyes. His brother drove him nuts. Always had. "Both."

"You take on responsibility for everyone and everything. You always have. But this is the right thing to do. I'm glad you made the deal, and I support you."

A weight lifted from Aaron's shoulders. He grabbed his brother by the side of the neck. "Thank you."

Jordan nodded. "You're welcome."

"Can I ask you something?" He swallowed. Maybe his brother could help him.

"Anything."

"If I wanted to look into expanding our deli—"

"I'd tell you to look into opportunities in DC."

Aaron swallowed. Questions swirled, and none of them made it past the thick blockage in his throat.

His brother squeezed his shoulder. "I'm not a child and I'm not blind. There's no reason I can't put my business degree to good use in the family business. So, decide what you want to do, and I'll support you. No matter what."

He nodded, unable to speak but silently vowing he'd somehow show his brother how much he meant to him. However, before he could do that, the judge and lawyers returned to the courtroom.

"Before I rule on the prosecution's and defense's request, I'd like to hear from the defendant, Kevin Forsyth," the judge said.

Aaron leaned forward, curious about what the kid would say.

"Kevin, what do you have to say for yourself? What do you think you deserve?"

Kevin fiddled with his tie and gazed nervously at his

parents. At their nod of encouragement, he turned and addressed the judge. "My problem, sir, is I've never thought of myself as a racist—as anything other than privileged. Jews, black people, LGBTQ people—they all live knowing people hate them. I've never felt that way or experienced it. So, I don't know what I deserve, other than punishment. I'm not sure what to say except I'm sorry for the damage I've caused. I watched when I should've stopped my friends. That's what upsets me the most. It's what disappoints me the most. I should have stopped them, no matter how hard it was." The boy looked down for a moment and swallowed hard. "I did learn one thing—when you witness someone doing the wrong thing, you have to speak up. No matter what. Otherwise, you're as bad as they are." He took a deep breath. "I know I deserve to be punished, and I'm ready to face it. Whatever you think is best."

The judge nodded as Kevin sat.

Aaron frowned. The young man's sincerity impressed him. Maybe Dave was right. He looked over at his friend, who nodded.

"This court accepts the request of the prosecution and defense," the judge said. "Kevin Forsyth will receive two years' probation, including mandatory education on discrimination and anti-Semitism, five hundred hours of volunteer work, and a ten-thousand dollar fine for his part in the damages, to be paid in full by the end of his probationary term."

The judge dismissed the court, and Aaron joined the line of people filing out of the courtroom.

Behind him, Dave patted him on the back. "This is for the best. You'll see."

The police chief stopped Aaron and the rabbi, with his wife and Kevin beside him. "Thank you for agreeing with this sentence."

"Thank you, sir, Rabbi," Kevin echoed.

The rabbi nodded. "You're welcome. Come to my office tomorrow afternoon—let's say—at four, to discuss what you can do."

Aaron stepped closer. "Then come to my deli and we'll talk."

He shook the police chief's hand. He would make Kevin work for his forgiveness.

Chapter Eighteen

Sarah stood outside the Jewish Federation offices and stared at the bronze statue depicting a Jewish star. Her interview had gone well, and they'd offered her the job on the spot. The work she'd do—educating the community in times of crisis—was exactly the type of fulfilling work she missed in DC. And the people she'd met while at her interview also seemed like people she might enjoy socializing with. She had a future here if she wanted it.

She thought about her friends—Caroline, Emily and Jessica. In the time she'd been here, she'd realized what she'd missed. Emily had put aside her jealousy, and Jess held her accountable, as always. Sure, she had friends in DC, but there was no one who "got her"—who understood who she was at her core—like the people from home. She had friends in DC, but they were mostly superficial. There was no one whose friendship she'd retain if she moved.

She thought about her family. As much as her parents

sometimes annoyed her, she'd missed them. The closeness between her and her mother was special. Her father's quiet humor warmed her, and she wanted to be here for them as they aged—to help them as they'd helped her. Ten years ago, she hadn't recognized or appreciated the responsibility she had to them. Now, she did.

She thought about the town. It was quirky and diverse and loyal. Everyone pulled together in times of need. Look what they'd done with the deli. These were the types of people she wanted around her, wanted to work with. Bad things could happen anywhere, but home was special.

Huffing, she walked to her car. It was obvious, even to her, she'd made her decision. But what about Aaron? Could she live here without him? He'd made it clear during their last interaction that he didn't see a future for them. With time, maybe they could get back on better footing. But maybe not. He had an idea in his head of who she was. But she'd changed, and he resisted change. She wasn't going to mold herself into anyone's idea of the "perfect Sarah," no matter how attracted to Aaron she might be, or how much she loved him.

Her body hummed as she remembered having sex with him. His kiss, his touch, his smell. She touched her lips. She wanted him. She loved him. But until he came around—if he came around—she'd learn to be alone. Her heart pounded at the possibility of him falling in love with someone else. It was a chance she'd have to take.

Aaron looked up from his desk when the bell over the front door of his deli jingled. The new security monitor showed Kevin walk in. His blond hair was combed neatly, and his jeans and shirt were clean and tidy. He stuffed his hands in his pockets and looked around, his expression pensive. Taking a deep breath, Aaron rose and stepped into the public area. Kevin straightened his shoulders, held out his hand and stepped toward Aaron.

"Hi, Mr. Isaacson." His voice cracked and he cleared his throat. "I want to thank you again for everything you did for me. I know I have a lot to prove, and I don't deserve your trust, but I hope to earn it back. You asked to see me?"

Aaron shook Kevin's hand, impressed by the teen's manners and presence. "I'm glad you came."

Kevin nodded. "I have a lot to make up for, and not showing up wouldn't have helped my cause."

"True." Aaron looked around the deli. "So, you've got community service hours to do, right?"

Kevin nodded. "Yes, sir. I'm splitting them between the temple and your deli. If you tell me what you'd like me to do, I can start as soon as you'd like."

"How many hours a week are you giving to the temple?"

"The rabbi asked me to help out in the religious school. I work there Wednesday afternoons and Sunday mornings."

"The religious school?" Aaron raised a brow. "But you're not Jewish."

Kevin's face colored. "I'm shadowing students, teachers and some of the assistants and doing whatever grunt work they need. I guess I'm learning about the Jewish religion as I go."

Interesting. "What kinds of school commitments do you have?"

"Well, I was supposed to play football, but the coach suspended me because of what I did." Kevin swallowed and held Aaron's gaze for a few seconds. "I have more time this fall than I thought I would. I might play basketball this winter, but I'm not sure yet."

"And you have homework."

Kevin nodded. "I'm willing to do whatever you want me to do. I'll figure out how to study around what you need."

Sympathy welled in Aaron's chest. This kid was trying. "I don't want you to fail out of school. How about you come here on Mondays and Thursdays after school. I can use help cleaning up, prepping food and stocking inventory. We'll see how things go from there."

"Yes, sir." He nodded.

"It's Aaron. You can call me Aaron."

"Yes, sir. I mean, Aaron." Kevin gave him a small smile. "I appreciate your giving me a second chance."

Aaron gave him a stern look. "Don't let me down."

"No, sir." Kevin shook his head as he backed toward the door.

Aaron smiled. "Good. I'll see you Monday."

"Monday." He nodded. "I'll be here."

Second chances. Aaron stared blindly out the window after Kevin left the store. All around him, things were changing. Jordan and Gabriel had their own lives, but they'd pitched in willingly—and in some cases, demanded their right to do so—when they were needed. They'd shown him he didn't have to shoulder the burden alone. Kevin had committed terrible crimes, but he was willing to learn from his mistakes and make the necessary changes to improve his life and fix what he'd done.

He rubbed the back of his head. He hated change, but sometimes it was necessary, and sometimes it resulted in good things. It was better than sitting around passively wondering what to do next.

Sarah had also changed. He snorted. If everyone else could do it, he could, too. Even if it meant changing his life for the woman he loved. Because he did love her. Despite everything that had happened. In fact, he'd never stopped. Love didn't just mean sacrifice. It meant compromise, too. Yeah, he had a responsibility to his family and to this deli, but not to the exclusion of everything else. He'd established a great community here, but it was nothing without Sarah. If Sarah couldn't be a part of his community, maybe he could be a part of hers.

He owed their history a second chance.

Chapter Nineteen

"And when you're done unloading the boxes, you can sweep and wash the floor in the storeroom," Aaron said.

Kevin nodded and walked away. This was the second week that Kevin had reported to work for him, and Aaron couldn't fault the kid for anything. He arrived at three in the afternoon every day he was scheduled and completed all the work Aaron gave him without complaint. He never asked to leave, only leaving when Aaron told him to go. He paid close attention and was a terrific worker. He did everything he was told, and he'd proven himself trustworthy. In fact, the last time he was in, he'd found a wallet a customer left behind and turned it over to Aaron right away. Although the sight of him still made Aaron tense, he was starting to soften. Maybe. A little.

The truth was, he'd been on edge ever since the holidays. Sarah had returned to DC and his world was off-kilter. He'd spent the better part of these last two weeks working with his family to find a better balance. He used to work from the moment he awoke until he couldn't stay awake anymore. Now, he'd relied more on Jordan, and it felt good. He'd broached the idea of opening a second store in DC with his parents, and they favored the idea. He and Jordan had stayed up late many nights, working out a business plan, researching optimal locations, and figuring out a timeline. Until he had everything in place, he didn't want to contact Sarah. The wait was killing him.

The bell jingled, and Sarah's mom walked in. The timing made his breath hitch.

"Hi, Aaron." She took a quick glance around. "You'd never know anything happened here."

He nodded toward Kevin. "Well, almost."

She smiled at the teen. "Good for him for being here. How's it working out?"

"So far, so good. He's a diligent worker. What can I get you?"

"Ever since the holidays, I've been craving your potato kugel. So, two pieces of that, a half dozen bagels and some lox."

He packed her order and his neck tingled. Should he ask? He clenched his teeth. It would be rude not to.

"How's Sarah?"

"She's doing well. She sold her apartment and is getting organized for her new job. How are you?"

She sold her apartment. His insides clenched. She was moving? And she had a new job? His neck went cold and hot. Damn, if he wanted a chance with her, he had to hurry.

"Uh, great. Thanks. That'll be twenty dollars."

Sarah's mother handed him a twenty-dollar bill and he walked her bag around the counter and placed it in her hands. She smiled her goodbye and left him standing there in a half stupor as she walked out of his store.

Forget about waiting. If he didn't act now, Sarah would move on without him. Her life didn't include him. His ears rang. The room tipped, and he braced himself against the counter. His chest tightened until he couldn't take a deep breath. To hell with planning for every possible scenario. He couldn't let her go. Not without a fight. He counted to ten before making a quick call to Jordan.

"Kevin!"

His raised voice brought the teen running.

"Yes, sir? I mean, Aaron?"

"We're closing early today. Or rather, I'm leaving early. My brother will stop by and lock up at seven. Can you help him out?"

"Yes."

Aaron stared at the kid for a moment. He was solemn and responsible, plus his brother would be here. It would be fine. "Thank you."

And with that, Aaron headed for his car and drove to DC.

Sarah surveyed her empty apartment. The movers had loaded most of her things onto their truck, and with another item checked off her to-do list, new energy invigorated her. She was about to close her door after the moving guys when the elevator dinged. She glanced toward it.

Aaron stood in the middle of the hallway.

Her breath froze in her chest. For a moment, joy suffused her. The overhead lighting made his brown hair glow, giving him a halo. Ha! Aaron as an angel. On closer inspection, however, he was pale.

Her joy faded and her stomach clenched. She closed her eyes and pulled in a deep breath before opening them again. When she did, he stood in exactly the same spot, watching her.

"What are you doing here?" It wasn't the first question that entered her mind, but it was the easiest one to voice.

"Trying to convince myself I'm not a *schmuck*."

She flinched. It wasn't the response she'd expected. "You're not a *schmuck*. But you're stubborn as hell."

She turned and walked into her apartment, leaving the door to shut behind her. But it didn't click. Instead, it smacked. Actually, *something* smacked it. She swung around.

A hand. A large, masculine hand with squared-off nails. A work-roughened hand that was gentle on her skin.

Aaron's hand.

She folded her arms across her body to keep from touching his hand and watched as the rest of him blocked her doorway. He didn't enter her apartment but stood with the door resting against his back.

"May I come in?" His tone was reasonable, and his voice slid like silk around her, heightening every nerve ending. But silk, though pretty, was hard to care for.

"Why?"

"Because I want to talk to you."

"You haven't talked to me in weeks. Why now?"

He studied her, his expression serious. She shouldn't want to kiss him or drown in those vivid blues. Drowning meant surrender, and there was too much they needed to work out between them for her to give up.

"Will you let me explain?" he asked.

"I've never stopped you."

"Let me in, Sarah."

"Let you in? Of all the…" Sarah's face turned beet red with anger. "You've *been* inside me, twisting my insides and my feelings, and squeezing them until I can't breathe. And when I tried to get you to let *me* in, you refused. I don't want you inside me any longer, Aaron."

Hurt flashed in his eyes, but he seemed to shake it off. "I meant your apartment."

The life went out of her. She couldn't win. She had no idea why he was here or what he wanted, but he spoke in riddles, and she was tired of playing the fool. She'd allowed it with Matthew, but she'd be damned if she'd allow it with Aaron, too. After so many days of wanting to talk to him but thinking he needed space, now—when she finally had the chance—everything jammed inside of her and she didn't know what to say. She stepped aside.

His footsteps echoed in the empty apartment. He ran his hands over the few remaining boxes, smoothing over tape. She didn't want his hands on her things. She needed to keep things separate. It would be hard enough moving home and knowing he was there, out of reach. If he touched her possessions, she'd have to deal with his ghost in her home, too.

"Why are you here, Aaron?"

"For you."

Time stopped—like she was in a movie and the viewer had pressed pause. She waited for the movie, the one in which she starred but had no script, to resume.

When it didn't, she spoke. "You had me. You let me go."

"I was wrong. I was hurt and confused and too proud to talk about it. I'm sorry." His gaze pierced hers, begging her forgiveness.

"God, your damned pride is going to kill...*everything*!"

"I know. I was angry."

Confusion rippled through her. She wanted him but she was no longer a woman who accepted men without question.

She narrowed her gaze. "Join the club. If that's all you came to say, you can leave." Her arm shook as she pointed toward the door, but she didn't care if he saw it.

He rammed both hands through his hair. "We meant something to each other at one point—you still mean something to me now. I can't let you go without seeing this through. Please."

Emotions swept her away, and she reached for the wall to brace herself. She nodded and slid down the wall to the floor. He joined her, the space between them electrified with everything that had happened between them.

Aaron gripped his knees. His strong hands, the ones she couldn't help but react to every time he touched her, whitened. "I've been so afraid—afraid of disappointing my parents if I didn't take over their deli, afraid of depriving my brothers of a promising future if I asked them for help and afraid of forcing you to give up your dreams if I fought for you and asked you to stay. But deep down, it all boiled down to the same thing—I was afraid of change."

Her heart thudded in her chest. "I know. I've always known, and I should have given more thought to your feelings. I was selfish and caught up in what I was discovering about myself."

Regret flashed on Aaron's face. "Maybe, but I was the selfish one. Every time I thought I'd have to change, I shut down." He turned to face her, his expression serious. "I've made so many mistakes. I'm not going to make them again. I'm not perfect, and I still hate change, but I've also realized some change is good."

"I'm sorry I didn't try harder to fix things with you," she said. "I should have placed more value on what we had. I was so convinced I had to go somewhere else to make a difference, and the power of making positive change was heady."

He reached for her hand, but she wasn't yet ready for his touch. It was hard to think when they connected, and if she was to stand up for herself, she needed a clear head. She made a fist at her side, and Aaron withdrew his hand.

He stared at the ceiling. "I should have remembered the type of person you were, but I couldn't think straight. I need you to know how proud of you I am. You're amazing at what you do, and I don't want you to sacrifice yourself for me, or for us. I won't let you. I never want you to stop being you."

A kernel of hope grew in her chest. "I broke up with Matthew."

He reached for her and squeezed her hand hard, like a reflex. But this time, she didn't pull away. And this time, she would say everything she needed to and get it all in the open. She owed him that.

"I think all along I was looking for a way out of that relationship. Matthew cheating on me was my wake-up call. I was beginning to realize the engagement wasn't right, that our relationship was stifling, and kissing you made me see what I was missing. Learning he cheated was the *kaka* on the bottom of my shoe."

"I wish you'd told me sooner," he said. "I've spent so much time trying to reconcile the new Sarah with the old one. Trying to figure out if you could want someone like me."

He whispered the last part, and Sarah's heart broke at the hurt expressed in those few words. Background noises disappeared, and her focus narrowed until it was only the two of them. She had one chance to get this right, to smooth over the hurt she'd caused and pave the way for him to do the same. It wasn't all her fault, of course, but she needed to make amends for her part if they were ever to have a chance at a new start.

"I'm sorry I hurt you," she said. "I wanted to tell you right away, but every time we were together, something happened. You walked away, and I thought you needed space to sort out your feelings. I needed time to figure out who I was and what I wanted. I'd spent so long making myself into Matthew's perfect version, I didn't know who I was anymore."

"And do you know now?"

She nodded. "I'm starting to. You and the rabbi and my parents, and people I met in town or at the synagogue, were so impressed by what I do. But more than being impressed, you valued my knowledge and made me remember I'm good on my own, not because of Matthew or any guy."

Aaron pulled away. "You've always been smart, Sarah. And independent. Those are some of the qualities I love most about you."

"Well, I forgot about it. But being home reminded me."

"I need to know if somewhere, in all that self-discovery, there's room for me. I've been researching opportunities for me here in DC. I want to open another deli here so you can keep following your dreams, but maybe with me at your side this time. I was going to wait until I had everything lined up before I told you, but your mom told me you have a new job and a new apartment, and I was afraid I'd run out of time. I didn't want to lose you again—"

She placed a finger over his lips and the kernel of hope spread. Her heart thudded in her chest. "My new job is at home working for the Federation."

"What?" He paled.

She nodded and squeezed his hand again, running her thumb across his knuckles.

"You're sure that's what you want? You won't miss DC? I don't want you giving up your dreams for me, Sarah."

"I miss home, and there's so much good I can do there."

"When do you start?"

"Next week. I'm going to live with Emily. Her apartment is big enough for a roommate."

Aaron rose and paced the empty apartment, staring out the windows. The set of his shoulders told Sarah something wasn't right, but she didn't know what was bothering him.

He clenched his hands at his sides and took a deep breath before kneeling in front of her and framing her face in his hands. "Sarah, I love you. I don't think I ever stopped, even though I tried. I've figured out a way to bring more balance to my life and let others help shoulder some of the responsibility with me. I don't care where I live or work—home, DC, the moon. The only thing I care about is being with you. If you're willing."

Joy filled her.

His chest rose and fell.

Her temperature dropped everywhere except her cheeks, which were warm from his palms. Her breathing echoed in her ears. Her heart pounded in her chest. "I don't think there are a lot of Jews on the moon." *Way to go, Sarah. He finally tells you he loves you, and this is what you say?*

"So, we'll be the first." He leaned forward until his breath fanned her forehead. He ran a hand along the side of her head and finally, finally, pulled her against him. His heart pounded against her ear. He was warm and solid and hers.

He tipped her chin up and kissed her. Their lips met, and she poured her apology into the kiss.

"I love you, Sarah," he whispered. "I always have."

She melted into him. "I love you, too."

Their kiss deepened. She opened her mouth and his tongue plundered hers. Their bodies molded to each other as if they'd never parted. She ran her hands over his shoulders and played with the hair at the nape of his neck. He wrapped his arms around her waist and held her against him. Desire washed over her, and she moaned as she arched against him.

He lifted her and she wrapped her legs around his waist. "Bedroom?"

Using her body to direct him, she continued kissing him as they made their way down the hall and into her bedroom. Falling onto the air mattress, she stared at him, memorizing his features. She saw nothing but desire and love.

Limbs tangled as they removed each other's clothing.

"You still have this." She rubbed the gold star pendant hanging from a chain around his neck.

"You gave it to me for graduation." He brushed a strand of hair behind her ear. "I've never taken it off."

"Even when you hated me?"

He nibbled her ear. "I never hated you. I wanted to. I even tried convincing myself I did and tried moving on. But deep down, you're as much a part of me as…my liver or spleen."

She smacked his chest. "Ew, that's gross!"

Laughing, he grabbed her hand and kissed each finger. "My kidney?"

She groaned. "You're terrible at this, you know that?"

With a sigh, he let go of her hand. "My heart. You're as much a part of me as my heart. Is that better?"

Something in her settled. "Much." She trailed kisses across his chest, moving her way toward his pelvis where she stopped and unbuttoned his jeans. His hands fumbled as he did the same with her clothes, and she writhed when his fingers dipped beneath the silk of her panties.

"Condom," she panted. "Crap, all my things are packed." She pulled away from him, but he held tight.

"I've got one." His voice was rough with need.

He pulled his wallet from his back pocket and removed

the foil package before pulling his jeans off. He handed her the condom and removed her pants.

"You're beautiful," he murmured as he stopped to watch her, his cheeks ruddy.

The boy she'd loved had grown into a man. He was the same, yet different, and her hands itched to explore the changes.

She unwrapped the foil package and slid the condom onto him. His hiss when she touched him heightened her need. She ran her hands up his broad chest, admiring the sculpted muscles she'd never seen before. He was here, and he was hers.

He massaged her backside and pulled her on top of him. She wanted to taste his skin. She leaned over and licked his nipples. They pebbled, tasting salty on her tongue. Beneath her, he hardened. He pulled her toward him, but she wanted to go slow this time. She rocked against him, maintaining control. Trailing her lips up his neck, she bit his earlobe.

He swore and bucked his hips.

"Not yet." Her voice was shaky, her need was as potent as his.

They kissed again, teeth and tongue, moans and whimpers, pulses racing, blood rushing in her ears. He was strong and powerful, his arms like bands of steel. White lines of strain bracketed his mouth.

She rocked against him once more before pulling away and staring down at him, her eyes dark with desire. "I need to know you'll stay. Even if things change. Even if *I* change. Because I'm learning new things about myself, and I want to share them with you, just as I want you to share yourself with me. I want to know we have a future together."

Without warning, he pulled her against his chest and flipped them over until she lay beneath him. "I will always stay. I'll never stop you from changing or following your dreams, so long as you save me a place beside you."

She nodded.

He rested his forehead against hers for a moment, then rose above her, ready to enter. She was warm and wet for him, and with one last look for consent, he thrust inside of her. Her body stretched and accommodated him like they'd been made for each other. He pulled out and thrust again, each time going a little deeper until he was completely sheathed inside her. They rocked, slow at first, then faster, their breaths rushing in time to their movements. Above her, his neck corded with strain. She trailed a finger along the bulging vein, ran her hand across his back and rode the waves of pleasure coursing through her as her need built and she approached the edge. She wanted to wait for him, though. This time, they needed to climax together.

As if he read her thoughts, he shut his eyes tight before opening them and staring at her. When she nodded, he made one last, deep thrust and she toppled over the edge. Flames engulfed her, wave after wave of pleasure crashing through her as he shouted her name. When they calmed, he collapsed on top of her, his breath deep and coarse like a racehorse after the Preakness.

Rolling to his side, he took her with him and cradled her in his arms. "Unless you ask—and if you do, you better have a damned good reason—I'm never letting you go, Sarah."

She nuzzled his neck, smiling into his warm skin that smelled of him and sex. "You won't have to because I'm not going anywhere without you. I don't feel like I'm sacrificing anything." She paused. "Well, maybe one thing."

"What's that?"

"Black clothing."

Laughter rumbled deep in his chest. "Congratulations

on your new job. You're going to be amazing. But I want you to know one thing."

"What's that?"

"I would have given up the deli for you. If you wanted to stay here, or move somewhere else, I'd go with you. Because my life is not the same without you."

At a loss for what to say in response, she kissed him instead, pouring all her dreams and love into that one kiss. When she came up for air, his eyes twinkled.

"As soon as we get home, I'm taking you shopping," he said.

"Oh really? For what?"

"Anything, as long as it comes in a color."

* * * * *

COMING NEXT MONTH FROM

ⓗ HARLEQUIN®
SPECIAL EDITION™

HSECNM0823

Get 3 FREE REWARDS!

We'll send you 2 FREE Books <u>plus</u> a FREE Mystery Gift.

FREE Value Over **$20**

Both the **Harlequin® Special Edition** and **Harlequin® Heartwarming™** series feature compelling novels filled with stories of love and strength where the bonds of friendship, family and community unite.

HARLEQUIN
PLUS

Try the best multimedia
subscription service for romance
readers like you!

Read, Watch and Play.

Experience the easiest way to get
the romance content you crave.

Start your **FREE TRIAL** at
<u>www.harlequinplus.com/freetrial</u>.